THE PEOPLE
OF
SPARKS

Also by Jeanne DuPrau

THE CITY OF EMBER

THE PEOPLE
OF
SPARKS

Jeanne DuPrau

RANDOM HOUSE NEW YORK

www.randomhouse.com/kids

Library of Congress Cataloging-in-Publication Data
DuPrau, Jeanne.
The people of Sparks / by Jeanne DuPrau. — 1st ed.
p.   cm.
SUMMARY: Having escaped to the Unknown Regions, Lina and the others
seek help from the village people of Sparks.
ISBN 0-375-82824-9 (trade) — ISBN 0-375-92824-3 (lib. bdg.) —
ISBN 0-375-82825-7 (pbk.)
[1. Fantasy.]   I. Title.   PZ7.D927Pe 2004   [Fic]—dc22   2003020760

Printed in the United States of America   10 9 8 7 6 5 4   First Edition

RANDOM HOUSE and colophon are registered trademarks of Random House, Inc.

Contents

"*Darkness cannot drive out darkness;*
only light can do that.
Hate cannot drive out hate;
only love can do that.
Hate multiplies hate, violence multiplies violence,
and toughness multiplies toughness
in a descending spiral of destruction."
—*Martin Luther King, Jr.,*
"*Strength to Love,*" 1963

THE PEOPLE
OF
SPARKS

The Message

Dear People of Ember,

We came down the river from the Pipeworks and found the way to another place. It is green here and very big. Light comes from the sky. You must follow the instructions in this message and come on the river. Bring food with you. Come as quickly as you can.

Lina Mayfleet and Doon Harrow

PART 1

Arrival

CHAPTER 1

What Torren Saw

Torren was out at the edge of the cabbage field that day, the day the people came. He was supposed to be fetching a couple of cabbages for Dr. Hester to use in the soup that night, but, as usual, he didn't see why he shouldn't have some fun while he was at it. So he climbed up the wind tower, which he wasn't supposed to do because, they said, he might fall or get his head sliced off by the big blades going round and round.

The wind tower was four-sided, made of boards nailed one above the next like the rungs of a ladder. Torren climbed the back side of it, the side that faced the hills and not the village, so that the little group of workers hoeing the cabbage rows wouldn't see him. At the top, he turned around and sat on the flat place behind the blades, which turned slowly in the idle summer breeze. He had brought a pocketful of small stones up with him, planning on some target practice:

he liked to try to hit the chickens that rummaged around between the rows of cabbages. He thought it might be fun to bounce a few pebbles off the hats of the workers, too. But before he had even taken the stones from his pocket, he caught sight of something that made him stop and stare.

Out beyond the cabbage field was another field, where young tomato and corn and squash plants were growing, and beyond that the land sloped up into a grassy hillside dotted, at this time of year, with yellow mustard flowers. Torren saw something strange at the top of the hill. Something dark.

There were bits of darkness at first—for a second he thought maybe it was a deer, or several deer, black ones instead of the usual light brown, but the shape was wrong for deer, and the way these things moved was wrong, too. He realized very soon that he was seeing people, a few people at first and then more and more of them. They came up from the other side of the hill and gathered at the top and stood there, a long line of them against the sky, like a row of black teeth. There must have been a hundred, Torren thought, or more than a hundred.

In all his life, Torren had never seen more than three or four people at a time arrive at the village from elsewhere. Almost always, the people who came were roamers, passing through with a truckload of stuff from the old towns to sell. This massing of people on the hilltop terrified him. For a moment he couldn't move. Then his heart started up a furious pounding, and he scrambled down off the wind tower so fast that he scraped his hands on the rough boards.

"Someone's coming!" he shouted as he passed the workers. They looked up, startled. Torren ran at full speed toward the low cluster of brown buildings at the far end of the field. He turned up a dirt lane, his feet raising swirls of dust, and dashed through the gate in the wall and across the courtyard and in through the open door, all the time yelling, "Someone's coming! Up on the hill! Auntie Hester! Someone's coming!"

He found his aunt in the kitchen, and he grabbed her by the waist of her pants and cried, "Come and see! There's people on the hill!" His voice was so shrill and urgent and loud that his aunt dropped the spoon into the pot of soup she'd been stirring and hurried after him. By the time they got outside, others from the village were leaving their houses, too, and looking toward the hillside.

The people were coming down. Over the crest of the hill they came and kept coming, dozens of them, more and more, like a mudslide.

The people of the village crowded into the streets. "Get Mary Waters!" someone called. "Where's Ben and Wilmer? Find them, tell them to get out here!"

Torren was less frightened now that he was surrounded by the townspeople. "I saw them first," he said to Hattie Carranza, who happened to be hurrying along next to him. "I was the one who told the news."

"Is that right," said Hattie.

"We won't let them do anything bad to us," said Torren. "If they do, we'll do something worse to them. Won't we?"

But she just glanced down at him with a vague frown and didn't answer.

The three village leaders—Mary Waters, Ben Barlow, and Wilmer Dent—had joined the crowd by now and were leading the way across the cabbage field. Torren kept close behind them. The strangers were getting nearer, and he wanted to hear what they would say. He could see that they were terrible-looking people. Their clothes were all wrong—coats and sweaters, though the weather was warm, and not nice coats and sweaters but raggedy ones, patched, unraveling, faded, and grimy. They carried bundles, all of them: sacks made of what looked like tablecloths or blankets gathered up and tied with string around the neck. They moved clumsily and slowly. Some of them tripped on the uneven ground and had to be helped up by others.

In the center of the field, where the smell of new cabbages and fresh dirt and chicken manure was strong, those at the front of the crowd of strangers met the village leaders. Mary Waters stepped to the front, and the villagers crowded up behind her. Torren, being small, wriggled between people until he had a good view. He stared at the ragged people. Where were *their* leaders? Facing Mary were a girl and a boy who looked only a little older than he was himself. Next to them was a bald man, and next to him a sharp-eyed woman holding a small child. Maybe she was the leader.

But when Mary stepped forward and said, "Who are you?" it was the boy who answered. He spoke in a clear, loud voice that surprised Torren, who had expected a pitiful voice from someone so bedraggled. "We come from the city of Ember," the boy said. "We left there because our city was dying. We need help."

Mary, Ben, and Wilmer exchanged glances. Mary frowned. "The city of Ember? Where's that? We've never heard of it."

The boy gestured back the way they had come, to the east. "That way," he said. "It's under the ground."

The frowns deepened. "Tell us the truth," said Ben, "not childish nonsense."

This time the girl spoke up. She had long, snarled hair with bits of grass caught in it. "It isn't a lie," she said. "Really. Our city was underground. We didn't know it until we came out."

Ben snorted impatiently, folding his arms across his chest. "Who is in charge here?" He looked at the bald man. "Is it you?"

The bald man shook his head and gestured toward the boy and the girl. "They're as in charge as anyone," he said. "The mayor of our city is no longer with us. These young people are speaking the truth. We have come out of a city built underground."

The people around him all nodded and murmured, "Yes" and "It's true."

"My name is Doon Harrow," said the boy. "And this is Lina Mayfleet. We found the way out of Ember."

He thinks he's pretty great, thought Torren, hearing a note of pride in the boy's voice. He didn't look so great. His hair was shaggy, and he was wearing an old jacket that was coming apart at the seams and grimy at the cuffs. But his eyes shone out confidently from under his dark eyebrows.

"We're hungry," the boy said. "And thirsty. Will you help us?"

Mary, Ben, and Wilmer stood silent for a moment. Then Mary took Ben and Wilmer by the arms and led them aside a few steps. They whispered to each other, glanced up at the great swarm of strangers, frowned, whispered some more. While he waited to hear what they'd say, Torren studied the people who said they came from underground.

It might be true. They did in fact look as if they had crawled up out of a hole. Most of them were scrawny and pale, like the sprouts you see when you lift up a board that's been lying on the ground, feeble things that have tried to grow in the dark. They huddled together looking frightened. They looked exhausted, too. Many of them had sat down on the ground now, and some had their heads in the laps of others.

The three village leaders turned again to the crowd of strangers. "How many of you are there?" Mary Waters asked.

"About four hundred," said the boy, Doon.

Mary's dark eyebrows jumped upward.

Four hundred! In Torren's whole village, there were only 322. He swept his gaze out over this vast horde. They filled half the cabbage field and were still coming over the hill, like a swarm of ants.

The girl with the ratty hair stepped forward and raised a hand, as if she were in school. "Excuse me, Madam Mayor," she said.

Torren snickered. Madam Mayor! Nobody called Mary Waters Madam Mayor. They just called her Mary.

"Madam Mayor," said the girl, "my little sister is very sick." She pointed to the baby being held by the sharp-eyed woman. It did look sick. Its eyes were half closed, and its mouth hung open. "Some others of us are sick, too," the girl went on, "or hurt—Lotty Hoover tripped and hurt her ankle, and Nammy Proggs is exhausted from walking so far. She's nearly eighty years old. Is there a doctor in your town? Is there a place where sick people can lie down and be taken care of?"

Mary turned to Ben and Wilmer again, and they spoke to each other in low voices. Torren could catch only a few words of what they said. "Too many . . ." ". . . but human kindness . . ." ". . . maybe take a *few* in . . ." Ben rubbed his beard and scowled. Wilmer kept glancing at the sick baby. After a few minutes, they nodded to each other. Mary said, "All right. Hoist me up."

Ben and Wilmer bent down and grasped Mary's legs. With a grunt they lifted her so that she was high enough to see out over the crowd. She raised both her arms and cried, in a voice that came from the depths of her deep chest, "People from Ember! Welcome! We will do what we can to help you. Please follow us!" Ben and Wilmer set her down, and the three of them turned and walked out of the cabbage field and toward the road that entered the village. Led by the boy and the girl, the crowd of shabby people followed.

Torren dashed ahead, ran down the lane, and got up onto the low wall that bordered his house. From there, he watched the people from underground go by. They were strangely silent. Why weren't they jabbering to each other? But they seemed too tired to speak, or too stupid. They stared at everything, wide-eyed and drop-jawed—as if they had never seen a house before, or a tree, or a chicken. In fact, the chickens seemed to frighten them—they shrank back when they saw them, making startled sounds. It took a long time for the whole raggedy crowd to pass Torren's house, and when the last people had gone by, he jumped down off the wall and followed them. They were being led, he knew, to the town center, down by the river, where there would be water for them to drink. After that, what would happen? What would they eat? Where would they sleep? Not in my room, he thought.

CHAPTER 2

Out from Below

The people from the dying city of Ember had come up into the new world only a few days before. The first to arrive had been Lina Mayfleet and Doon Harrow, bringing Lina's little sister, Poppy, with them. From a ledge high up in the great cave that held their city, they'd thrown down a message, hoping someone would find it and lead the others out. Then they'd waited. At first they'd explored the wonders around them. But as the hours passed, they began to worry that their message had not been found and that they would be alone in this world forever.

Then, in the late afternoon of the next day, Doon suddenly shouted, "Look! They're coming!"

Lina grabbed Poppy by the hand. All three of them ran toward the mouth of the cave. Who was it? Who was it coming from home? A woman emerged from the darkness first, and then two men, and then three children, all of them squinting against the bright light.

"Hello, hello!" Lina called, leaping up the hill. She saw who it was when she got closer: the family who ran the Callay Street vegetable market. She didn't know any of them well—she couldn't even remember their names—and yet she was so glad to see them that tears sprang to her eyes. She flung her arms around each one in turn, crying, "Here you are! Look, isn't it wonderful? Oh, I'm so glad you're here! And are more coming?" The new arrivals were too breathless and amazed to answer, but it didn't matter, because Lina could see for herself.

They came out from the cave, shading their eyes with their hands. They came in bunches, a few of them and then minutes later a few more, stumbling out into a light a thousand times brighter than any they'd ever seen. They stared in astonishment, walked a few steps, and then just stood, dropping the sacks and bundles they carried, gazing, blinking. To Lina and Doon, who felt already that they belonged here, the refugees from Ember looked strange in this bright landscape of green grass and blue sky. They were so drab and dingy in their heavy, mud-colored clothes, their coats and sweaters in colors like stone and dust and murky water. It was as if they had brought some of Ember's darkness with them.

Doon suddenly leapt away, shouting, "Father! Father!" He threw himself against his stunned father, who fell backward, sat down on the ground, and burst into a combination of laughter and weeping to see his son again. "You *are* here," he gasped. "I wasn't sure. . . . I didn't know. . . ."

All afternoon they came. Lizzie Bisco came, and others from the old High Class, along with Clary Laine from the greenhouses, and the doctor who had helped Lina's granny, and Sadge Merrall, who had tried to go out into the Unknown Regions. Mrs. Murdo came, walking in her brisk, businesslike way, but giving a cry of joy when she saw Lina hurtling toward her. People came whose faces Lina recognized but whose names she didn't remember, like the shoe repair man from Liverie Street, and the little puffy-faced woman who lived in Selverton Square, and the tall, black-haired boy with blue-gray eyes so light they looked like glints of metal. What was that tall boy's name? She spent a second trying to recall it, but only a second. It didn't matter. These were her people, the people of Ember. All of them were tired and all of them were thirsty. Lina showed them the little stream, and they splashed the water on their faces and filled their bottles there.

"What about the mayor?" Lina asked Mrs. Murdo, but she just shook her head. "He's not with us," she said.

Some of the older people looked terrified to be in such a huge place, a place that seemed to go on without borders in all directions. After they had stared nervously about them for a while, they sat down in the grass, hunched over, and put their heads to their knees. But the children ran around in ecstasy, touching everything, smelling the air, splashing their feet in the stream.

By evening, 417 people had arrived—Doon kept track. As the light began to fade from the sky, they shared the food they had brought, and then, using their coats as blankets and their bundles as pillows, they lay down on the warm, rough ground and slept.

The next morning they got ready to leave. Lina and Doon, when they first arrived, had spotted a narrow gray line that ran along the ground like a pencil stroke in the distance. They thought it might be a road. So the people of Ember, having no other clue about where to go, picked up their bundles and set out in that direction, a long, straggling line trailing across the hills.

It was on this walk that Mrs. Murdo told Lina and Doon about leaving Ember. The three of them walked together, Mrs. Murdo with Poppy in her arms. Doon's father walked behind them, leaning forward now and then to hear what Mrs. Murdo was saying.

"I was the one who found your message," Mrs. Murdo said. "It fell right at my feet. It was the day after the Singing. I was on my way home from the market, feeling sick with worry because you and Poppy had disappeared. Then there was your message." She paused and looked up at the sky. She was keeping a couple of tears from falling, Lina saw.

Mrs. Murdo composed herself and went on. "I thought it would be best to tell the mayor first. I wasn't sure I trusted him, but he was the one who could most easily organize the leaving. I showed him your message, and then I waited to hear the city clock ringing out the signal for a meeting."

Mrs. Murdo paused to catch her breath. They were going uphill, over rough clumps of earth—hard walking for city people, whose feet were accustomed to pavement.

"And was there a meeting?" Lina asked.

"No," said Mrs. Murdo. She plucked some burs off her skirt and shifted Poppy to her other shoulder. "Mercy," she said. "It's terribly hot." She stood still for a moment, breathing hard.

"So there was no meeting?" Lina prompted.

Mrs. Murdo started walking again. "Nothing happened at all," she said. "The clock didn't chime. The guards didn't come out and start organizing people. Nothing. But the lights kept flickering on and off. It seemed to me there was no time to lose.

"So I went to the Pipeworks and showed your message to Lister Munk. We followed the directions, and we found the rock marked with E right away— because people were there already."

"But how could they be, if they didn't have the directions?" Doon said. "Who was it?"

"It was the mayor," said Mrs. Murdo grimly, "and four of his guards. Looper was there, too, that boy who used to keep company with your friend Lizzie. They had huge, bulging sacks with them, piled up on the edge of the river, and they were loading the sacks into boats. The mayor was shouting at them to work faster.

"Lister yelled, 'What are you doing?' but we didn't need an answer. I could see what they were doing. They were going first. The mayor was making sure that he would get out, along with his friends and his loot, before anyone else."

Mrs. Murdo stopped talking. She trudged along, wiping sweat from her forehead. She frowned up at the hot, bright sky. Poppy whimpered.

"Let me carry the child for a while, Mrs. Murdo," said Doon's father.

"Thank you," Mrs. Murdo said. She stopped and passed the squirming Poppy to Doon's father, and they walked on.

Lina waited a minute or so, and then she couldn't wait any longer. "Well, what happened?" she said.

"It was awful," Mrs. Murdo said. "Everything happened at once. Two of the guards looked up at us and lost their balance and fell into the water. They grabbed hold of the loaded boats, which made the boats tip and dump their load into the river. The other guards and

Looper knelt down and tried to reach them, but they were pulled in, too. In the midst of all this, the mayor jumped onto the one boat that was still upright, but as soon as he hit it, it turned over and he plunged into the river." Mrs. Murdo shuddered. "He screamed, children. It was a horrible sound. He bobbed in the water like a giant cork, and then he went under. In just a few seconds, he and his guards were swept away. They were gone."

They walked in silence for a while, going downhill now. After a few minutes Mrs. Murdo went on.

"So Lister and I went back up into the city, and we had the Timekeeper ring the bell for a public meeting. We tried to explain what to do, but as soon as people heard the first bit—that a way out of Ember had been found, and that it was in the Pipeworks—everyone began shouting and rushing around. Things turned into a terrible mess. People were in too much of a hurry even to ask questions. Hundreds of them poured through the streets of the city all at once, and outside the door of the Pipeworks a huge crowd pushed and shoved to get in, so many people, so panicky, that some were trampled and crushed."

"Oh!" cried Lina. "How horrible!" These were people she knew! It was too awful to think about.

"Horrible indeed," said Mrs. Murdo. She frowned out across the vast landscape surrounding them, where there were no people in sight at all. "It was impossible to control them," she went on. "They rushed to the stairway—some people lost their footing and fell all the way down the stairs. Others ran right over them. And then when they realized that they were going to have to get into these little shells and float on the river, some people were so frightened that they turned around and tried to go up the stairs again, and some were so eager to get going that they jumped into the boats and capsized them and fell into the river and were drowned." She raised her eyes to Lina's. "I saw everything that happened," she said. "I'll never forget it."

Lina looked behind her at the citizens of Ember toiling across the hills. These were the ones who had made it out. "How many do you think were—left behind?" she asked Mrs. Murdo.

Mrs. Murdo just shook her head. "I don't know," she said. "Too many."

"And have the lights gone out forever now?"

"I don't know that either. But if they haven't, they will soon."

Hot as she was, Lina shuddered. She and Doon exchanged a look. They were thinking the same thing, she was sure: their city was lost in darkness now, and anyone left there was lost, too.

Later that day the refugees from Ember came to the road they had seen from afar. It was potholed and weed-cracked, but easier to walk on than the rough ground. It led alongside a creek that flowed swiftly over round, smooth rocks. In all directions, they saw nothing but endless expanses of grass. They shared the food they had brought with them, but it wasn't much. Some of them soon grew weak with hunger. They grew faint from the heat, too, which was hard to bear for people used to the constant chill of Ember. Poppy cried when she was set down on her feet, and her face looked flushed and hot.

Night came in the strange, gradual way so different from the sudden lights-out that signaled night in Ember. The travelers lay down on the ground and slept. They walked the next day, too, and the day after that. By then the food they had brought with them was gone. They traveled more and more slowly, stopping often to rest. Poppy was listless; her eyes were dull.

Finally, around the middle of the following day, they trudged up still another hill, and from there they saw a sight that made many of them weep with relief. Farmed fields lay below them in a wide valley, and beyond the fields, where the stream they'd been following joined a river, was a cluster of low brown buildings. It was a place where people lived.

Like the others, Lina was glad to see it. But it wasn't a bit like the city she had imagined, the one she'd drawn pictures of back in Ember, the one she'd hoped to find in this new world. The buildings of that city had been tall and majestic and sparkling with light. That city must be somewhere else, she thought as she started down the hill. She'd find it—not today, but someday.

CHAPTER 3

Through the Village

The woman who had greeted them led the people of Ember into the town. They went down a dusty street, past buildings that looked as if they'd been made out of the same brown earth that was underfoot. They were heavy-looking, imperfect buildings: their walls were fat and lumpy, rounded smooth at the corners. Lina saw cracks in the walls and crumbled places where bits of a window ledge or a step had fallen away.

Paths and alleys and strips of garden wound between the houses. It was clear that no one had planned this place, not the way the Builders had planned Ember. This town must have grown, one bit added to the next and another bit added to that. Plants grew everywhere. In Ember, the only plants were in the greenhouses—unless you counted mold and fungus, which grew on the trash heaps and sometimes in kitchens and bathrooms. Here, flowers and vegetables grew together beside every house. Plants sprang up alongside the streets, climbed walls, crawled over fences, pushed up through cracks in stairways, tumbled out of big pots and over windowsills and even down from roofs.

There were animals, too—huge, amazing, terrifying animals. In a fenced-in place at the edge of the town, Lina saw four brown animals much bigger than she was, with squarish heads and long, tasseled tails. Farther on, tethered to a post in front of a house, was a yellow-eyed creature with two spikes poking out of its head. When she walked by, it suddenly said, "Ma-a-a-a," and she skittered away in fright.

She turned to look for Doon, who had fallen a little behind. She found him stooping over, peering at some yellow flowers growing next to a wall. "Look at this," he said when she came up beside him. He pointed to a flower's tube-shaped center. "There's a spider in there the exact same yellow as the flower."

There was. Only Doon would notice such a thing. Tugging at the sleeve of his jacket, she said, "Come on. Stay with us," and she hurried him up toward the front of the line to join his father and Mrs. Murdo and Poppy.

These four people—Poppy and Mrs. Murdo, Doon and his father—were Lina's family now, and she wanted them close around her. Only Poppy was really related to her. But Mrs. Murdo was like a mother; she had taken Lina and Poppy into her house when their granny died, and she would have kept them with her if they hadn't had to leave the city. Doon's father was part of her family just because he was Doon's father. And Doon himself—he was the one who'd been Lina's partner in finding the way out of Ember. There was a tie between the two of them that could never be broken.

On they walked, down one street and up another, around curves and down through narrow passages. Everywhere, people stared at them. Some leaned from open windows. Some sat up on roofs, their legs dangling over the side. Some stood still in the midst of work they'd been doing, their shovels or brooms in their hands. These people were taller and browner than the people of Ember. Were they friendly? Lina couldn't tell. A few children waved and giggled.

After a while, the refugees came out from the narrow streets into a wide-open area. This must be like Ember's Harken Square, Lina thought, a place in the center of town where people gather. It wasn't square, though. It was more like a rough half circle paved in dusty brown brick.

"What is this place called?" Lina asked Mary Waters, who was walking just ahead of her.

"The plaza," Mary said.

Plah-zuh. Lina had never heard that word before. It was her first new-world word.

On one side of the plaza was the river. On the other side were stalls with thatched roofs and small buildings with display racks out in front holding faded-looking clothes, shoes with thick black soles, candles, brooms, pots of honey and jam, along with plenty of things that Lina didn't recognize.

A bigger building stood at the plaza's far end. It had wide steps in front, a double door, and a tower with windows up high that looked out over the plaza. Next to it was a tremendous plant of some kind—a great pole, much higher than the building, with branches like graceful, down-sweeping arms and leaves like bristles.

"What is that?" Lina asked a woman who was standing at the edge of the plaza, watching them go by.

The woman looked startled. "That's our town hall," she said.

"No, I mean the big plant next to it."

"Big plant? The pine tree?"

"Pinetree!" said Lina. "I've never seen a pinetree." Her second word: *pinetree.*

The woman gave her an odd look. Lina thanked her and walked on.

"Step this way, please," said Mary, who was trying to keep the unruly refugees in order. "There's plenty of water for you here—both in the river and in the fountain." She pointed to the middle of the plaza, where there was a pool of water circled by a low wall.

The water in the middle of the pool jumped up into a column of bubble and spray that splashed back down and jumped up again constantly.

The people of Ember surged forward. Dozens ran to the edge of the river and bent down to bathe their faces with water. Dozens more crowded around the pool. Children splashed their hands in it, crawled up on the rim, and tried to reach the leaping water in the middle. Some of the children jumped in and had to be hauled out by their parents. People at the rear of the crowd pushed forward, but people at the front weren't ready to be pushed. Suddenly there was yelling and jostling and water sloshing out onto the pavement. Lina slipped and fell down, and someone tripped over her and fell, too.

"Please!" shouted Mary, her deep, loud voice rising above the uproar.

"Order! Order!" shouted a man's voice. Lina heard other voices, too, as she struggled to her feet, the voices of the villagers crowding in at the edges of the plaza.

"Get back, Tommy, get away from them!"

"Where did you say they came from? Under the *ground*?"

"Are they people like us, Mama?" a child said. "Or some other kind?"

Of *course* we're like you, thought Lina. Aren't we? Are there more kinds of people than one? She got to her feet and wrung out the hem of her sweater, which was sopping wet. She spotted Mrs. Murdo on the other side of the plaza and headed toward her.

The commotion finally subsided. The people of Ember, their thirst quenched, gazed about them in wonder. Everything was strange and fascinating to them. They stood with their heads craned back, gazing at the towering plants and the peeping creatures that flitted around in them; they stooped down to touch the bright flowers; they peered in doorways and windows. Children ran down the grassy bank to the river, tore off their shoes and socks, and dunked their feet in the water. Old people, exhausted from their long walk, lay down behind bushes and went to sleep.

The three town leaders began moving among the people of their village, talking with them in low voices for a minute or two, then nodding and moving on. Lina saw these townspeople glance at the new arrivals with worried looks; they didn't seem to know what to say. Lina could understand why. What would the mayor of Ember have done, for instance, if four hundred people had suddenly arrived from the Unknown Regions?

By this time, the sky was beginning to darken. A few townspeople started calling the refugees together. "Come this way! Call your children! Please sit down!" They stood at the edges of the crowd with their arms stretched out and nudged people inward, until finally all four hundred people were squeezed into the plaza, gathered around the wide steps in front of the town hall, where the three leaders were standing.

Mary Waters raised her arms above her head and stood that way without speaking for several seconds. She looked powerful, Lina thought, even though she was very short. The way she stood, with her feet planted slightly apart and her back straight, made her seem almost to be growing out of the ground. Her black hair was streaked with gray, but her face was smooth and strong-boned.

Gradually people fell silent and turned their attention to her.

"Greetings!" she cried. "My name is Mary Waters. This is Ben Barlow. . . ." She pointed to one of the men standing next to her, a wiry man with a stiff, gray, box-like beard jutting from his chin. He had two wrinkles, like the number eleven, between his eyebrows. "And this is Wilmer Dent," she said, pointing to the other man. He was tall and thin, with wispy, rust-colored hair. He smiled a wavering smile and waggled a few fingers in greeting. "We are the three leaders of this village, which is called Sparks. Three hundred and twenty-two people live here. I understand that you come from a city three days' walk away. I must say, this is a . . . a surprise to us. We have not been aware of any post-Disaster settlements nearby, much less a city."

"What does 'post-Disaster' mean?" Lina whispered to Doon.

"I don't know," Doon said.

Mary Waters cleared her throat with a gruff sound and took a breath. "We will do our best for you tonight, and then tomorrow we will talk about . . . about your plans. Some of our households are willing to take in a few of you for the night—those with young children, and those who are old or ill. The rest of you may sleep here in the plaza. Those who go with the householders will share in their evening meal. Those who stay here will be given bread and fruit."

There was a scattering of applause from the people of Ember. "Thank you!" several voices cried out. "Thank you so much!"

"What's 'bread'?" Lina whispered to Doon.

He shrugged his shoulders.

"Will all those who most need shelter for the night please stand?" Mary Waters called. "As I said—those with children, and the elderly and ill."

A rustle swept through the crowd as people got to their feet. Voices murmured, "Stand up, Father," "You go, Willa," "No, I'm all right, you go," "Let Arno go, he's sprained his foot." Because of Poppy, Lina and Mrs. Murdo stood up. Doon remained sitting, and so did his father.

The brilliant yellow ball in the sky was traveling downward now, and the shadows grew longer. Night was coming, and with the gathering darkness Lina's spirits grew darker, too. She thought of the green-and-blue bedroom she'd moved into back at Mrs. Murdo's house in Ember, the lovely room she had been so glad to have. She was homesick for it. Right now, she would have been happy to have a bowl of turnip soup and then crawl between the covers of the bed in that room, with Poppy next to her, and Mrs. Murdo out in the living room tidying up, and the great clock of Ember about to strike nine, the hour when the lights went out. She knew that this place—the village of Sparks—was alive, and that Ember was dead, and she would not want to go back there even if she could. But right now, as the air grew chilly and whispered against her skin, and a strange bed in a stranger's house waited for her, she longed for what was familiar.

Mary Waters was calling out names. At each name, someone from the village stepped up and said how many people that household could take.

"Leah Parsons!"

A tall woman in a black dress came forward. "Two people," she said, and Mary Waters pointed at an old couple at the front of the crowd of refugees, who picked up their bags and followed the tall woman.

"Randolph Bonito," called Mary, and a big, red-faced man said, "Five." The Candrick family, with their three small children, went with him.

"Evers Mills." "Four."

"Lanny McMorris." "Two."

"Jane Garcia." "Three."

It went on for a long time. The sky grew darker and the air cooler. Lina shivered. She untied her sweater from around her waist and put it on. Light and warmth must go together here, she thought: warm in the day, when the bright light was in the sky, and cool at night. In Ember, the lights made no heat at all, and the temperature was always the same.

At the edges of the plaza, someone was raising a flame-tipped stick and lighting lanterns that hung from the eaves of buildings. They glowed deep yellow and red.

Mary was pointing at Mrs. Murdo now. "You, ma'am," she said. "Your child looks the sickest of anyone. We'll send you home with our doctor." She beckoned to a woman standing nearby, a tall, bony old woman with bushy gray hair chopped off just below her ears. She was wearing loose pants of faded blue and a rumpled tan shirt that was buttoned crookedly, so one side hung down lower than the other.

"Dr. Hester will take you," Mary said. "Dr. Hester Crane."

Lina stood up. She turned to Doon. "Will you be all right here?" she said. It made her uneasy to be separated from Doon and his father.

"We'll be fine," Doon said.

"No need to worry," said his father, spreading a blanket on the ground.

The doctor stooped down to look at Poppy, who drowsed in Mrs. Murdo's arms. She put a hand on Poppy's forehead—a big, knuckly hand, with veins like blue yarn. She pulled down the underside of Poppy's eye. "Um-hm," she said. "Yes. Well. Come along, I'll do what I can for her."

Lina cast an anxious glance at Doon.

"Come and find us in the morning," Doon said. "We'll be right here."

"This way," the doctor said. "Oh, wait." She scanned the mostly empty plaza. "Torren!" she called.

Lina heard the slap of footsteps on brick and saw a boy running toward them out of the darkness.

"We're going home now," the doctor said to him. "These people are coming with us."

The boy was younger than Lina. He had a strangely narrow face—as if someone had put a hand on either side of his head and pushed hard. His eyes were round blue dots. Above his high forehead, his light brown hair stood up in an untidy tuft.

He glared sideways at Lina and said nothing. The doctor headed up the road beside the river, walking with a long stride, her hands in her pockets and her head bent forward as if she were looking for something on the ground.

Staying close beside Mrs. Murdo, who was carrying the sleeping Poppy, Lina followed. The chilly evening air crept in through the threads of her sweater, and an insect hovering near her ear made a high, needle-like whine. The homesick feeling swelled so big inside her that she had to cross her arms tightly and clench her teeth to keep it from coming out.

CHAPTER 4

The Doctor's House

The sky had turned a deep blue now, almost black. At one edge shone a streak of brilliant crimson. In the houses of the village, one window and then another began to glow with a flickering yellow light.

They walked and walked. Each time they came to a doorway, or a gate in a wall, or stairs leading upward, Lina hoped this might be the house. Back in Ember, where she'd had the job of messenger, she'd been a tireless runner; running was her greatest joy. Tonight it was hard just to walk. She was so tired her feet felt like bricks. But Dr. Hester walked on and on, with the boy trotting ahead of her sometimes, and sometimes lagging back to stare at Lina and Mrs. Murdo and Poppy, until they came to the outer edge of the village. There, standing somewhat apart, was a low-roofed house. Except for a glimmer of light on its two windows, reflected from the reddening sky, it was in darkness, huddled beneath a great brooding plant the shape of a huge mushroom.

"Is that a pinetree?" Lina asked the doctor.

"Oak tree," the doctor said, so Lina understood that "tree" must mean all big plants, and they came in different kinds.

A path led to a wooden gate, which the doctor opened. They came into a shadowy, leaf-littered courtyard paved with uneven bricks. On three sides were the three wings of the house, like a square-cornered U. The eaves of the roof sloped down to form a walkway all around. In the failing light, Lina could just see that the courtyard was crowded with plants, some growing in the ground and some in pots of all sizes. Vines wound up the columns of the walkway and crawled along the edge of the roof.

"Come inside," the doctor said. She led the way to a door in the central part of the house. She and the boy went in. Lina stopped just inside the doorway, and Mrs. Murdo came up behind her, Poppy in her arms. They stood peering into the gloom. There was an odd pungent smell—like mushrooms or leaf mold, only sharper.

The doctor disappeared for a moment, and when she came back she held a lit candle. She moved around the room lighting more—two candles, three candles, four, until a wavery light filled the central part of the room. The corners remained in darkness.

"Come in, come in," the doctor said impatiently.

Lina moved forward. She felt grit beneath the soles of her shoes, and the tickle of dust in her nose. She was in a long, low room with clutter everywhere—clothes draped over the backs of armchairs, a shoe on a saggy couch, a plate with some bits of food on it sitting on the windowsill. At one end of the room were two doors, both of them closed. At the back, a stairway rose into a dark square hole in the ceiling. At the other end of the room, in the corner, was an open doorway—leading, Lina guessed, to the kitchen. Beside this doorway was a kind of hollow in the wall, framed by stones and containing some sticks and scraps of paper.

The doctor stooped down before this hollow place and held her candle to the sticks and paper there. In a moment, a flame leapt up. It was a bigger flame than Lina had ever seen, like a terrible orange hand, reaching up and out. Lina's heart knocked hard against her ribs. She stepped backward, bumping into Mrs. Murdo. They stood staring, Mrs. Murdo with a hand clutching Lina's shoulder.

The doctor turned around and saw them. "What's the matter?" she said.

Lina couldn't speak. Her eyes were fixed on the flames, which leapt higher and crackled.

Mrs. Murdo tried to answer. "It's, ah, it's—" She inclined her head toward the end of the room, where the first flame had become a dozen flames, licking upward, sending out flashes of orange light.

"Oh!" said the doctor. "The fire? You're not used to fire?"

Mrs. Murdo managed to smile apologetically. Lina just stared.

"It stays in the fireplace," the doctor said. "Not at all dangerous."

In Ember, there was never fire unless there was danger—someone's electric wiring had frayed and ignited, or a pot holder had fallen on a stove's electric burner. The only fire Lina had seen that wasn't dangerous was the tiny flame of a candle. This fire scared her.

In the window glass, reflections glimmered. The windows were set so deeply into the walls that there was a ledge at the bottom, wide enough to sit on. The boy, Torren, hiked himself up on one of these ledges and sat there, kicking his feet against the cabinet set in the wall below it. "Afraid of fire," he said in a low, scornful voice.

"Come in," the doctor said. "You can sit over there, if you like." She pointed to some chairs at the other end of the room, far from the fire, so that was where Lina and Mrs. Murdo sat. Poppy woke up enough to give a weak wail, and then she slumped into Mrs. Murdo's lap. "This will likely be the last fire of the season, anyway," said the doctor. "Nights will be getting warmer soon. We won't need one."

A creak sounded from outside, and then rapid foot-steps. Someone pounded on the door. Lina clutched Mrs. Murdo's hand.

But the doctor only sighed and moved to answer the knock. "Oh, it's you, William," she said. "What do you need?"

"Some of that ointment," said a man's voice. "I need it right now. My wife cut her hand. It's bleeding all over."

"Come in, come in, I'll get it," the doctor said, and she went into another room and rummaged around while the man stood shyly just inside the door, looking out of the corners of his eyes at Lina and Mrs. Murdo.

The doctor brought him his jar of ointment, and he went away. No more than ten minutes later, another knock came, this time from a young woman who wanted some willow bark medicine for her sister, who had a pounding headache. Again the doctor rattled around in the other room. She came out with a small bottle, and the woman hurried off with it.

"Are you the only doctor here?" Mrs. Murdo inquired.

"Yes," said Dr. Hester. "It's a never-ending job." She suddenly looked worried. "Did I give William the right jar? Yes, yes, the one on the third shelf, I'm sure I did." She gave a frazzled sigh. "Now let's tend to your little girl. Put her down here." She patted the couch that stood against the wall. "And wrap her in this." She retrieved a knitted blanket that had fallen on the floor, gave it a shake, and handed it to Mrs. Murdo. "I'll give her a swallow of medicine."

Poppy accepted two spoonfuls of medicine—it was something reddish that Dr. Hester poured from a jar—and spit out the third, whimpering. Lina's heart ached to see Poppy so sick. Most of the time, Poppy was a ball of energy, so quick and curious you never knew what she'd do next. She might chew up a valuable document, for instance, or trot off on an exploration of her own at exactly the wrong moment. Now she was limp and pale, like a little sprout that hadn't been watered.

Mrs. Murdo laid her on the bed. Lina sat by her and stroked her hair, and quite soon she went to sleep. The doctor disappeared into the kitchen, and Torren climbed the stairs and vanished into the room above.

All at once Lina was overcome with tiredness. The disorderly house, the unfriendly boy, the fire . . . all of it was strange and disturbing. And Poppy was terribly sick, which worried Lina so much that she felt a little sick herself. She sat down by Mrs. Murdo and laid her head on Mrs. Murdo's lap. She was vaguely aware of clattering and chopping noises coming from the kitchen, and then she dozed off into a confusing dream of lights and shadows. . . .

"Dinner!" shouted Torren. Lina bolted upright,

and he laughed. "Have you heard of food?" he said. "Have you heard of eating?"

They sat at the table, all of them but Poppy, and the doctor ladled out something from a big bowl. Lina wasn't sure what it was. Cold potatoes, she thought, and something else. She ate it because she was hungry. But when she had eaten she suddenly became so tired again that she could hardly move.

"Quite tasty," said Mrs. Murdo. "Thank you."

"Well," said the doctor. "Certainly. You're welcome." She started to stand up, then sat down again, looking flustered. "Maybe you'd like to read? Or . . . walk around? Or . . ."

"We're a bit tired," said Mrs. Murdo. "Perhaps we could go to bed."

Dr. Hester's face brightened. "Bed, yes," she said, standing up. "Of course, why didn't I . . . Let's see. Where will we put you?" She looked around, as if an extra bed might be hidden in the mess. "The loft, I suppose."

"No!" cried Torren. "That's my room!"

"It's the only place with two beds," said Dr. Hester. Picking up a candle, she made her way through the clutter to the stairway.

"They'll touch my things! And Caspar's things!" cried Torren.

"Don't be silly," said Dr. Hester, starting up the stairs.

"But where will I sleep?" Torren wailed.

"In the medicine room," said Dr. Hester. Tears had appeared in Torren's eyes, but the doctor didn't notice. She disappeared into the loft, and for a few minutes Lina heard thumps and scrapes from above.

"Come on up," the doctor called.

Lina climbed the stairs, and Mrs. Murdo came after, carrying Poppy. By the light of the doctor's candle, Lina saw two beds under a sloping ceiling. There was a chest at the foot of each bed. Some clothes hung from hooks, and some boxes were neatly lined up on the sill of the one window.

"Two beds, but three of you," said the doctor, frowning. "We could . . . hmm. We could put the baby . . ."

"It's all right," Lina said. "She'll sleep with me."

And a few minutes later, she was in bed, Poppy in the crook of her arm, covers drawn over them. "Good night," Mrs. Murdo said from the other bed, and the candle was blown out, and the room went dark—but not as dark as the rooms in Ember at night. Lina could still see a faint gray rectangle where the window was, because of the lights in the sky, the silver circle and the bright pinpoints. What are they called? she wondered. And who is Caspar? And how can the doctor stand to have that huge, awful fire right there on the floor of her house?

Everything here was the opposite of Ember.

Ember was dark and cold; this place was bright and hot. Ember was orderly; this place was disorderly. In Ember, everything was familiar to her. Here everything was strange. Will I learn to like it here? she wondered. Will I ever feel at home? She held Poppy tight against her and listened to her snuffly breathing for a long time before she fell asleep.

The First Town Meeting

While Lina slept, the three town leaders were holding a meeting. They sat at a table in the tower room of the town hall, which looked out over the plaza. Mary's hands were clasped tightly in front of her. Ben scowled, his gray eyebrows bunched together, deepening the two lines between them. Wilmer pulled nervously on one ear and looked from Mary to Ben and back to Mary.

"They can't stay here," said Mary. "There are too many of them. Where would we put them? How would we feed them?"

"Yes," said Wilmer. "But where can they go?"

No one spoke. They had no answer for that question. Outside the settlement of Sparks, the Empty Lands stretched for miles in all directions.

"They could go up to Pine Gap," said Wilmer. "Maybe."

Mary snorted and shook her head. "Don't be

ridiculous," she said. "That's at least two weeks' walk away. How could these feeble people travel that far? How could they carry enough food with them? Where would they *get* enough food, unless we emptied our storehouse and gave them everything?"

Wilmer nodded, knowing she was right. The people of Sparks knew of only three other settlements, and they'd heard from the roamers that those places were smaller and poorer than Sparks. Their inhabitants wouldn't want extra mouths to feed, either.

The three of them gazed out the window and down at the moonlit plaza, filled with strange sleeping people from a city under the earth. Four hundred of them, with no food, no possessions to speak of, and nowhere to go.

"What I fail to understand," said Ben, "is why this particular misfortune has happened to us." He paused, looked into the air to his left, and frowned. This was a habit of his; he seemed to need a pause and a frown every now and then to put together his thoughts. Wilmer and Mary had gotten used to waiting through these pauses. "I don't see that we deserve it," Ben went on after a few seconds, "having labored as diligently as we have. And just when we are starting to prosper at last, after so many years of . . . well, adversity is a mild word for it."

The others nodded, thinking of the hard years. There'd been winters when people shivered in tents and ate chopped-up roots and shriveled nuts. There had been years of drought and plagues of tomato worms and devastating crop failures that meant people had nothing to eat for months but cabbage and potatoes. There had been times when people had to work so hard to stay alive that they sometimes died just from being too tired to go on. No one wanted to go back to those times.

"So what do we do," said Mary, "if they can't stay and they can't go? What is the right thing to do?"

The others sat silent.

"Well, there's the Pioneer," said Wilmer. "As a temporary solution."

"True," said Ben.

"A good thought," said Mary, and Wilmer beamed. "So what about this," Mary went on. "We'll let them stay in the Pioneer. We'll give them water and food— we do have some extra in the storehouse. In exchange, they work—they help in the fields, they help with building, they do whatever there is to do. We'd have to teach them how. As far as I can see, they know nothing. After a while, when they're stronger, and when they know better how to get along, they can move on. They can set up their own village somewhere else."

"We'll have to watch them carefully if we let them stay," said Ben. "They're strange. We don't know what they might do."

"They seem fairly ordinary to me," said Mary.

"Except for the business about living in a cave."

"You believed that?" said Ben.

Mary shrugged. "The question is, shall we let them stay?"

"How long would we have to keep them," asked Wilmer, "before they were ready to go?"

"I don't know. Maybe six months? Let's see. It's near the end of Flowering now." Mary counted out the months on her fingers. "Shining, Burning, Browning, Cooling, Falling, Chilling. They could stay through the summer and fall seasons and leave at the end of Chilling."

"That would mean they'd be on their own for the winter," Wilmer pointed out.

"That's right," said Ben. "Are you suggesting we should keep them even longer? We'll be stretching ourselves to keep them at all."

They fell silent again, considering this.

Finally Mary spoke. "Shall we let them stay for six months, then?" she said. "And teach them as much as we can?"

No one really liked this idea. They thought of the food the refugees would need, which would mean less for their own people, and the bother of teaching them all the skills they'd need to survive on their own. Each one—Mary, Wilmer, and especially Ben—wished the unfortunate cave people would simply vanish.

But they weren't going to vanish, and the leaders

of Sparks knew that they must for the sake of their consciences do the right thing. They wanted to be wise, good leaders, unlike the leaders of the past, whose terrible mistakes had led to the Disaster. So they would be open-minded. They would be generous.

With this in mind, the three leaders voted:

Mary voted yes, the cave people should stay.

Ben voted yes, reluctantly.

Wilmer voted yes.

So it was agreed: They would give them a place to stay. They would help them for six months. After that, the strangers would have to take care of themselves.

Mary, Ben, and Wilmer shook hands on this agreement, but none of them said out loud what they were thinking: that even after six months, the people of Ember would be hard-pressed to start a town. The founders of Sparks had known carpentry and farming, and even so it had taken them two years just to build rough shelters and get the rocks out of the fields. They had known how to manage animals and build good soil, but still their animals sometimes died of disease and hunger in the many years when the crops failed. They had known to expect harsh weather, wolves, and bandits, and still they suffered losses from all three.

The town leaders knew in their hearts that in this vast, empty country, where there were a thousand dangers the people of Ember did not understand, they would *never* be able to take care of themselves.

CHAPTER 5

The Pioneer

In the village the next morning, criers ran through the streets calling to the people of Sparks. They told them to bring out all their old blankets, pillows, towels, and rags, and any clothes they no longer needed. They were to heap these on the street in front of their houses. From the storehouse, people collected food—things that didn't need to be cooked, like apples from the prior fall, and dried apricots, and bread, and big hunks of cheese. Doon, who had gotten up at the first sign of light in the sky, watched these preparations with rising excitement.

By midday a caravan was moving southward out of the village. It was composed of strange vehicles that the villagers called "truck-wagons," or just "trucks." They were made of rusty metal and had four fat black wheels. At the front was a boxy part, like a metal chest with a rounded top, and behind that was a higher box with two seats in it where the drivers sat. The back of the truck was flat; this was where the crates of supplies were loaded. Attached to each of these trucks by sturdy ropes were two big, squarish, muscular animals, by far the most enormous animals Doon had ever seen. They made snuffling noises, and sometimes a low sort of groan.

"What are they?" Doon asked someone walking near him.

"Oxen," the man answered. "Like cows, you know? That milk comes from?"

Doon had never heard of cows. He had thought milk came as powder in a box. He didn't say this, of course. He just nodded.

"And what does 'truck' mean?" he asked. He understood the "wagon" part.

The man looked surprised. "It just means 'truck,'" he said. "You know—what people used to drive in the old times. There are millions of them, trucks and cars, everywhere. They used to run on their own, without oxen. They had engines in here." He rapped on the front of the truck. "You poured stuff called gasleen on the engine, and it made the wheels turn. Now, since we don't have gasleen anymore, we take the engines out, and that makes the trucks light and easy to pull."

Doon didn't ask what "gasleen" was. He didn't

want to show his ignorance all at once. He'd spread his questions around, find out just a few things from one person at a time.

He and his father walked along together beside one of the trucks. Doon had expected Lina to be with them, but by the time the caravan left she hadn't come. That was all right. She'd easily find out where they'd gone and come later.

Doon's father still had sore muscles from the long walk of the days before, so Doon soon went ahead of him. He was bursting with energy and joy and simply could not walk slowly. He took deep breaths of sweet-smelling morning air. Over his head, the sky was a deep, clear blue, a thousand times bigger than the black lid that had covered Ember, and around him the green-and-golden land seemed to stretch away without end. Doon kept wondering where the edges were. He made his way to the front of the procession and asked Wilmer, who was trotting along with his arms swinging jauntily.

"Edges?" said Wilmer, glancing down.

"Yes. I mean, if I were standing way over there"— he pointed to the horizon, where the sky seemed to meet the land—"would I be at the edge of this place? And what's beyond the edge?"

"There is no edge," said Wilmer, looking at Doon as if he must have something wrong with him. "The earth is a sphere—a huge, round ball. If you kept going and going, you'd eventually come back to where you started."

This nearly knocked the breath out of Doon, it was so strange and hard to comprehend. He thought at first that Wilmer was playing a joke on him, thinking he was a fool. But Wilmer's expression was plainly puzzled, not sly. He must be telling the truth.

There were a million mysteries here, Doon thought. He would explore them all! He would learn everything! That morning, he'd already learned the words *sun, tree, wind, star,* and *bird.* He'd learned *dog, chicken, goat,* and *bread.*

He had never in his life felt so good. He felt as huge as the land around him and as clear and bright as the air. No laboring in dank tunnels here; no running through dark streets to escape pursuit. Now he was out in the open, free. And he was powerful, too, in a way he hadn't been before. He had done something remarkable—saved his people from their dying city— and, along with Lina, he would be known for that deed all his life. He gazed around at this new world full of life and beauty, and he felt proud to have brought his people here.

The road passed the last houses of the village and ran along the river, which was wide and slow, with grasses bending along its banks. The trucks rattled. Clouds of dust billowed from their wheels. All around Doon rose a babble of voices as people pointed things out in tones of astonishment.

"Look—something white floating in the sky!"

"Did you see that little animal with the big tail?"

"Do you feel that? The air is *moving!*"

Children darted every which way, daring each other to touch the broad sides of the oxen, plucking blossoms from the brambles at the edge of the road, jumping onto the trucks for a quick ride until they were shooed off again.

And the sun shone down on everyone. The people of Ember loved the strange feeling of heat on the tops of their heads. They put their hands up often to touch their warm hair.

The road went up a gentle rise and around a clump of trees. "Here we are!" cried Wilmer, sweeping his arm out proudly. "The Pioneer Hotel!"

At the crest of the slope stood a building bigger than any Doon had ever seen. It was three stories high and very long, with a wing at each end perpendicular to the main part. Windows marched in three rows across its walls. In the center, overlooking a long field that sloped down to the river, was what must once have been a grand entrance—wide steps, a roof held up by columns, a double doorway. But the building was grand no more. It was very old, Doon could tell; its walls were gray and stained, and most of the windows were no more than dark holes. The roof had sagged inward in some places. Grass grew right up to the steps, and far down at the other end, Doon could see that a tree had fallen against the building and smashed a corner of it.

Ben Barlow strode across the wide, weedy field in front of the hotel and climbed the steps. Wilmer followed. He leaned against a column, and Ben took a position on the top step and waited for the crowd of refugees to assemble before him. Doon wove among the people until he found his father again, and they stood together.

Ben held up both hands and called, "Attention, please!" The crowd grew silent. "Welcome to your new home, the Pioneer Hotel," he said.

A cheer arose from the crowd. Ben frowned and held up both hands, palms out, and the cheer died away. "It is a *temporary* home only," he said. "We cannot, of course, keep you here in Sparks on a permanent basis. To do so would severely strain our resources and no doubt cause resentment and deprivation among our people." Ben cleared his throat and frowned into the air. Then he went on. "We have decided you may stay here for six months—through summer and fall, to the end of the month of Chilling. After that time, with the training you'll receive from us, you will go out into the Empty Lands and found a village of your own."

The people of Ember glanced at each other in surprise. Found their own village? Some of them smiled eagerly at this idea; others looked uncertain. The city of Ember had been constructed *for* them. All they'd ever had to do was repair work as the buildings got older. They'd never built anything from scratch. But, Doon said to himself, thinking about all this, I'm sure we could learn.

Ben went on. "The Pioneer Hotel has seventy-five rooms," he said, "plus a big dining room, a ballroom, offices, and a lobby. There will be adequate space for everyone."

Excited murmurs swept through the crowd. Doon started doing the math in his head. Four hundred and seventeen people divided by seventy-five rooms equaled five or six people per room. That sounded crowded, but maybe they were big rooms. And then there were the dining room and the ballroom, whatever that was, maybe those would hold ten or twenty people. . . .

"Now, of course this building is somewhat less than fully functional," Ben went on. "You won't have water pumps here, as we do in the village. But the river is close, just down this slope, and the water is clean. The river will provide water for drinking, bathing, and washing clothes. Your toilets will be outside—you'll start digging them tomorrow, once we've organized you into work teams. Today you'll settle into your rooms." He paused, frowning. The two lines between his eyebrows deepened. "There's not much furniture left in the rooms," he said. "Maybe a few rooms still have beds, but I think we've taken most of them by now. You'll be sleeping on the floor."

"Sleeping on the floor!" The voice came from somewhere behind Doon. Its tone was somewhere between outrage and amused disbelief. Doon turned around to see whose it was. In the middle of the crowd he spotted a tall boy, a young man really, who seemed to be standing up on something—maybe a rock or tree stump—so he could look out over people's heads. He was handsome in a sharp-edged way. His jaw was square-cornered. His shoulders were straight as a board. His dark hair was combed back from his face and slicked down, so his head looked neat and round and hard, and his eyes were as pale as bits of sky.

Doon recognized this boy, though he didn't know him—his name was Mick, or Trick, or Mack, or something like that.

"On the floor, yes," said Ben. "But we'll give you as many blankets as we can."

The boy's sharp voice came again, rising above the others. "One more question, sir: What about food?"

The question rippled through the crowd: Yes, food. What will we eat?

Ben raised his voice. "Please listen!" he shouted. "Listen!" All faces turned toward him again. Doon could see that Ben's eyes were fixed on the boy with the sharp voice. Ben had the look of a teacher speaking to a slightly unruly class. "Eating will work this way," he said. "You will be assigned to households in the village—four or five people to each house. At noontime, you'll go there for your main meal." He paused and frowned. "As for breakfast and dinner—your lunchtime family will give you food to take away with you, some to eat in the evening, and some to save for the next morning. They will be as generous as they can. But remember—we do not have an *abundance* of extra food. Your arrival means less for everyone." He gazed at the crowd for a moment and took a breath. "Is that clear?" he said. "Any questions?"

No one spoke for a moment, and then the tall boy said, "No, sir. Lead on."

So Ben led the way into the lobby of the ancient Pioneer Hotel. Doon and his father stayed close together, stepping carefully. It was hard to see. The only light came from the doorway behind them and from a hole in a great dirt-encrusted glass dome three stories above their heads. The floor was littered with chunks of fallen plaster and gritty with dirt that had blown in over the years.

"This place needs work," Doon whispered to his father.

His father brushed a spiderweb away from his face. "Yes," he said. "But we're lucky to be here. We could be sleeping on the ground."

Ben led them down a hall to the left, to a vast

room with high windows, where dusty sunshine slanted across the broken tiles of the floor. "This was the dining room," Ben called out. Doon saw only a few chairs, lying on their sides, most of them with a leg broken or missing.

Beyond the dining room was a room even more immense, with a raised platform at one end, a high ceiling, and a wooden floor. "The ballroom," Ben said. "In earlier years, before the Disaster, musicians sat up there on the stage. People danced out here." At the great high windows hung tatters of faded rose-colored cloth that had been curtains years ago.

"Smells moldy in here." It was that boy again. His clear, sharp voice carried over other voices even though it wasn't much louder. "Reminds me of home."

People laughed. It was true—the smell of mold was common in the underground city of Ember. There was a bit of comfort in it.

Doon suddenly remembered the name of this tall boy who kept speaking out. It was Tick—Tick Hassler. In Ember, Doon recalled, Tick had been a hauler. He had pulled carts full of produce from the greenhouses to the stores, and garbage from the stores out to the trash heaps. Doon hadn't known him then, but he remembered seeing him, pulling his loaded cart with his whole long body slanted forward and a fierce grin of effort on his face. He'd pulled his carts faster than anyone else.

Ben led them to the stairs, and they climbed to the floors above. Long, dim corridors lined with doors stretched the length of the building. Some of the doors were open. Doon looked through them as he passed. All the rooms were more or less the same: windows across one wall, a stained and faded carpet, a couple of broken lamps lying on the floor. A few of the rooms had beds, and several had other furniture—chests with their drawers hanging crookedly out, end tables, a chair or two. He stepped into some of the rooms and found that they had bathrooms as well, with rust-stained sinks and bathtubs that were homes to spiders.

For the next couple of hours, people swarmed through the corridors and up and down the stairs, calling to each other as they chose their rooms and decided who to share them with. People grouped together, chose a room, then changed their minds and teamed up with another group. Shouts rang through the halls.

"Jake! Down here!"

"No, this one is better, it has a chair!"

"Mama! Where are you?"

"This room's full! No more people!"

Doon heard Tick's voice ringing out over the others now and then. He wondered which room he was choosing, and who he was choosing to live with.

Finally everyone was settled. Doon and his father chose a room on the second floor, room 215, along with two other people. One was Edward Pocket, who had been Ember's librarian. He was a friend of Doon's, in a way. He was old and often crabby, but he liked Doon, who had been a frequent visitor to the library. The other was Sadge Merrall, the man who had tried to venture out into the Unknown Regions beyond the city of Ember. For a while after that experience, he'd gone out of his mind with fright and raved in Harken Square about monsters and doom. He'd recovered somewhat since then. In spite of his terror, he'd managed to climb into one of the boats that took people out of the city to the new world. But he was still a fearful, trembling sort of person. Nearly everything about this unfamiliar place scared him. He refused to go near the window of their new room. "Something might come in," he said. "There are things here that fly."

The four of them set to work fixing up the room. It was full of cobwebs, two of its three windows were broken, and bits of dry leaves and splinters of glass littered the carpet. It also had a dresser with three drawers, a padded armchair with a sunken seat, and two end tables with lamps.

They took their socks off and used them as dust rags to sweep away the cobwebs. They picked up the leaves and glass and tossed them out the windows. They put the lamps out in the hall—they were useless, of course, since there was no electricity—and they lined up the dresser and end tables in the middle of the room to make a sort of wall dividing the space in two. There was enough room for Doon and his father to spread their blankets on the floor on one side, and Sadge to spread his on the other. Edward Pocket, who was very short, decided to spread his blanket on the floor of the large closet, which had a sliding door. He said he didn't mind being slightly cramped; he liked the privacy.

That night, Doon didn't sleep much. He lay on his folded blankets and stared up through the window at the dark sky. His mind teemed with possibilities—so much to do, so much to learn! He felt suddenly older and stronger, though it had been less than a week since he'd left Ember. But he was a new person in this new world. He would do new things and be friends with new people. Maybe, he thought, remembering the voice that had stood out above the others that day, he'd be friends with Tick.

CHAPTER 6

Breakfast with Disaster

Lina's first morning in the doctor's house did not go well. Poppy was still sleeping when she awakened, and so was Mrs. Murdo, so she got up quietly, put on the same pricker-stuck clothes she'd been wearing the day before, and went down the stairs. The doctor was standing by the table in what must have been her nightgown—a patched brown sack that hung to her knees. The hair at the back of her head was sticking up. She was leafing through a big book that lay on the table.

"Oh!" said the doctor, seeing Lina. "You're up. I was just looking for . . . I was trying to find . . . Well. I suppose it's time for breakfast."

The doctor's kitchen looked like a complete mess to Lina. In Ember, the kitchens had been spare, stocked with only what was needed—some shelves, an electric stove, a refrigerator. But in Dr. Hester's kitchen there were a thousand things. Wide wooden counters ran along two sides, and on the counters was a jumble of jugs and pans and tubs and pitchers, big spoons and knives and scoops, and jars and bottles full of things that looked like pebbles and brown powder and tiny white teeth. There were baskets piled with vegetables Lina had never seen before. In the corner squatted a bulging black iron box. She thought it might be a cabinet, since there was a door in its front.

"We'll see if we have any eggs this morning," said Dr. Hester. "That would be a start."

Torren appeared suddenly from the other room. "Eggs!" he cried. "I want one!"

Eggs? Lina didn't know what that meant. She followed the doctor and Torren through a door that led outside. Beyond the door was a place like an open-air version of the Ember greenhouses, only the plants growing here were far bigger and wilder, curling and twining and shooting upward with tremendous energy. Lina recognized some of them: bean vines climbed up frames of netting, tomato vines grew on wooden towers, chard and kale plants spurted up like big green fountains.

In among the rows of plants, some fat, fluffed-up, two-legged creatures of the kind she'd seen on her way into town yesterday waddled along, poking at the ground with a sharp thing like a tooth that stuck out from their faces.

"What are those?" asked Lina.

"Chickens," said the doctor. "We'll check their nests and see if they've left us anything." She bent down and went through the door of a wooden hut in the back of the garden, and when she came out she had spiderwebs in her hair and a white ball in her hand—not a round ball, but one that looked as if it had been stretched sideways. "Just one today," she said.

"I want it!" cried Torren.

"No," said the doctor. "You've had plenty of eggs. This one is for our guest." She handed the egg to Lina, who took it gingerly. It was smooth and warm. She had no idea what it was. It felt more like a stone than food. Was it some sort of large bean? Or a fruit with a hard white peel?

"Thank you," she said doubtfully.

"See, she doesn't even want it!" Torren said. "She doesn't even know what it is!" He gave her a hard shove, making her stagger sideways.

"Quit that!" cried Lina. "You almost pushed me over!"

"Torren—" said the doctor, stretching out a hand. But Torren ignored her.

"I'll push you again," he said, and he did, harder.

Lina stumbled backward and caught herself just in time to keep from falling into the cabbage bed. She felt a flash of fury. She raised her arm and threw the egg at Torren, and it hit him on the shoulder. But instead of bouncing off, it broke open, and a slimy yellow mess dripped down his shirt.

"Now look what you've done!" Torren screamed. "It's ruined!" He put his head down as if to run at Lina and butt her, but the doctor grabbed his arm.

"Stop this," she said.

Lina was horrified. Disgusted, too. That yellow goop was something people ate? She was glad she didn't have to. But she felt stupid for what she'd done. "I'm sorry I wrecked the egg," she said. "I didn't know what it was."

"You wrecked my shirt, too!" shouted Torren, wriggling in the doctor's grasp.

"But you *pushed* me," Lina said.

"Well, yes," said the doctor in a weary voice. "That's how it goes, doesn't it? Someone pushes, someone pushes back. Pretty soon everything's ruined."

"Everything?" said Lina. "But can't his shirt be washed?"

"Oh, yes, of course," the doctor said. "I didn't mean that. Never mind." She let go of Torren. "I guess we'll have bread and apricots for breakfast."

Mrs. Murdo had come downstairs now, leaving the still-sleeping Poppy in bed. They all had breakfast together. Lina ate five apricots. She loved them for their taste and for the feel of them, too—their rosy-orange skins were velvety, like a baby's cheek. She also liked the bread, which was toasted and crunchy, and the jam, which was dark purple and sweet. Mrs. Murdo kept saying, "My, this is tasty," and asking questions about what bread was made of, and what a blackberry looked like, and why apricots had a sort of wooden rock in the middle. Dr. Hester seemed a bit flummoxed by these questions, but she did her best to explain. She was nice, Lina decided, but distracted. Her mind seemed to be elsewhere. She didn't notice that Torren was putting all his apricot pits into his pocket, for instance—or maybe she didn't care.

When breakfast was over, Torren went up to the loft and came back down carrying a bulging bag. "These are my *things*," he said loudly. "I don't want anyone touching them." He knelt down and opened the doors of the cabinet under the window seat and thrust the bag inside. "Caspar gave them to me, and anyone who touches them gets in *big* trouble." He closed the cabinet doors and glared at Lina. What an awful boy, Lina thought. How could nice Dr. Hester have such a horrid son?

Lina had thought she'd go back to the plaza and find Doon right after breakfast. But she changed her mind when she went upstairs to waken her little sister. Poppy seemed so sick that Lina was frightened. She didn't want to leave her. She brought her downstairs, and all that morning, Poppy lay on the couch, sometimes sleeping, sometimes wailing, sometimes just lying much too still with her mouth open and her breath coming in short gasps. Lina and Mrs. Murdo sat on either side of her, putting cool cloths on her forehead and trying to get her to drink the water and the medicine the doctor provided. "I don't know what's causing this child's fever," the doctor said. "All I can do is try to bring it down."

After all the walking of the days before, Lina was glad to sit still. She settled into a corner of the couch, her legs tucked under her, and watched the doctor dither about. She seemed to have a hundred things to do and a hundred things on her mind. She'd stand for a second staring into the air, murmuring to herself, "Now. All right. First I must look up . . . ," and then dart over to her enormous book and shuffle through its pages. After a second or two, she'd suddenly set the book down and hurry off to the kitchen, where she would take a bottle of liquid or jar of powder down from a shelf and measure some of it into a pot. Or she'd dash out to the garden and come back with an armload of onions. Or she'd vanish out the back door and appear again with a sheaf of dried stems or leaves. It was hard to tell what she was doing, or if she was really accomplishing anything at all. Every now and then she would come back to Poppy and spoon some medicine into her mouth or put a cold, damp cloth on her forehead.

"What is that enormous book?" Lina asked her.

"Oh!" said the doctor. She always seemed a little startled to be spoken to. "Well, it's about medicine. A lot of it is useless, though." She picked up the book from the floor and riffled its pages. "You look up 'infection' and it says, 'Prescribe antibiotics.' What are antibiotics? Or you look up 'fever' and it says, 'Give aspirin.' Aspirin is some kind of painkiller, I think, but we don't have it."

"We had aspirin in Ember," said Mrs. Murdo, rather proudly. "Although I believe it had nearly run out by the end."

"Is that so," said the doctor. "Well, what we have is plants. Herbs, roots, funguses, that sort of thing. I have a couple of old books that tell about which ones to use. Sometimes they work, sometimes they don't." She ran a hand through her short, wiry hair, making it poke out on one side. "So much to know," she said, "and so much to do . . ." Her voice trailed off.

"I suppose your son is a help to you," said Mrs. Murdo.

"My son?"

"The boy, Torren."

"Oh," said Dr. Hester. "He's not my son."

"He's not?" said Lina.

"No, no," the doctor said. "Torren and his brother, Caspar—they're my sister's boys. They live with me because their parents were killed in an avalanche years ago. They were in the mountains, on an ice-gathering trip."

"And the boy has no other relatives?" asked Mrs. Murdo.

"He has an uncle," said the doctor. "But the uncle didn't want the trouble of bringing up the boys. He offered to have this house built for me if I'd take them on." The doctor shrugged. "So I did."

"What is an avalanche?" Lina asked. "What are mountains?"

"Lina," said Mrs. Murdo. "It's not polite to ask too many questions."

"I don't mind," the doctor said. "I forgot that you wouldn't know these things. You really lived underground?"

"Yes," said Lina.

Dr. Hester scrunched her gray eyebrows together. "But why would there be a city underground?"

Lina said she didn't know. All she knew was what was in the notebook she and Doon had found on their way out. It was a journal kept by one of the first inhabitants of Ember, who told of the fifty couples brought in from the outside world, each with two babies to raise in the underground city. "They thought there was some danger," Lina said. "They made Ember as a place to keep people safe."

"It was that long ago, then," said the doctor. "Before the Disaster."

"I don't know," said Lina. "I guess so. What disaster?"

"The Disaster that just about wiped out the human race," said Dr. Hester. "I'll tell you about it sometime, but not right now. I have to go and see to Burt Webb's infected finger."

"Can I ask one more question?" said Lina.

The doctor nodded.

"Why is this place called Sparks?"

"Oh," said the doctor, smiling a little. "It was the People of the Last Truck who gave it that name—our twenty-two founders. They were among the very few people who survived the Disaster. For a while they found food by driving around from one place to another in the old towns, using cars and trucks that still had a sort of energy-making stuff called gasleen—'gas' for short."

Cars and trucks? thought Lina. Gasleen? But she didn't want to interrupt, so she didn't ask.

"When food and gas began to run out," the doctor went on, "they decided it was time to start a new life somewhere else. They found one last truck that still had gas, and they loaded it up with supplies—food in cans and boxes, tools, clothes and blankets, seeds, everything useful they could find. Then they drove east, out across the Empty Lands, staying close to the river. Right here, the truck broke down. When they opened the hood, a great spray of sparks shot up out of the engine. So they decided to settle in this spot, and they named it Sparks." The doctor stood up and looked around for her medicine bag. "It turned out to be a fitting name in another way," she said. "Sparks are a beginning. We are the beginning of something here, or trying to be, the way a spark is the beginning of a fire."

"But fires are terrible," said Lina.

"Terrible or wonderful," said the doctor, who had found her bag behind a chair and was heading out the door. "They can go either way."

Lina never did go down to the plaza that day. She didn't think Doon would worry—he knew Poppy was sick, and he'd figure out that Lina had stayed with her. She would go and look for him tomorrow, she decided, and find out then what was happening to the people of Ember.

Late in the afternoon, Lina went outside and sat on a rickety bench in the courtyard of the doctor's house, waiting to see if anyone was going to make dinner. It seemed unlikely. The doctor was off treating someone's toothache, and Mrs. Murdo was up in the loft with Poppy, who had started crying an hour ago and still had not stopped.

A door opened, and Torren came outside. He sauntered over to Lina and stood in front of her.

"Your sister is probably going to die," he said.

Lina jerked back. "She is *not.*"

Torren shrugged. "Looks like it to me," he said. "Looks to me like she has the plague." He sat down on a wooden chair, where he could stare straight into Lina's face. He was wearing a sort of undershirt—it was white and looked like a sack with holes for neck and arms—and his thin legs stuck out from baggy shorts of the same material. He had combed his hair so that it stood up like a tuft of grass at the top of his forehead, making his long, narrow face look even longer.

"I don't know what you're talking about," Lina said.

"You don't know about the Three Plagues?" said Torren in a tone of exaggerated surprise. "Or the Four Wars? You've never heard of the Disaster?"

"I've heard of it," said Lina. "But I don't know what it is. I don't know about anything here."

"Well, then, I'll tell you," he said. "You can't go around being so ignorant."

She said nothing. She didn't like this boy's superior attitude, but she wanted to know everything there was to know. She would let him tell her, but she wasn't going to ask him to.

"It was a long time ago," he said. He spoke in a precise, teacherly voice. "There were millions of people in the world then. They were all geniuses. They could make their voices travel around the world, and they could see people who were miles away. They could fly."

He paused, waiting, no doubt, for Lina to be amazed.

She *was* amazed, but she wasn't going to show it. Besides, he was probably lying. She just nodded.

"They could make music come down out of the air. They had thousands of smooth roads and could go anywhere they wanted, really fast. They had pictures that moved." He waited again. He took a few apricot pits from his pocket and rattled them idly in the palm of his hand.

All right, she would ask. "What do you mean, pictures that moved?"

"Didn't think you'd know that one," Torren said with a tight little smile. "They were huge pictures, taller than a house. They were called movies. You'd look at a wall and see a story happening on it, with voices and other sounds."

"How do you know all this?" asked Lina. She thought he might easily be making it up.

"We learn it in school," said Torren. "They teach us *a lot* about the old times, so we won't forget."

"Have you seen a moving picture, then?"

"Of course not," he said. "You have to have electricity. There hasn't been any for a long time." He chucked one of the pits at a bird that was about to drink from the water dish. The splash scared it away.

"We had electricity," Lina said, glad to score a point over him. "We had it in Ember, until it ran out.

We had street lights, and lamps in our houses, and electric stoves in the kitchen."

For a moment Torren looked dismayed. "But did you have *movies*?" he said.

Lina shook her head. "Anyway," she said, "what does all this have to do with my sister?"

"I'm about to tell you, if you'd just let me." The important tone came back into his voice. "So there were all these billions of people, but there got to be too many of them. They messed up the world. That was why the Three Plagues came. But before the Three Plagues, they had the Four Wars." Once again he paused and looked at her in that infuriating way, lifting his thin eyebrows.

"Just tell me," she said. "Don't look at me like that."

"You don't know about the Four Wars?"

"No. War—what's that?"

"A war is when one bunch of people fights with another bunch, when both of them want the same thing. Like for instance if there's some good land, and two groups of people want to live there."

"Why can't they both live there?"

"They don't *want* to live there *together*," he said, as if this were a stupid question. "Also you could have a war because of revenge. Say one group of people does something bad to another group, like steal their chickens. Then the first group does something bad back in revenge. That could start a war. The two groups would try to kill each other, and the ones who killed the most would win."

"They'd kill each other over chickens?"

"That's just an example. In the Four Wars, they were fighting over bigger things. Like who should get some big chunk of land. Or whether you should believe in this god or that god. Or who got to have the gold and the oil."

All of this was enormously confusing to Lina. She didn't know the meaning of "god" or "gold," and she wasn't sure what he meant by "oil." "You mean," she said, thinking of the jars that had once been stocked in the storerooms of Ember, "the kind of oil you cook with?"

Torren rolled his eyes. "You *really* don't know anything," he said. He flung the rest of the pits he was holding at three little red-headed birds pecking at the weeds between the bricks, and the birds scattered, cheeping. "This was really beautiful, valuable oil. Everyone wanted it, and there wasn't enough of it to go around, so they fought over it."

"They hit each other?"

"Much worse than that," said Torren. He leaned forward, elbows on his knees, and in a low, husky voice told Lina about the weapons they had had in those days, the guns that let you kill people without even getting near them, and the bombs that could flatten and burn whole cities at once. "They set the cities on fire all over the world," Torren said. His small eyes glittered. "And afterward came the plagues."

"I don't know what a plague is," Lina said.

"A sickness," said Torren. "The kind where one person catches it from another person, and it spreads around fast before you can stop it."

"We had one of those," Lina said. "The coughing sickness—it would come sometimes and kill a lot of people and then go away again."

"We had three," said Torren, as if three plagues were better than one. "There was the one where you wither away, like you're starving to death; the one where you feel like you're on fire and you die of heat; and the one where you suddenly can't breathe. No one knew where they came from, they just rose up and swept over the whole world like a wind."

Lina shuddered. She was tired, all at once, of listening to Torren, who took such pleasure in describing horrors and saying words she didn't understand.

"So," Torren said. "The Four Wars and the Three Plagues—those together were the Disaster. When it finally got over with, hardly any people were left. That's why we had to start all over again." He stood up and brushed away a twig that was clinging to his shorts. "We don't have war anymore," he said. "Our leaders say we must never have war again. And besides, there's no one to fight against. But if we ever *do* have to have one, we'll win, because we have the Terrible Weapon."

"The Terrible Weapon?" said Lina. "What's that?"

But just then Mrs. Murdo came out the door with Poppy in her arms. Lina jumped up and ran over to her. "Is she better?"

"She's a little better." Poppy lay against Mrs. Murdo's shoulder, her head turned sideways, her eyes dull. "Wy-na," she said in a small voice. Lina ruffled her fine brown hair.

Torren cast an indifferent glance at Mrs. Murdo and walked away across the courtyard. The gate clattered behind him.

"Poppy doesn't have a plague, does she?" Lina said.

"A plague? Certainly not," said Mrs. Murdo. "Whatever gave you that idea?"

"That boy," said Lina. "That horrible boy."

CHAPTER 7

A Day of New People

The next day, back in the plaza, Ben Barlow organized the residents of the Pioneer Hotel into teams. The teams would work together and eat lunch together. Each team would be led by someone from Sparks, who would decide where that team's labor was most needed each day. Some days a team might work with the people of Sparks at the bakery or the shoe workshop or the wagon yard; other days they might do a job on their own, such as repairing a fence or digging a ditch. Sooner or later, nearly everyone would have done nearly every kind of work. This was the best way for them to learn, Ben said.

Doon's team included his father, two teachers from the Ember school (Miss Thorn and Mrs. Polster), Clary Laine, the greenhouse manager, and Edward Pocket, the librarian, who would join them for lunch but not work with them because he was so old.

Doon found Lina in the crowd—the first time he'd seen her since they arrived. He told her about the Pioneer Hotel; she told him about the doctor's house and what she'd learned from Torren about the Disaster. Lina and Mrs. Murdo were told they'd be a team of two with the job of helping Dr. Hester, since they were staying at her house. They were sent home, and all the other work teams went off to their first project: digging the hotel toilets.

They went out into the scrubby woods behind the Pioneer. The work leaders had brought picks and shovels from town; they gave each person a tool. "You'll dig fifty holes," one of the leaders said, "each one six feet deep. Then you'll build a shelter of scrap lumber around each one."

But the people of Ember had never done much digging or picking. They had to be shown how to put a foot on the shovel's edge to drive it into the dirt, and how to lift the pick over their shoulders and bring it down hard. At first they scraped and hacked awkwardly at the hard, dry earth, grunting with effort, dislodging only a few crumbs of dirt with each stroke. After ten minutes of hard work, they'd made hardly more than shallow dips in the dirt. They were breathing fast. "Did you say six *feet* deep?" someone called out.

"That's right," came the answer.

So the Emberites set themselves to the task, which

was for most of them the hardest work they'd ever done. After an hour, Doon had blisters on both hands and a kink in his neck. Some of the others had given up entirely and had flopped down onto the ground, dripping with sweat and aching in every muscle. Doon made himself keep going, but he was glad when the work finally stopped at noon and the team leaders marched them back into the town. He heard people murmuring to each other as they walked. "Do you think we'll have to work like this *every day*?" "It'll make us strong, I guess." "Or else kill us."

Each team was assigned to a different household for lunch. Doon's team went with the Parton family. Through the streets of the village, they followed a stout, cheerful woman named Martha Parton, whose wide rear end wagged from side to side as she walked. "Here we are," she said after a few minutes. She opened an unpainted wooden door and ushered her six guests inside. "Welcome to our home," she said.

Doon looked around the low-ceilinged room. At one end was a long wooden table; at the other, a couple of benches stood before a niche in the smoke-stained wall. Sitting on the benches were two people, who got up and came forward as Martha introduced them. "My husband, Ordney," Martha said. He was tall and narrow, with a mustache like a brown toothbrush under his nose. "And my son, Kensington."

Kensington was a little younger than Doon, a

skinny boy with yellow hair, big ears, and a freckled nose. He kept his eyes on the floor, except for a couple of quick, curious glances. "Hi," he said to the floor in a soft, shy voice.

"And these," Martha Parton said to her family, sweeping her arm in the direction of the guests, "are the people from underground." She raised her eyebrows at them. "You're lucky to have found your way here," she said. "The only other settlements we know of are little miserable ones hundreds of miles away. Everything else is just hard, rocky dirt, and ruins, and grass."

"And you've not only come to the right place," added Ordney. "You've come at the right time. It's taken years of hard work, but Sparks is finally doing well."

"Now!" said Martha, clapping her hands. "Time to eat!"

They sat down at the big table, and Martha brought out dishes of food. "I suppose you've never tasted anything like this," she said, handing around a bowl of fresh peas. "Just picked this morning. And this is pumpkin bread, made from what I canned of last year's crop. Good, isn't it? Did you have pumpkin bread where you came from?"

"No, indeed," said Doon's father.

"We did have peas, though," said Clary. "Grown in our greenhouses."

"And very fine they were," said Mrs. Polster loyally. "Though slightly smaller than these."

"Probably you haven't had pickled carrots, either," Martha said, passing the dish around. "These are from my mother's famous recipe."

"We did have carrots," said Mrs. Polster. "A nice pale orange, some of them fully four inches long."

"Is that right," said Martha. "Ours are twelve inches, usually."

Miss Thorn picked delicately at her food, making a polite comment now and then. Edward Pocket ate with such a vigorous appetite that he had no time for talking. Kensington ate steadily and silently. Every time Doon glanced his way, he found the boy staring at him, but as soon as their eyes met, Kensington looked back at his plate.

Ordney Parton cleared his throat. Apparently this meant he was going to speak, because his family all instantly looked at him. "I never knew," he said, "that there was a kind of people who lived underground. Must feel strange to you here on the surface."

"Actually," said Doon, "we aren't a different kind of people. This place feels familiar, in a way, because we came from here originally."

"From here? Oh, I don't think so," said Martha. "You don't look a bit like us. You're so much—well, smaller, if you'll pardon my saying so. And paler."

"True," said Clary, "but I suppose that's because of

living in a dark place for so long. Everything is bigger and brighter here."

"But why do you think you came from here?" Martha asked.

"Because of a notebook we found," Doon said. "It was written by someone from this world who went to live in Ember right at the beginning. All the people of Ember came from this world."

"Is that so," said Martha, eyeing Doon skeptically. "Well, I must say, it's the strangest thing *I've* ever heard."

Doon's father changed the subject. "You have such a fine, solid house," he said. "What is it made of?"

"Earth," said Martha.

"Pounded," said Ordney. "Strong as stone."

"Thick walls," said Martha. "They make it cool in hot weather and warm in cold." She reached for another pickled carrot. "I suppose you lived in—what? Some sort of burrows?"

"Stone houses," said Edward Pocket, suddenly joining the conversation because his plate was empty. "Two stories. Extremely sturdy. Never too warm."

There was a silence.

"Such a lovely lunch," said Miss Thorn in a small voice.

"Perfectly delicious," Mrs. Polster declared. The others chimed in, and Martha beamed.

They all rose from the table. Martha scurried into

the kitchen and came out with a basket full of cloth-wrapped parcels. She handed one to each of her guests. "Your supper," she said, "and breakfast."

"Thank you," said Doon's father. "You're very generous."

They filed out the front door. Doon was the last to leave. Just as he stepped outside, he felt a light tap on his shoulder. He turned to see Kensington standing behind him, his eyes wide.

"Aren't you the one who found the way out?" he whispered.

Doon nodded.

"I thought so," the boy said. He made a curious gesture—stuck out his hand with the fingers curled and the thumb straight up. Doon didn't understand it, but he thought it must mean something good, because a shy smile went with it. "Call me Kenny," the boy said, and he darted back through the door.

Doon followed his father and the others down the street. He's heard of me, he thought. He felt a pleasant sort of glow. Of course, Kenny was just a little boy; it was natural for a young boy to admire an older one.

All afternoon, they worked on the toilet holes. Doon was ready to drop by the end of the day. When the work leaders let them go, he walked down the long slope of ground in front of the Pioneer Hotel to the river. Large stones bordered the water at this point; he found one that was flat on top and sank onto it, tired to his bones. The sun was setting; the western sky glowed pink. The trees on the other side of the river cast long, thin shadows across the ground. He sat for ten minutes or so, just gazing, his thoughts swirling slowly.

It was going to take the people of Ember—all four hundred of them—several days just to build their outhouses. And already they were exhausted. How long before they got used to doing this kind of work? Doon couldn't imagine feeling so tired day after day. He had blisters on his hands, his wrists and shoulders ached, and the back of his neck felt hot and sore, as if it had been burned. And he was strong and young! What about the older people and the younger children? Of course they'd all have to work if they expected to be fed, but—

His thoughts were interrupted by footsteps crunching behind him.

He turned. There was Tick Hassler, walking toward him across the field. Doon's pulse quickened a little. Tick moved through the grass with a long stride, and when he came to the rocks alongside the river, he stepped from one to the next easily, never slipping or losing his balance. He raised a hand in greeting, and Doon waved back.

"Thinking deep thoughts?" Tick said, coming up beside Doon and smiling down at him.

"Not really," said Doon. "Just watching things."

"Ah," said Tick. He put his hands on his hips and gazed out across the river. The setting sun shone on his face, making it glow, and draped his long shadow over the rocks. Doon wished he would sit down and talk. After a while, Tick said, "I'll tell you something."

Doon glanced up quickly. Tick's eyes were a blue so light it was almost startling.

"This is a very fine place you've brought us to," Tick said.

"Yes," said Doon, pleased at being given the credit.

"You deserve a lot of respect," Tick said. "You may be just a kid, but you took action when things got desperate. You were brave."

Ordinarily, Doon didn't pay much attention to what other people thought about him, but there was something about Tick that made it pleasing to have his good opinion. Somehow, he didn't even feel insulted at being called "just a kid." "Thank you," he said. He thought surely Tick would sit down on the rock next to him now, and they would talk, but instead he stepped onto another rock, closer to the water, so that he had his back to Doon.

They both gazed for a while at the reddening sky. Then Tick turned around and said, "Really a wonderful place. Just look at all this!" He swept his arm in a wide arc, taking in the groves of trees, the fields, the river, and the glowing red ball of the sun.

"Yes," said Doon. "It *is* wonderful."

"We just need to get ourselves a little more comfortable," Tick said. "I have ideas already. We could fix up this old building, first of all. Get people organized and working together. Get new glass for the windows, maybe. Pipe some water in from the river. What do you think?"

"Sure," said Doon.

"Chet Noam wants to work with me," Tick said. "Lizzie Bisco, too, and Allie Bright. How about you?"

"Sure," said Doon again, a little disappointed that Tick had talked to all these other people before him.

"You'll be great on the pipe project," Tick said, "because of your experience."

Doon nodded. Actually, there were lots of things he'd rather do than work with pipes again, as he had in the Ember Pipeworks. But it might actually be fun to work on a plumbing project with Tick. Energy blazed from Tick's keen blue eyes.

"There's so much we can do . . . ," said Tick, and Doon waited to hear the end of his sentence, to hear what else he thought they could do, but Tick didn't say any more. He just bent down, plucked a stone from between the bigger rocks, turned back to face the river again, and threw the stone with all his might. It sailed high up, a black dot against the scarlet sky, and came down with a splash in the shallow water on the far side of the river.

Then he twisted around and smiled at Doon, an exuberant, radiant smile. "See you," he said, and he stepped across the rocks, climbed up the riverbank, and went back toward the hotel.

When he was gone, Doon picked up a stone and flung it as hard as he could. It plunked down in the middle of the river—not a bad throw, but not as good as Tick's.

CHAPTER 8

The Roamer and the Bike

Several days passed. Poppy would get a little better and then a little worse, and Lina and Mrs. Murdo stayed with her nearly all the time, putting cool rags on her forehead and trying to get her to drink the medicine the doctor gave her. When Mrs. Murdo wasn't caring for Poppy, she was prowling around the medicine room, inspecting the doctor's jumbled collection of herbs and potions and powders, making notes in a tiny notebook, and rearranging things, trying to create some order.

Dr. Hester was often gone, seeing patients in the village, and when she was in the house she was doing ten things at once, or trying to, and being interrupted by patients who came to the door at all hours. It seemed to Lina that the people of Sparks were constantly cutting themselves, spraining their muscles, getting rashes, and falling ill. The doctor would give them medicine or bandage their wounds, and a few days later the patients would bring something in return—a basket of eggs, a jar of pickles, a bag of clean rags.

Lina had never seen anyone so disorganized as the doctor. She peeked into the medicine room once when the doctor was out and was amazed at the clutter in there—shelves and cupboards and tables piled with stuff in bottles and stuff in boxes and stuff in jars, all higgledy-piggledy. How Dr. Hester found anything she couldn't imagine.

It took the doctor a couple of days even to get organized enough to figure out how Lina could help her. But when she did, she began giving her one chore after another, and sometimes several all at once, often forgetting that Lina didn't know how to do them.

"Could you go and water the asparagus?" she'd say. Then before Lina could ask what asparagus was, and where to find it, and what to put the water in, she'd say, "And then can you rip some of those rags in the kitchen basket into strips for bandages? And when you've done that, maybe you could wipe the floor in the medicine room—I spilled something the other day, I think over by the window. And the chickens, the chickens—they need to be fed." And then she'd be out the door, leaving Lina to remember the string of tasks and figure out how to do them.

Everything here seemed extremely *inconvenient* to Lina. To get water, you had to go outside the gate to a pump and work a stiff handle up and down. To go to the bathroom, you had to go out in back of the house to a little smelly shed. There was no light at night except for candles, and at first she'd thought there was no stove to cook on. "Oh, yes," said the doctor, "that's the stove there"—she pointed to the thing like a black iron barrel in the corner of the kitchen—"but I hardly ever use it in the summer. Too much trouble to keep the fire going, and it's too hot anyway. We mainly eat cold food in summer."

When she did want to cook something—boil a pot of water to cook an egg, for instance, or make tea—the doctor had to squat down, stuff some dry grass and twigs into the stove's belly, and set them alight. Sometimes she used a match; sometimes she hit what looked like two rocks together until they made a spark and the grass caught fire. Then she had to feed in bigger and bigger twigs until the fire was finally hot enough. This fire seemed fairly safe to Lina, though she didn't like to get too close to it; at least it was contained in its iron box. It wasn't free to leap out at her like the fire in the fireplace. Fortunately, the doctor didn't make another fire in the fireplace after that first night. As the days grew hotter and hotter, the nights were no longer cool. Extra warmth was the last thing they needed.

One day—a week or so after Lina first came to the

doctor's house—a patient came with news to tell as well as a wound to bind. She was a scrawny young woman with brownish teeth. She had a bad scratch on her wrist where she'd scraped it against some rusty wire. "There's a roamer in the village," she said. "Just arrived this morning."

"What's a roamer?" Lina asked.

The doctor, tying a rag around her patient's wrist, said, "Roamers go out into the Empty Lands and bring things back."

"From the old places," added the patient. "The ruined places."

"My brother Caspar is a roamer!" said Torren. "And when I'm old enough, I'm going to be a roamer, too, and we're going to be partners."

This was the first time Lina had sensed real happiness in Torren. His little eyes shone with hope.

"That will be exciting," Lina said. "Is it dangerous to be a roamer?"

"Oh, yes. Sometimes you run into other roamers trying to get the same things you want. Sometimes you're attacked by bandits. You have to fight them off. Caspar has a whip."

"A whip?"

"A great long cord! As long as this room, almost. If people get in his way, he lashes them." He lifted his arm overhead and brought it down as if he were lashing something. "Whhhhtt! Whhhhtt!" he said.

"Now, stop that," said the doctor absently, tying the final knot in the rag. The patient left, and Lina and the doctor and Torren, along with Mrs. Murdo, carrying Poppy, went down to the market plaza to see the roamer.

A crowd had assembled in the plaza. Lina looked for Doon, but she didn't see him. She saw only a few Emberites, in fact; most of them must have been working in other places. But a great many villagers were there, clustered around a big truck. The truck was loaded with barrels and crates, and on it stood a brown-skinned woman with wiry muscles in her arms and legs. "I have been in the far north," she cried out in a shrill, strong voice, "out in remote corners of the Empty Lands. I have traveled roads where I saw no human being for weeks on end. And in these distant regions, I came across houses and farms that had never before been searched. I have treasures for you today." She beckoned with a long brown arm. "Step up and look."

The crowd pressed forward. Apparently this roamer was known to the villagers. Some people called out greetings and questions.

"Did you bring us any writing paper this time, Mackie?"

"What about seeds?"

"What about tools?"

"And matches?"

"And clothes? I'm so tired of wearing homemade patchwork!"

"I have all that and more!" the woman called. "Come close. Special things first." She bent over an open crate and rummaged around for a moment. When she stood up again, she was holding a blackened iron cooking pot, so big she had to use both hands to lift it. "What am I offered?" she cried.

"Half a bushel of dried apricots!"

"A bushel of peas!"

"Barrel of cornmeal!"

The woman listened, cocking her head, her eyebrows raised. She waited until the offers stopped, and then she pointed at a tall young woman with shiny black hair who had offered five loaves of apricot cornbread. "Done!" she said, and she lowered the pot into the young woman's hands.

For the next special thing, the roamer reached into a big cardboard box. She brought out a smaller box colored blue and held it high. "Soap flakes!" she cried. "Twenty-four boxes of them!"

Dozens of people bid for these. They were all gone in minutes. Then came more cooking pans, two thick jackets of shiny material, rolls of rope, garden tools, books, a pair of scissors, some doorknobs, some nails. There were a few odd, useless things, too. For half a dozen carrots, one woman bought a pair of faucets, one with an H and one with a C. "What will you do with them?" asked Lina. People here got their water from long-handled pumps that stood at certain spots in the village. No one had indoor running water. "I'll turn them upside down," said the woman. "They'll make good candle holders."

When the roamer brought out a handful of jewels, Lina gasped. She had never seen such things—necklaces and bracelets made of gleaming stones and silver chains. But only a few people seemed interested in them, and they bid hardly anything—one girl bid a couple of potatoes, but a man got them for a slightly used pair of sandals. "If my wife doesn't want them," he said, "I'll use them to pretty up my oxen."

The roamer brought out the last of her wares—packets of paper, boxes of safety pins, some spoons and forks. The doctor stepped up to buy a set of small glass bottles.

"Dr. Hester!" the roamer said. "Good to see you!"

"And you, Mackie," said the doctor. "It's been a long time."

"I was hoping you'd be here," the roamer went on. "I ran into your nephew the other day."

"Caspar?" cried Torren in a voice so piercing that several people looked up, startled. "Where is he?"

"He was up in the apple country," said Mackie. "I told him I was coming down here, and he said to tell you he's heading for home."

"Is that right," said the doctor. She was clearly not as excited as Torren. "We haven't seen him for quite a while."

"One year, ten months, and nineteen days," said Torren. "When will he be here? Did he say?"

"Should be soon," said the roamer. She was putting the little bottles into a cloth bag. "I'd guess within the next two weeks or so."

When the roamer's sale was over, Lina walked home along the river road with the doctor and Mrs. Murdo and Poppy, who was asleep in Mrs. Murdo's arms. Torren leapt ahead, his thin legs splaying out sideways. He bounced off steps, jumped onto walls, leapt up to grab branches of trees, and swung from them.

As they neared the doctor's house, Torren, who was way ahead of them by now, suddenly turned around and raced back. "You have to get out of our room!" he said to Lina and Mrs. Murdo. "My brother will want his own room, and he'll want to be with me. You all have to move."

"Fine," said Lina. "We will. We'll go live with our own people as soon as Poppy's well enough."

Torren's narrow face lit up. "Good, good, good!" he cried. "When are you leaving?"

"Not *today*," said Lina. "Not right this *minute*."

"But soon!" Torren cried. He skipped ahead of

them again, through the gate and across the courtyard.

The doctor said not to mind Torren, he was being rude because he was so excited. But it seemed to Lina that Dr. Hester didn't see clearly when it came to Torren. He wasn't rude just when he was excited, he was rude nearly all the time. The doctor was so preoccupied with her work that she hardly noticed him. Maybe if she'd pay him more attention, Lina thought, he wouldn't be so awful.

But he *was* awful, and Lina would be glad to get away from him. Two weeks, she thought. Then we'll meet Caspar the Great, and if Poppy is well by then, Torren can have his room back and we'll go and live with Doon and the others.

Now and then, Lina saw people on wheels going by on the road in front of the doctor's house. The only wheeled vehicles Lina had ever seen were the heavy wooden carts in Ember. But these people were riding beautiful, slender devices, two big wheels per person. They glided by, their feet going round and round. She wanted to do it, too! So *badly,* she wanted to. "What are they?" she asked the doctor.

"Bikes, of course," said the doctor. "You've never seen one?"

"No," said Lina, looking at a bike with longing. If she could have a bike, she thought, she could go even faster than when she ran. She could go so fast and so far. . . . She looked out toward the endless rolling hills. She could go everywhere. She could go to wherever the roads ended.

"I wish I could ride one," she said.

"Well, you can, if you want," said the doctor. "There's an old one out behind the toolshed. I suppose it still works."

"There is?" Lina nearly dropped the basket of eggs she had just gathered. "May I get it now?"

"I guess so," said the doctor. "But would you mind watering the parsley first? And if you could just shell these peas . . . and maybe wash that spinach . . ."

Lina did these tasks in a fever of impatience, and when she was finished she dashed out to the shed. The bike was leaning against the shed wall. It was old but beautiful—made of wires and slender pipes and rods, some of them silver under their coat of dust, and some of them red. Thin, weedy vines wove among the spokes of the bike's wheels, and cobwebs draped its seat. Lina took hold of the two handles and pulled the bike from its nest. She wheeled it out onto the road in front of the house and brushed the cobwebs and dry leaves and bits of grass off it, and then she swung one leg over and settled herself on the seat.

Now what?

She spent the rest of the morning figuring it out. She pushed on the pedals, rolled forward, tipped over sideways, and had to put her feet down. She rolled forward again but didn't know how to turn. She fell off. She heaved the bike upright and tried again. She fell off again. After an hour or so of this, she gave up and went inside for a while.

And later, when she tried again, something had changed. She had the feel of it in her legs now, or somewhere in her. She rolled forward, she put a foot on the pedal and pushed, she rolled farther, she brought up the other foot, and magically, her body understood for a second what to do. She was sailing; her feet were going round and round. A smile broke over her face. She held on, feet going round, breathless, breeze against her face—a whole long distance, maybe five yards, before suddenly she was nervous and dragged her feet along the ground to stop. She stood holding the handlebars, her mouth open in amazement.

And by the end of the day she had it. She could ride back and forth on the road, she could stop whenever she wanted to. She could even turn around corners without putting a foot down.

"I'm going to see Doon," she told Mrs. Murdo. She was longing to see Doon, longing to talk to someone she really knew. Mrs. Murdo was fine, of course, but she was a grown-up. Lina wanted to be with a *friend*. She got on the bike and rode, sweeping down the river road, into the plaza, where she asked someone for directions, and out the other side of the town to the hotel.

When she got there, she stopped for a moment just to stare. The enormous old building looked to her like a wonderful place to live. She felt a sudden longing to have her own room there, back among her old friends and neighbors.

It was nearly evening by then. People were sitting on the hotel steps in the last rays of the setting sun, eating their dinners from their food parcels and talking. Some were down by the river, cooling their feet, splashing water onto their faces. Over by the farthest wing of the hotel, a few boys were gathered around another boy, who was sitting on a fallen tree talking to them. Maybe Doon was over there.

She wheeled her bike toward them—the ground here was too rough and weedy to ride on. Her old friends and neighbors called out to her as she passed, and she waved at them, glad to be back among people she knew.

When she got closer to the group of boys, she saw that Doon was among them. He and a couple of others were listening to that tall dark-haired boy—what was his name, Tigg? Tim? He'd been a cart puller in Ember, she thought. He laughed as she came up, a ringing, confident laugh, and all the other boys laughed, too.

She went up behind Doon and tapped him on the shoulder. He turned around. She grinned at him. "Look, Doon!" she said. "I have a bike!"

He seemed astonished to see her. "Oh!" he said. "Lina!"

"Come and talk to me," she said.

His eyes shifted back toward the tall boy. "Okay," he said, but he didn't move.

"Come on!" said Lina, tugging at his jacket.

They walked down toward the river. Lina leaned the bike against a tree, and she and Doon sat facing each other on the ground.

"What a huge place!" she said, waving an arm at the Pioneer Hotel, and talking fast in her eagerness. "What's it like? Will you show me around? Poppy is a little better, and maybe in a couple of weeks we can come and live here, too. With you. And with everyone."

Doon nodded. "That would be good," he said.

"It's kind of lonely at the doctor's house," Lina went on. "There's a boy there who doesn't like us, and the doctor is so busy she can hardly think, and her house is a mess, and I have to do a million chores." She paused for breath. "Today we saw a roamer, Doon."

"A roamer?"

She explained what a roamer was. Doon listened, but she saw his eyes veer back toward the group of boys.

"Who is that boy?" she asked. "The one who's talking?"

"Tick Hassler," said Doon.

Lina turned around and looked at him. He was handsome, she thought. His black hair was thick and glossy, and his face was all sharp angles, as if it had been carved from wood. "Is he a friend of yours?"

"Sort of," said Doon. "I mean—I'm just getting to know him."

"Oh," said Lina. "Do you know which room Lizzie is in?"

Doon said he didn't. "I don't stay inside very much," he said. "It's kind of dark and dismal in there. What I like is being outside." He pointed up into the branches of the tree, where little fluttery things were hopping around. "Remember when we first saw those?" he said. "When we'd just come up from Ember? I learned that they're called birds. When you start really looking at them, you see there's all different kinds. I've seen ones with a yellow chest, and ones with stripes on their wings, and ones with red heads. There's even one that's bright blue." He gazed upward. "It's strange, isn't it? Why have all these different kinds, I wonder? Just for the fun of it?"

A burst of laughter came from the group of boys around Tick Hassler. Doon glanced over at them.

"Do you like it here, Doon?" Lina said. "In the village of Sparks, I mean?"

"I do," said Doon. "I like it a lot."

"Me too," said Lina. "Mostly."

"But it sort of worries me that we have to leave in six months," Doon said. "There's so much we need to learn."

"Well, I guess so," said Lina. "But maybe if we leave . . . I mean, I still wish . . ."

"Wish what?" said Doon when she trailed off.

"Oh, I don't know." She'd been going to say she wished they'd found the city she used to dream of. But she was afraid Doon might think that was silly.

The sun was going down. Shadows grew longer. "Show me your room before I have to go," Lina said, "so I'll know where to find you."

Tick was walking away, and the other boys were following him. Doon gazed after them. "I can't right now," he said. "I will next time you come."

"All right," Lina said. She got up from the ground and swatted the leaves off her pants. She picked up her bike. "I'll see you sometime," she said, and she rode back to the doctor's house feeling lonelier than she had before.

CHAPTER 9

Hard, Hungry Work

Instead of getting easier as the days went on, work for the people of Ember got harder. It wasn't just the work—it was the heat they had to work in. Every day was hotter than the last. Doon had never felt this warm in his life—it was like being cooked. All the people of Ember felt this way. They sweated, their skin turned red and stung and peeled off, and the brightness of the sky hurt their eyes. They got terrible headaches. Sometimes one of them would drop to the ground in a faint, just from being too hot. At times like these, people thought, This is a dreadful place we have come to. They put their hands over their eyes, missing the familiar darkness.

The team leaders tried to be understanding when their workers drooped and fainted. But the people of Sparks were used to the heat; beside them, the people of Ember seemed like weaklings. A few times, Doon saw the leader of his team press his lips together and drum his fingers against his leg when one of the Emberites had to sit down and rest.

Doon's team leader was Chugger Frisk, a big, stubble-jawed man who didn't talk much except to give directions. Every day he sent his team wherever it was most needed. Doon did all kinds of jobs over the next few weeks. He dug ditches for the pipes that conducted water from the river to the crops in the fields. He repaired the wagons that hauled the produce home from the fields. He milked the goats out in the goat pasture and made sure the water troughs for the oxen were full. He picked fruit, built fences, planted seeds, stirred vats of soap, and dug chicken droppings into the cabbage field.

Except for being so hot, he didn't mind the work. He was getting strong, and he *liked* being strong. He liked feeling the muscles in his arms getting harder, and he liked being taller (he knew he was taller, because his old pants were too short). The feeling of being a new person in this new world stayed with him. He would be thirteen soon—not a child anymore. Work was making him sturdy and ready for anything.

Besides, as he worked he was finding out all kinds of things he wanted to learn. How did the pumps work that brought water up from the river to the fields? How was cheese made, and shoes, and candles? Where did they get the ice that kept things cold in their big ice house? What were the bushy-tailed animals that scurried up trees, and the long, rope-like animals that he sometimes almost stepped on in the grass? He wanted to know how houses were built, and what glass was made of, and how bicycles worked. It was exciting, having so much to learn. But every time he remembered that he and his people had less than six months to learn it—less than six months to master all the skills they'd need to build a town of their own—a worm of fear twisted in his stomach.

Chugger wouldn't answer questions. He was too busy giving directions or working. So Doon often asked his questions at lunch. Sometimes Ordney answered him, sometimes Martha did. Ordney's answers were more like lectures, and Martha's were more like boasts. After a while it was clear that both of them were getting tired of questions, so Doon asked fewer of them. One day, Kenny followed him outside after lunch and stretched up to whisper in his ear. "I can show you where there's answers to your questions," he said. "Want me to?"

"Sure," said Doon.

"Right now?" said Kenny.

"Okay," said Doon.

Kenny led him through the streets of the village,

going first toward the river and then away from it, along a street that led out away from the houses and into a grove of oak trees.

"There," said Kenny, pointing ahead.

At first Doon saw only the long line of a roof above the trees. Then the street opened out into a big empty space that, he could see, had once been covered with pavement. Now the pavement was cracked and weeds grew up through it. To the left of this span of pavement stood a huge building—a rectangular structure so tremendous it could have held both the Ember school and the Gathering Hall. At the end facing them were two massive wooden doors, which Kenny walked toward. "In the ancient days," Kenny said, "you didn't have to open these. They were made of glass, and they had eyes and opened as soon as they saw you."

"That can't be," said Doon.

"It was, though," Kenny said.

Above the doors was a sign missing most of its letters. It was a long sign, so you could tell whatever it used to say was a long word, but now all it said was UPE ARK.

"What does that mean?" Doon asked, pointing to the sign.

"I don't know," Kenny said. "We just call it the Ark. It's our storehouse. We're going around to the back."

He led the way around the side of the building to a small door in the back wall, which he opened.

He had to push hard, because something was behind the door that had to be shoved out of the way.

Doon peered into the darkness. At first he couldn't make out what he was seeing. Lumpy mountains appeared to fill the room to the ceiling and spread from wall to wall. He took a step forward, but his foot jammed against something hard on the floor.

"There's answers to everything in here," said Kenny.

As his eyes adjusted to the dimness, Doon saw that the room was full of—was it boxes? No, they almost looked like books. They lay in toppling stacks, giant heaps, sliding mounds, as if they had been dumped in from an enormous bucket. Some of them lay open, with their pages crumpled. Some were so warped that their covers curved. A smell of ancient dust and mold arose from them. He reached down and picked one up. Its cover was furred with dust. He opened it and saw pages of tiny neat printing. It *was* a book, yes. Not like the books of Ember—these were much bigger and sturdier, and had much more writing. He riffled the pages—more dust flew up—but he couldn't tell what the book was about. One page said, "Chapter XV. The Thermodynamics of Aluminum." He had no idea what that meant.

"This is amazing," said Doon. "Can I take some back to the hotel?"

"I guess so," said Kenny. "No one will notice."

Doon set down the book about thermodynamics. He brushed his smudged fingers against his pants. He felt like a hungry person who had been led to an immense banquet, far more food than he could eat in his whole life. He was starving, all of a sudden, for the knowledge hidden in these books. He reached out and chose three of them blindly, not even looking at the titles.

"Don't you want some?" he said to Kenny.

"No," said Kenny. "I already read four books in school. That was enough. We learned about history. Pre and post."

"Pre and post?"

"Pre-Disaster and post-Disaster."

"Oh," said Doon. "What do you like to do, then?" he asked.

"Just poke around," said Kenny. "I poke around in the woods. You could come with me sometime," he said, looking up at Doon with hopeful eyes. "If you want."

"Maybe I will," Doon said, though he was thinking probably he wouldn't. He had so many other things in mind to do. Besides, Kenny was a little young to be his friend.

During the first week after the Emberites arrived, Martha Parton had showed off her cooking skills at lunch every day. She made mashed potato pie, fresh peas with chives, walnut croquettes, mushroom gravy, cheese popovers, red-onion-and-bean dumplings, scrambled eggs with tomato jam, apricot pudding, and apple butter cookies. Every time she brought in a new dish, she said, "I don't imagine you had these where you came from," or "This will be new to you," and the Ember guests would say, "You're right, we've never had this! We've never tasted anything so delicious! It's wonderful!" and Martha's mouth would crimp into a small, pleased smile.

As time went on, however, the food at lunchtime became plainer. Martha got tired of making something new every day to impress her guests. What they found in their dinner and breakfast parcels became less interesting, too—usually it was some chunks of cornbread, ten or twelve carrot sticks, and a few slimy bits of goat cheese. If they were lucky, there might be a hard-boiled egg. Martha took to mentioning, as if it were a little joke, that even though the Partons were given extra food from the storehouse because of the extra people, it *seemed* as if they had less! Wasn't that odd!

Doon started to feel hungry a fair amount of the time, and he knew others did, too. His father never spoke of it, but Edward Pocket griped about the food every evening. "I know I'm old and small," he'd say, polishing off the last crumbs of both his dinner and his breakfast, "but that doesn't mean I can live on air."

One day Ordney made a disturbing announcement. The cabbage crop, he said, was going to be smaller than expected. Worms had got into it. They'd have only about two-thirds of the cabbage they had last year.

After this, not only was the food at lunchtime plainer, but there was less of it. One week, they had string beans, last year's pickled cabbage, and goat's milk pudding for lunch four days in a row, and when they opened their baskets at dinnertime, they found only a bottle of cold potato soup to serve as both dinner and breakfast.

Clary had started a garden just a few days after the Emberites arrived at the Pioneer Hotel. She cleared a patch of ground about forty feet square not far from the riverbank and planted seeds that she had brought from Ember. Children who were too little to go to work in the village helped her pull weeds and fetch buckets of water from the river. Old people sat in the shade giving her advice. After a while, green shoots appeared in rows on the patch of dirt, and Clary was out there every morning and every evening, tending them. In several weeks, there would be a little extra food for the people of Ember out in their own front yard.

But it wouldn't be nearly enough. Some people were already grumbling about their skimpy dinner parcels. One night, when Doon was in room 215 eating with his father and the others, he heard voices in the hall and went out to see a cluster of people a few doors down. Lizzie was there—Doon spotted the red cloud of her hair. Tick was there, too. His voice carried above the rest. "Well, I got three carrots, a plum, and a chunk of sour cheese," he said. "Lucky me. That ought to keep me going for a while."

A few people laughed drily at this. Doon heard Lizzie giggle.

"It'll keep you going for maybe half an hour," someone said. "I don't know how they think we can work, with nothing but scraps to eat."

Along the hall, other doors opened, and other voices joined in.

"All I got was some limp green beans and a few clumps of porridge!"

"I've had carrot soup three days in a row!"

Some people counseled patience. "We shouldn't complain," someone said. "It's hard for them to give us food. We should be grateful for—"

"I'm tired of being grateful!" someone else broke in. "They promised to feed us, but they're starving us instead!"

"It seems to me," said Tick, "that we should do something about this. I think maybe I'll mention the problem at lunch tomorrow. Maybe we *all* should. Maybe we should tell them it's very hard to work when you're hungry."

"I'll tell them!" cried Lizzie's high voice, and other voices rose in agreement. An excited, angry babble filled the hallway, drowning out those who spoke for patience. "I'll speak up!" "We have to protest!" "Tick is so right!"

"Tick for mayor!" someone shouted, laughing.

For a second Tick looked surprised. Then his eyes glowed with pleasure. He raised a fist in the air. "We'll stand up for ourselves!" he said, and the people around him roared and raised their fists, too.

Doon turned to his father and Edward and Sadge, who had all come to the door to see what was going on. "We should tell the Partons," he said. "If we're working, we need enough to eat. It's only fair."

"Of course, they don't *have* to give us *anything*," said Doon's father. "They're giving what they think they can spare." He looked sadly at the dry chunk of cornbread in his hand. "But I suppose it can't hurt to mention it," he said, "without being rude, of course. I imagine they're doing the best they can."

Mrs. Polster agreed to be the one to bring the matter up. She did so at lunch the next day. They were having cold spinach soup.

"I have a request," she said firmly. She set down her soup spoon.

Everyone looked toward her. Doon felt a jitter in his stomach.

"We have noticed," said Mrs. Polster, "that the food parcels you so generously give us have become considerably *smaller* lately. We find that when we have eaten what is within, we are still, to be frank, *hungry*. This is a difficulty for us."

There was silence. Everyone stared at Mrs. Polster, who sat very calmly with her hands in her lap, waiting for an answer.

"What?" said Martha Parton at last. "Did I hear right?"

"I believe so," said Mrs. Polster, "unless you have ear trouble. I said we are not getting quite enough to eat."

Martha laughed a one-note laugh, a laugh of disbelief. Kenny stopped chewing and looked frightened. Ordney drew himself up and cleared his throat. "I am surprised," he said. "I had thought you people understood the situation."

"We do, indeed," said Doon's father hastily. "We're very grateful for what you've done for us. It's just that . . ."

"We're working quite hard," said Clary.

"It's a very small amount . . . ," said Miss Thorn timidly.

"For both dinner and breakfast," added Edward Pocket.

"Last night," said Doon, "I had a boiled egg and

three carrots for dinner. And nothing for breakfast this morning."

There was a silence again, a terrible, vibrating silence.

Then Ordney leaned forward, gripping the edge of the table with his fingertips. "Now, listen here," he said. "We're doing the best we can with what has been asked of us. And I must say, a great deal has been asked. Suddenly we're supposed to feed twice as many people as before! More than twice as many!" He glared at the Emberites, shifting his eyes to each one in turn. "And yet we do not have twice as much food as we did before. It's true that each family is being given a little extra from the storehouse for this emergency. But not much. *Sparks village just does not have enough for four hundred extra people.* Are we supposed to feed you instead of our own families? Why should we? Who *are* you, anyway, you strangers from some city no one's ever heard of?"

By the end of this speech, Ordney's face was a deep red and his voice was shaking with rage.

Doon felt frozen. All he could think was, *He's right. Of course he's right. But we're right, too.*

Everyone else must have been thinking the same thing. They finished their soup in silence. At the end of the meal, Martha dumped the food parcels on the table instead of handing them out. They each took one, but Doon's father was the only person who said thank you.

Later, when Doon opened his parcel, he found a wedge of cabbage leaves turning yellow at the edges and a hunk of some sort of bean cake. His stomach clenched. They're tired of helping us, he thought. What are we going to do?

CHAPTER 10

Restless Weeks

Poppy was now almost well. She still slept more than usual, but when she wasn't sleeping she tromped around the doctor's house pulling spoons off the table and spilling cups of water and crumpling pages of books. That is, she was almost her old self. So Lina often asked Mrs. Murdo if it wasn't time for them to go and live with the others at the Pioneer Hotel. Mrs. Murdo always said she wasn't quite ready. They'd wait until the brother came, she said. Lina had a feeling the real reason was that she liked helping the doctor. She was always poring over the doctor's big medicine books, and helping her pick her herbs and mix her remedies. So they stayed on.

And Lina worked for the doctor. It wasn't that she didn't like working. But in Ember, she'd had an adventurous job, an important job. She'd run with her messages all over the city—running the way she loved to run, so fast she almost flew. It was hard for her to stay in one place all day. She felt restless and bored.

She did a huge amount of cooking—well, not cooking exactly, since the doctor rarely wanted to bother making a fire in the stove, but chopping and peeling and slicing and mixing. She wiped up spilled medicines and herbal solutions from the counters, she swept dirt from the floor, she pulled down cobwebs from the ceiling. There were always rags to be torn into bandages. There were always herbs to be pounded into powder and bottles to be labeled and plants to be watered. While everyone else was out in the village, doing new, interesting things and meeting new people, Lina was stuck doing *housework*.

One day she asked the doctor if there was any extra paper she could use for drawing. There wasn't, the doctor said, but if she could find blank pages at the backs of books, she could use those. So Lina tore out eight blank pages, the doctor gave her a pencil, and she began drawing whenever she had a few minutes of free time.

Out of habit, she drew the city she had always drawn—she hardly knew how to draw anything else. But she thought that since she was here in the real world, she should be able to imagine the city much better than before. She remembered the first drawing she'd done with her colored pencils, back in Ember, when she'd made the sky blue instead of its normal black. She had thought it was just an imaginary thing, a little crazy, to draw a blue sky. But now look! The sky really was blue! She must have known it somehow, in some secret place in her mind. Something in her was a little bit magic, maybe—she could see beyond what was right in front of her eyes to things that used to be, or things that could be in the future.

So she shut her eyes and tried to look deep into her imagination. But the old version of the city, the one she'd drawn so many times, seemed to be stamped inside her eyelids. She kept drawing the same thing— the tall buildings, the lighted windows. She added a few extras: some trees, a couple of trucks with their oxen, a chicken. But it didn't look quite right. Would the buildings be taller than the trees? How much taller? Would there be chickens in the city? She felt discouraged. So she set aside her city drawings and tried to draw what she saw around her.

She drew the lemon tree outside the doctor's back door. She drew her bike. She drew the front of the doctor's house, and the gate, and the grapevine over the door. Once a truck parked a little way up the road to unload some crates, and she dashed out with her paper and pencil and drew the truck and its oxen.

But none of these gave her quite the same thrill as drawing the city. There was a feeling that went with drawing the city, a feeling of longing and excitement and mystery. It was as if her drawings of the city were a half-open window, a glimpse of something she couldn't quite see clearly.

Torren sometimes came up behind her when she was drawing and peered over her shoulder. Now and then he would point out some part of the picture that didn't look right, but most of the time he didn't comment at all. He was hopping with impatience these days, waiting for his brother to come home. "He'll be bringing me something," he said one day. "Every time he comes home, he brings me something." He went to the window seat and took his bag of treasures from the cabinet underneath. "I'll show you these," he said to Lina, "if you promise not to touch them."

Lina wandered over. She didn't want to appear too interested, since Torren was certainly never interested in anything *she* did, but she was curious about these prized possessions he'd been hiding.

He reached into the bag and took out one thing at a time, placing it carefully on the window ledge. There were six things, all different. Lina could not identify a single one of them.

"Caspar brought me these," Torren said. He lined them up, making tiny adjustments to their positions until he got them just right. "They're all extinct."

Lina took a step closer and bent down to look.

"Don't touch them!" Torren cried.

"I'm not," said Lina irritably. "Well, what are they?"

Torren pointed to the first thing, which was shaped like a T and made of scratched silver metal. "An airplane," Torren said. "It carried people through the air."

"Oh, come on," said Lina. "It's not even a foot long."

"Real airplanes did," Torren said. "This is just a *model* of a real airplane."

He pointed to the next one. "A tank," he said. "It runs over people and crushes them."

"What's the point of that?" Lina asked.

Torren sighed at Lina's stupidity. "It's for fighting enemies," he said.

The next thing looked like a short, chubby bike. "Motorcycle," said Torren. "It goes really fast." Then came a battered silver tube. "Flashlight. You push this button, and light comes out."

"Show me," Lina said.

"It doesn't *work,*" said Torren. "I told you, all these are extinct."

The next thing was a black rectangle with rows of small colored buttons. "Remote," said Torren.

"What's it for?"

"It makes things happen when you press the buttons."

"What kind of things?"

"Just things," said Torren. "I don't know. It's very technical."

The last thing was different from all the rest. It seemed to be an animal, made of some stiff grayish material. It stood about ten inches high, on four thick feet. "Elephant," said Torren. "As tall as a house."

"Tall as a *house*?" Lina tried to imagine it. "You mean if I stood next to one I'd only come up to here?" She pointed at the creature's knee.

Torren swatted her hand away. "It was the biggest animal on earth," he said. "If it wrapped its nose around you, you would die."

"I'd love to see one," Lina said.

"You can't. There aren't any more." Torren spread his arms out, hiding his treasures from view. "You have to go away now," he said. "You only get one look."

So Lina went out into the courtyard and picked a few green grapes, which turned out to be much too hard and sour to eat. Through the window, she could see Torren moving the tank and the motorcycle toward each other, and she could hear him making growling and crashing noises. What must the ancient world have been like, she wondered, with all these strange things moving around in it? Was it wonderful or terrible?

One afternoon, when Lina was in the village picking up some salt for the doctor, she saw a long line of people at a clothing shop. A few Emberites were among them. Lizzie was in the line, wearing the black scarf around her neck that she'd worn ever since she arrived, to show that she was mourning for Looper, her boyfriend back in Ember.

"Why are there so many people here?" Lina asked.

"They have eyeglasses!" Lizzie said. "A roamer brought in a special load of them yesterday."

"Glasses? But you don't wear glasses."

"These are *dark* glasses," Lizzie said. "They call them sunglasses. They make it so the light doesn't hurt your eyes as much."

Most of the people of Sparks already had sunglasses. A couple of the work leaders, understanding how much the light bothered the Emberites' eyes, traded some extra wooden crates for a couple of boxes of the glasses and gave them out for free. Lina tried some on but didn't like them because they made all the green look brownish. She also thought they made people look sneaky, as if they had evil secret plans.

Lina liked going to the market plaza. It was always alive with people and animals, and the markets had things she'd never seen before—sandals made of old truck tires, hats and baskets woven of straw. It was a noisy, bustling, interesting place. It was also very messy.

The animals made the mess. Goats and oxen, pulling carts in from the fields, left their big, smelly plops all over. These got cleaned up eventually—

someone came and scraped them into buckets and took them away—but often this didn't happen until halfway through the morning, and people had to step carefully until then and breathe in that powerful smell. This gave Lina a good idea. She would do a favor for the marketplace, she decided; everyone would appreciate it.

So the next morning, just at dawn, she rode her bike down to the plaza with a big bucket hanging from the handlebars. She scooped up a load of cow plops and goat plops and dumped it into the river. Back and forth from the plaza to the river she went, scraping up one smelly, squashy load after another, and when she was just about to dump the last load, one of the shopkeepers arrived. She smiled at him, expecting some words of approval. But instead his face twisted in rage.

"What are you *doing*?" he shouted. He started running toward her. "Dumping that good stuff in the river?" He seemed unable to believe his eyes. "What is the matter with you?"

Good stuff? thought Lina. What was he talking about?

He snatched the bucket out of her hand. "You people are—" He stopped. He pressed his lips together and closed his eyes for a moment. "All right," he said in a tight voice. "I suppose you didn't know. This stuff is precious. You do not throw it in the river!"

Lina took a step backward. She felt as if she'd been slapped. "Oh!" she said. "Then what do you do with it?"

"It goes out to the fields," the man said. "It goes into the rotting pile, and when it's ready they dig it into the ground. It's fertilizer. I guess you've never heard of it."

"No," said Lina. "I didn't know. I'm sorry. I was trying to be helpful."

"The most helpful thing you people could do would be to . . . well, never mind." He gave Lina a last disgusted look and walked away, leaving her with a half-filled bucket she didn't know what to do with. She carried it out of the village and up the road, and when no one was around, she dumped its contents at the side of a field.

It wasn't only Lina who got into this kind of trouble. As time went on, she heard about other people doing or saying the wrong thing and irritating the people of Sparks. Sometimes it was because they seemed stupid. People from Ember were frightened by chickens, had never seen a cloud, and didn't know the meaning of ordinary words like *storm* and *forest* and *cat* and *lemon*. They knew nothing about history. They'd never heard of other countries. They didn't even know that the earth was round like a ball. To the villagers, they seemed unbelievably dumb.

On the other hand, they sometimes acted a bit superior, boasting of the things they'd had in their underground city. The villagers didn't like hearing that in Ember people had had electric lights and flush toilets and hot and cold running water. Once when Lister Munk, who had been the Pipeworks supervisor, was telling a Sparks man about the generator, the man called him a liar. When Lister protested that he was telling the truth and implied that Sparks was a rather backward place compared to Ember, the man hit him. It took five people to break up the fight.

Worst of all was the ravenous hunger of the Emberites. The village families were pleased that these strangers were so impressed by their fruits and vegetables, but they were also worried. Their leaders had told them the newcomers were to be fed, and all households were being supplied with extra food for the purpose. But the people of Ember never seemed to get full. They cleaned every last crumb off their plates, asked for seconds, finished those off, and then sat there looking hungry. The villagers resented it. Lina sometimes overheard them talking in the markets. "It's too much to ask," she heard a woman grumbling. "And these cavepeople are going to be here nearly five more months! Am I going to have to give them some of my strawberry crop? I don't see why I should." And another woman was even more direct. "I wish they'd just get out," she said. "It's hard enough to feed your own family, much less a bunch of strangers."

Lina wasn't used to feeling unwanted. She didn't like it. There were plenty of things about this place she didn't like. The dust that coated her feet and legs, for instance, turning them a yellowish brown. The tiny bugs that bit her and made red itchy spots on her arms. The way the sun burned the back of her neck. This place wasn't so perfect, she wanted to tell those crabby villagers. In Ember, for instance, they didn't have so many mean, snotty people as they did here.

Lina sometimes rode down to the Pioneer Hotel to see Doon. He always seemed glad to see her, but it wasn't the same as it had been back in Ember, when they were involved in the desperate search for a way out of their doomed city. Doon showed her around the Pioneer, and he told her about the work he did and the people he ate his lunch with. But he seemed distracted, or troubled, as if he was trying to solve a problem that he wasn't telling her about.

Lina would ride back to the doctor's house after these visits with thoughts struggling against each other in her mind. She missed the old Doon, her clever, adventurous partner. And she herself felt different here, too. She didn't know what to do or how to be. Some of the people were trying to be kind, but there was so much unkindness mixed in with the kindness.

To the people of Sparks, the people of Ember were just a nuisance. How could they stay in a place where they weren't wanted?

This world was huge. There must be another place in it for the people of Ember.

CHAPTER 11

Tick's Projects

By the month of Burning, it was so hot that the people of Ember felt as if they were trapped in a huge oven. The sun blazed down, the grasses dried to a brownish yellow, the roads were deep in dust. People gasped and sneezed and wilted. All they wanted was to lie down in the shade, or wade deep into the cool water of the river. But the work went on as always—in the ferocious heat, they hauled garbage, cleaned out the goat pens, pulled weeds in the fields, shoveled manure. When they flopped down on the ground to rest or stopped every few minutes for a drink of water, the workers of Sparks glared at them and grumbled. They suspected them of being lazy, and that made the people of Ember angry. Resentment increased on both sides, until any little accident could flare up into a fight.

At the Pioneer Hotel, the mood grew more and more grim. At first, it had been rather fun to live there, especially for the smaller children, who explored the hidden corners of the huge old building, held races in the long corridors, and played colossal games of hide-and-seek. Lizzie Bisco liked going into the Ladies' Room on the ground floor, where there was still a large fragment of mirror attached to the wall. She could see almost her entire self in it, which pleased her on the days when she had just washed her hair in the river or found a bit of colored cloth to use as a ribbon.

But for the older people, the Pioneer Hotel quickly stopped feeling like a fine adventure. They didn't like sleeping on piles of pine needles and dry grasses wrapped in bedspreads. It annoyed them to have to go to the river for water, and to have no indoor bathrooms, only outhouses full of bad smells and spiders. They worried that the candles might set things on fire, and they wanted real windows, with glass, to keep the bugs out. Almost two months had passed since they'd arrived in Sparks. In about four months, they would have to leave. If they didn't like living in the hotel, they knew they'd like even less to start from nothing somewhere out in the wilderness. They imagined sleeping with no roof over their heads, having no protection at all from the sun or the bugs, and scratching through the grass for something to eat. No one liked the prospect. In the dim hallways, in the roofless, ruined lobby, and in the dusty ballroom, people gathered in little clusters and spoke to each other in worried tones, and sometimes their worry turned to anger and fear.

One person, however, did not stand around talking: that was Tick Hassler. When he saw a problem, he did something about it. He'd become a sort of leader around the Pioneer Hotel, just by the force of his personality. He started what he called the Pioneer Hotel Rehabilitation Project. He explained his ideas to anyone who would listen, and the way he explained them made them seem instantly exciting and fun.

"Here's what we'll do," he said, the night he announced the first project. It was late evening of a very hot day, nearly dark, and a few people were still sitting out on the steps of the hotel, hoping for a cool breeze. Tick never seemed much affected by the heat. Everyone else was disheveled and sweaty by the end of the day, but Tick always managed to look neat, his hair combed so flat it looked almost polished, his bare arms and legs smooth and brown, his clothes—a plain black T-shirt and black shorts—never torn or stained. He wore his sunglasses almost all the time, and they gave him a commanding and slightly mysterious look.

Doon was there the night Tick announced his first project. It was a relief, after a hard day, to be part of a group of people who were easy with each other, a group with a common purpose. Several of Doon's classmates from the Ember school were part of it, and some boys who had been cart pullers with Tick, and quite a few others. There were some girls, too. Lizzie was always somewhere around Tick, listening eagerly as he talked, or trotting off on an errand of some sort for him. She had stopped wearing the black scarf that signified her mourning for Looper. "I've been sad long enough," she told Doon. "Besides, Tick doesn't think black looks good on me." Now she wore her sunglasses all the time.

"What we're going to do," said Tick, sitting on the low wall that bordered the steps, leaning forward with his elbows on his knees, and speaking in a way that made you feel his words were meant just for you, "is get ourselves organized. There's a lot that needs to be done around here." People nodded. "The first thing we need," Tick went on, "is a gathering place, like the Gathering Hall back in Ember. And what's the perfect spot for it?" He held out his hands, palms facing the sky, waiting for an answer.

No one spoke.

"This field, of course!" He swept an arm out, taking in the whole of the big field in front of the hotel, with its rough, weedy ground, scrawny trees, and chunks of concrete and other rubble. "We're going to clear it out. We're going to make it into a grand plaza, better than the one in the village. We can have meetings here, with our leader speaking to us from these steps."

"We don't have a leader," someone said.

"But we will someday, once we decide who's best for the job," Tick said. "I'm going to start on it tomorrow—who wants to work with me?"

And although they had already worked a full day, nearly all of them flung their hands up and volunteered. Doon did, too. It wasn't so much that he wanted to clear the field and make a plaza; he wasn't sure they really needed such a thing. After all, they'd be leaving here before long. But he wanted to be part of this; he didn't want to be left out.

The project got off to a great start: twenty or thirty people were out there every evening, pulling up weeds, digging out rubble, and hacking down trees. Tick was always there, working twice as fast and hard as anyone else and telling them all what terrific progress they were making. It was hard work, but somehow it was fun, too.

Then one night Tick called everyone together and announced that he had a new idea. "We won't stop working on the field," he said, "but I'm going to take a team out to start on another project. We need to build a platform out over the river. It'll get us out toward the deeper part, where we can swim and catch fish and maybe even launch a boat someday. There might be lots of places to explore besides this one. Who wants to work with me?"

Of course everyone wanted to switch over to this

new project. It sounded much more interesting than clearing the field. And besides, people wanted to be on the project Tick was working on.

So a great many of them started helping with the new platform—the dock, Tick said it was called. They ripped boards off the old storage sheds behind the hotel, they piled up rocks in the river to make supports. The field project slowed way down. Hardly anyone was working on it anymore.

And as the weeks went on, Doon began to see that this was how Tick's projects went. He would have an idea and get everyone excited about it. They'd start in to work. Then after a while Tick would have an idea for a new project, and everyone would follow him to that one, while the old project withered away. What Tick seemed to like was the thrill of something new, and the power of being a leader. This slightly dimmed Doon's admiration for Tick. But no one was perfect, after all. Tick had far more energy than most people, and far more ideas, even though they weren't all good ones.

In addition to helping with Tick's projects, Doon had plenty of his own projects to keep him busy. In the early mornings, he helped Clary with the garden she'd put in near the river. He was working on a way to make watering easier for her. He'd seen a pump the villagers had constructed, which used the river's current to push water out into the channels that watered the fields. This pump was fairly simple—a deep hole in the riverbank, with an arrangement of pipes and valves at the bottom. He thought he could figure out how to make one.

In the evenings, by the last of the daylight, Doon read. He was choosing books from the room in back of the Ark every few days now. His choices at first were pretty random—he just grabbed whatever he could reach. But then he'd had a great idea for bringing some sort of order to this vast collection. One day, when he got back to room 215 after work, he'd found Edward Pocket standing by the window, frowning at the sky. Edward looked unhappy. His gnarled hands were tightened into fists, and his mouth was bunched up into a twisted knot.

"Are you all right?" said Doon.

"Oh, I'm fine," said Edward. "I just love sitting around all day doing nothing."

"You're bored," said Doon.

"Yes!" Edward cried. "Yes, yes, yes!" He raised both hands and grabbed wads of his frizzled gray hair and stretched his mouth into a mad grin. "They say I'm too old to work, but I'm not ready to freeze up and die. I don't want to spend my days *chatting*. Or *sleeping*." He said the words with contempt. "What am I supposed to do with myself?"

And of course Doon had the answer. It was so obvious he didn't know why he hadn't thought of it before. "I know exactly what you can do," he said, and he told Edward Pocket about the books.

Now Edward spent all the daylight hours in the book room, sorting and organizing and arranging the books. He often picked out ones he thought Doon would like and brought them back to the hotel. In this way, Doon learned about bird migrations, cowboys, basketball, whales, mountain climbing, Egyptian history, dog training, French cooking, car repair, and dinosaurs, among other things. Edward even found a book called *Science Projects,* in which there was a chapter that explained how to do an experiment that made electricity. The experiment required things Doon didn't have, but he kept the book anyway, in case he ever got them. You never knew what was going to turn up in the loads the roamers brought to town.

In the meantime, Tick carried on tirelessly with his projects. The dock never did get built. It kept getting torn apart by the river's current. But other projects succeeded. One of Tick's ideas was to hoist the flag of Ember over the Pioneer Hotel. Lottie Hoover, who had worked in one of Ember's city offices, had rolled the flag up and tucked it into her bag just before she rushed down into the Pipeworks to leave. Doon didn't really see the point of flying Ember's flag over the hotel—everyone knew that it was the people of Ember who lived there—but he helped with the project, sawing the limbs off a tall, thin tree to make a flagpole. Soon the flag of the city of Ember, deep blue with a yellow grid, flapped above the Pioneer.

"Beautiful," said Tick, gazing up at it. He turned to the people gathered around him. "We have to show them," he said, "that we're *proud* of being the people of Ember. They have all the advantages right now. They control the food. They control the work teams. They're taller than we are, and stronger. But we can't let any of that matter. If we want them to respect us, we have to respect ourselves."

Several days later, as Doon was walking through the plaza, he noticed that a flag was also flying from the tower of the town hall. It was black with a spray of orange dots rising from the corner—sparks, Doon thought. He wondered if they'd had this flag all along, or if someone had made it and put it up after seeing the one at the Pioneer Hotel.

CHAPTER 12

Caspar Arrives with a Surprise

Lina was sweeping the floor of the kitchen when she heard the thump and shuffle of hooves outside. There was a shout, in a man's voice—"Hello-o-o! Where is everyone?"—and then a shriek from inside the house, running footsteps, and Torren's voice screaming, "Caspar! Caspar! You're home!"

Lina flung down the broom and dashed to the door. There was Torren, clamped onto the front of a very large man, who was rumpling Torren's hair and thumping him on the back. Behind the man was his truck, an especially large one, piled high with boxes and crates, pulled behind two huge oxen with curved horns. They stood breathing noisily, their sides going in and out.

"Well, small brother," said Caspar. "Glad to see me?"

"Yes!" said Torren. He unwrapped his arms from

around his brother's trunk and gazed up at his face. "You were gone so long this time."

"I had to extend my route," said Caspar. "Quite far, in fact. *Quite* far. The work of a roamer gets harder every year."

Lina could see Caspar's resemblance to his brother, Torren—they both had the same small eyes and the same wispy light brown hair. But while Torren was narrow, Caspar was wide. He had a wide, round, rosy-pink face, with a glistening, round chin. It was almost a babyish-looking face, except for the tiny mustache on the upper lip, twisted at both ends into points.

Dr. Hester, who had been picking peas, came out from the side of the house. "Welcome back, traveler," she said.

"Auntie Hester!" cried Caspar, flinging his arms wide. He stood that way while Dr. Hester walked toward him, and when she came close he gave her a hug that lifted her feet in their dusty slippers off the ground.

"Don't do that," she said, her face squashed against Caspar's shoulder.

He dropped her back down. "Can't help it," he said. "You're light as a feather."

"I'm not, either," said the doctor, rubbing her neck. "You're just showing off your muscles."

"Well," said Caspar, "it's true that being a roamer builds muscles." He made a fist and flexed his meaty arm back and forth. "Heavy things to lift, you know.

Some *exceedingly* heavy. Out near the Camp Range foothills a few months ago, I got stuck in the mud and had to lift the whole back end of the truck, which was loaded at the time with—"

Torren jumped up and down at Caspar's side. "Did you bring me a surprise?"

Caspar looked startled. "A surprise?"

"Yes, the way you always do. A surprise for me!"

For a second Lina felt sorry for Torren; the look on his face was so hopeful. She had a feeling that Caspar was more important to Torren than Torren was to Caspar.

Caspar laughed. He had the oddest laugh— *hih-hih-hih-hih*, all on one high, squeaky note. It was hardly a sound of pleasure at all. "Well," he said, "as it happens, I did bring one surprise. It's more of a surprise for everyone, though." He looked back toward his truck. "Are you there?" he called.

"Right here," answered a gruff voice. From behind the truck stepped a woman almost as big as Caspar himself—a massive tree trunk of a woman, with swirls and tangles of red-brown hair falling to her shoulders. She was dressed in faded blue pants and a huge brown shirt. She looked at them, smiling slightly. Her eyes were blue and fierce.

"This is Maddy," said Caspar. "She's my roaming partner."

From Torren there was silence. Dr. Hester held out

her hand and said, "Welcome." The big woman pumped the doctor's hand firmly up and down three times, and then Dr. Hester glanced toward the house and saw Lina standing in the doorway.

"Caspar," she said, turning back to him. "Have you heard about what's happened since you've been gone? About the people who came here from the underground city?"

"I heard some tale like that," said Caspar.

"Lina is one of them," Dr. Hester said. "Come here, Lina."

Lina walked out toward Caspar, who squinted at her and then thrust a hand into the pocket of his pants and pulled out a pair of slightly bent glasses, which he put on. He peered at her through their cracked lenses as she approached. When she got close, he held out an enormous hand. Lina shook it.

"Underground, eh?" said Caspar. The cloudy glasses made his eyes look bigger and dimmer. "Some sort of mole people? But you've got no fur!" He laughed his squeaky laugh again. "Hih-hih-hih!"

Lina smiled politely at this stupid joke. Something about Caspar seemed to be slightly off, she thought.

"Lina's sister, Poppy, is with us, as well," Dr. Hester went on, "and their guardian, Mrs. Murdo."

During all this Torren had been standing very still. His narrow face had closed down: his eyes looked like tiny stones, and his mouth was pinched small. He was staring at Maddy. Suddenly he cried, "But *I'm* supposed to be your partner!"

Caspar blinked at him, as if he'd already forgotten he was there. "You?" he said. "You're much too young."

"I'm almost eleven!" Torren yelled. "I'm big enough!"

"Not quite, little brother," Caspar said. He grinned at Maddy, who gazed back at him calmly. She was like a big rock, Lina thought. Her face didn't move.

Torren scowled. "Don't call me little!" he shouted. He turned and ran toward the house.

Caspar watched him go, lifting his eyebrows slightly. "It's hard for children to accept change," he said. "But they must learn, mustn't they?"

Dr. Hester said, "Our three guests have been sleeping in the loft, Caspar. They'll have to sleep in the main room while you're here." She paused. "How long do you think you'll stay?"

"Just a night or two," said Caspar. His face took on a serious look. "I'm on a particular mission this time. Heading for the city."

The city? thought Lina. What city?

The doctor echoed her thought. "The city?" she said. "Why in the world would you go there?" She seemed astonished, as if she'd never heard before of anyone going to the city.

"Because of this particular mission," Caspar said. "Of a secret nature."

"I see," said Dr. Hester. "All right, then. It's nearly time to eat. Take your beasts down to the barn, and then come on in."

That night, Caspar talked a great deal about his exploits as a roamer. "In the northern forest lands," he said, "I came upon some old cabins that still had glass in the windows. It was quite a trick to get the glass out without breaking it—took four days—but I managed. Did cut my hand a bit." He extended his large hand and pointed out a tiny scar on the palm. "Quite a lot of blood from that. Then up near Hogmarsh, I found a very valuable item." He gazed around at them, smiling slightly.

"What was it?" asked Torren, who had forgotten for the moment to be mad at his brother.

"An ancient statue," said Caspar. "It depicts some very rare sort of bird, with a long neck and only one leg. You can see that it was once painted pink." He paused to let the wonder of this sink in.

"Pink, tink, stink," said Poppy. "Pinky stinky." She stared at Caspar and giggled.

"Hush, Poppy," said Lina.

"Then in Ardenwood," Caspar went on, idly twisting his tiny mustache, "I had to fend off a few bandits."

"Bandits?" cried Torren. "Really?"

"Well, they might as well have been bandits,"

Caspar said. "Turned out they had no weapons, but they were set on stealing from me, that's for sure. I got rid of them fast with a few well-placed lashes." Caspar sliced his arm through the air, as if he were cracking a whip. "And a good thing, too," he went on, "because not far from there I located another special thing—several boxes of authentic, pre-Disaster artificial flowers. They are made of very fine cloth, hardly faded at all."

"Artificial flowers?" said Lina, wondering why the people of Sparks would want fake flowers when they had real ones growing everywhere.

"Yes," said Caspar. "I have a sort of knack for finding unusual things."

Maddy didn't join much in the conversation. Once Mrs. Murdo, being polite, asked her if she too enjoyed being a roamer, but she only smiled a little and said, "I don't mind it. There are worse things to be."

Mrs. Murdo waited to hear about the worse things, but it seemed that was all she was going to say.

When it was bedtime, Caspar went up into the loft and Torren dashed up after him. Maddy took Torren's place in the medicine room, saying a brief good-night and closing the door firmly after her. The doctor helped Lina and Mrs. Murdo make up beds of pads and blankets on the couch and on the floor.

"It sounds interesting to be a roamer," Lina said.

"I suppose so," said the doctor.

"And Caspar has a special knack for finding things?"

The doctor bent over and spoke softly into Lina's ear. "He has a knack for finding the *wrong* things," she said. "He's always bringing loads of things people already have, and not finding the things people really need. Artificial flowers," she said wearily. "What are we going to do with artificial flowers?" The bed being made up, she went around the room and blew out all the candles but one. "He's always been a bit odd," said the doctor. "Looks as if he's gotten even odder since he was here last. He tries hard, though, you can say that for him. He has high ambitions. He wants to be a famous roamer. He doesn't know that he's a bit famous already, among the other roamers—but not famous the way he'd like."

She handed the last candle to Lina and stumped off to her room.

The next day was strange and unpleasant. Caspar sat in the big armchair telling stories about his adventures while Torren hovered around him asking questions. Lina listened for a while. She was curious about this work of roaming—it sounded exciting, like something she might want to do herself. But she soon got bored, because it seemed to her that Caspar never said much about the really interesting parts of his adventures. She wanted to hear what the faraway places were like, and how the old buildings looked, and everything that was in the buildings, but all Caspar talked about was how brave and clever he'd been to find the things he found, and what injuries he'd suffered in finding them.

Maddy didn't listen to Caspar; she spent most of her time in the courtyard or the garden, motionless and silent, gazing at the plants, her arms folded across her wide waist. Every now and then she plucked a leaf or blossom, rubbed it between her fingers, and sniffed it. Once she asked Lina what a certain plant was. "I'm not sure," Lina said. "I only know a few of them."

"Then you know more than I do," said Maddy, flashing Lina an unexpected smile. But other than that, she said almost nothing to anyone. She didn't seem angry or unhappy, just off in her own world. Lina wondered about her but felt far too shy to ask questions.

After a while, Caspar shooed Torren away, sat down at the table, and pulled some scraps of paper from his pocket. He spread them out and bent over them, and his jovial, boastful manner changed. He ran his finger along the lines of writing on the papers. He wrote on them with a stubby pencil. And as he did so, he frowned and muttered and mumbled to himself, words that sounded like nonsense to Lina except for an occasional string of numbers. "Mmmbgl bblbble 3578," he would say. "Throobbm wullgm fflunnnph

147

44209." She wandered up behind him and tried to look over his shoulder. After all, she had experience with torn documents and hard-to-decipher bits of writing. But Caspar twisted around and scowled at her, holding his hands over the papers. "Private! Private! Keep away," he said. He wouldn't let Torren see, either, so Torren sat on the window seat and sulked.

Around midafternoon, the doctor rushed in the door looking even more frazzled than usual. Her shirt was smudged with blood, and her shirttails were half tucked in and half not. "I'm out of clean bandages," she said. "Lina, did you do them? I need some. And I need that lavender extract—a bottle of it. No, I'd better get two bottles." She hurried into the medicine room.

Lina had forgotten all about the bandages. She dashed into the kitchen, pulled some rags from the basket, and tore them into strips. She took these to the doctor, who was on her knees, rummaging through a chest.

"And," said the doctor, "I'm going to have to make some mustard plasters tonight. You'll need to go out into the orchard and gather me some mustard flowers. I'll need a lot. Get the leaves, too, and the roots. I want the whole plant." She found her bottles of oil, thrust them into her bag along with the bandages, and rushed out the door again.

Lina felt her spirits sink down into her shoes. She didn't want to gather mustard plants. It was too hot. It was *ferociously* hot. She was sick of being hot, having her neck damp beneath her long hair and her clothes sticking to her back. She was sick of doing chores. She shuffled out into the courtyard, where a few of the doctor's seedlings were drying up in their pots. She trudged to the pump, filled a bucket, and splashed some water on each limp plant. Then she sat down in the shade of the grapevine and leaned against the wall beneath the window and thought about everything that was wrong.

She was mad at the doctor for giving her so much work to do and hardly noticing when she did it. She was mad at Mrs. Murdo for not moving them out to the Pioneer Hotel. And she was lonely. She missed being with people she knew. Especially, she missed being with Doon in the old way, the way they'd been together when they were partners in Ember. Now he seemed to care more for his new friends than he did for her. Every time she thought about him, she felt a thud of pain, like a bruised place inside her.

From the window just above her head, Lina heard Caspar's voice. "Not now!" he said. "I have to do some planning. I need quiet."

The door opened, and Torren stormed out. He threw a furious glance at Lina but didn't speak. He ran through the gate and up the road. He's mad, too, thought Lina. Everyone's mad.

From inside, she heard Caspar's voice again,

startlingly near. He was talking to Maddy, who must have come in the kitchen door. Lina realized they were standing by the window, just behind her.

"We'll head out day after tomorrow," said Caspar. "Starting early."

"Uh-huh," said Maddy in her low, growly voice.

"All those stories about germs still lurking there," Caspar said, "they're nonsense, you know. Those germs died out long ago."

"No doubt you're right," said Maddy.

They were talking about the city! Lina sat very still and listened harder.

"People talk about other kinds of danger there, too," Caspar went on. "Bandits and so on. Doesn't bother *me.*"

"Of course not," Maddy said.

"And anyway, even if there is danger," said Caspar, "it's worth the risk, because of what we're going to find."

"You sound very sure that we're going to find it," said Maddy.

"Of course I'm sure," said Caspar. "Aren't you?"

The answer to this was just a grunt.

They moved away from the window, and their voices grew fainter. Maddy spoke next. Lina couldn't hear all of what she said, but she caught the words "How far?" and in Caspar's answer she heard the words "day's journey." Then she heard steps clomping up the stairs to the loft, and the room went quiet.

Lina sat very still. Her bad mood faded. Other thoughts swirled in her mind. She was remembering the sparkling city whose picture she had drawn so many times, the great city of light, the city she had always believed in. Now Caspar was planning to go there. It wasn't dangerous anymore, and it was only a day's journey away.

She knew, of course, that the city Caspar was talking about had been damaged, like everything else, in the Disaster. The beautiful, shining city she had imagined must have been this city in the past, in the time before the Disaster. In her mind, she revised her vision of the city: some of the high towers would have toppled, and their windows would be broken. Stones from ruined buildings would have fallen into the street. Roofs would have caved in.

But the idea that struck her was this: maybe the people of Ember were meant to restore the city. Perhaps their great job—the reason they had come up into this new world—was to live in the city and rebuild it, so that once again it was the glorious, shining city of Lina's vision.

This was *such* a beautiful idea. That night, she lay in bed thinking about it, and the more she thought, the more sure she was, and the more excited.

CHAPTER 13

Taking Action

One evening Doon wandered off by himself toward the far corner of the hotel, where the trees grew thickly and the undergrowth beneath them was dense. He made his way into the woods, to a thicket of vines all woven together like thorny ropes. Little lumpy fruits, some red and some black, grew on these vines. Doon had already discovered that the red ones were hard and sour, but if left to ripen they turned black and sweet. He had been checking the vines regularly; each day there were more and more of the black ones. Today, he saw, there were more black berries than red. He began picking them. Some he ate right from the vine—they were sweet and juicy. Others he put in a basket he'd brought with him to take back to the others in room 215.

He heard footsteps behind him. A voice—he recognized it instantly—called out, "Doon!" He turned around, and there was Tick striding toward him, smiling his dazzling smile.

Doon stood up—he'd been squatting to reach for the berries on the lowest vines. "Look what I found," he said, holding out a handful of berries to Tick.

Tick took one and popped it into his mouth. His eyebrows shot up in surprise. "Terrific!" he said. He took the rest of them from Doon's palm. "So," he said, "are you going to save us again?"

"Save us?" said Doon, confused.

"Yes, from starvation. You're the hero of Ember. It's about time for you to save us again."

It flustered Doon to be called a hero. He wasn't sure if Tick was admiring him or making fun of him. He couldn't think what to say next.

Tick reached into the thicket and plucked a few berries for himself. "These are good," he said. "Mind if I take some?"

"They don't belong to me," said Doon. "Anyone can have them."

Tick hunted among the vines for a while, picking berries and popping them into his mouth. Then he said, "You know that building they call the Ark?"

Doon nodded.

"Ever been in it?"

"No," Doon said. "Just in the separate room at the back. They have books in there—you should see them, there must be thousands."

Tick didn't comment on the books. "I went in there the other day," he said. "They had me carry in a crate of pickled beets. It's their storehouse, you know. They say they're short of food. Hah!" Tick gave a laugh that was more like a bark. "That place is *full* of food."

"Really?" said Doon.

"Really," said Tick, tossing three berries into his mouth. "There's jars of preserved fruit, and sacks of dried fruit, and every kind of pickle, and bags of corn—loads and loads of food. And we get limp carrots for our dinners. I believe there's a bit of stinginess going on."

Doon frowned. He thought of his father, looking with dismay last night at the scanty contents of his dinner parcel. He thought about what Ordney had said at lunch the week before: *We just don't have enough for four hundred extra people.* Was this untrue after all?

Tick had moved a few steps away and found a patch that was thick with berries. He was picking them rapidly, eating each one. When he spoke, his words sounded a little juicy. "I don't know about you," he said, "but I don't like unfairness."

"I don't, either," said Doon. He walked over to Tick and offered him the handful of berries he'd just collected. Tick took them all.

"I believe an unfair situation needs to be corrected," Tick said.

"Corrected how?"

Tick wiped his red-stained fingers on his pants. "Well," he said, "that's something we have to figure out."

We, thought Doon. He liked that. Though he'd stopped taking part so often in Tick's projects, still he admired Tick's energy and felt his power. He was glad Tick had sought him out. He was glad that Tick seemed to consider him different from the others, smarter, more important. "You're right," he said. "We should do something."

Tick nodded. "I don't trust these Sparks people," he said. "In some ways, they seem very primitive. Do you know that they make fire by hitting two stones together?"

"They do?" Doon hadn't seen anyone starting a fire, since he was rarely in kitchens. He knew that the fire in the bakery was kept going all the time; he'd seen people going in there sometimes carrying candles that had gone out. "They don't have matches?" he said.

"Sometimes they do," said Tick. "But not always. Matches seem to be rare."

"We should give them some of ours," said Doon. All the people who'd come out of Ember had the matches that were supplied with the boats. The Emberites had hundreds of matches.

"Oh, I don't think so," Tick said quickly. "We need them. We have to keep those for ourselves."

Doon wondered why, when they had so many; but

he thought maybe matches figured somehow in Tick's plans.

"So you're with me?" said Tick.

"Sure," said Doon. Then he hesitated. "With you in what?"

"Action," said Tick. "You took action before, when there was an urgent situation. We may need to take action again pretty soon."

Doon still didn't know what Tick had in mind, but he asked no more questions. Tick had a way of letting you know that he'd given all the answers he was going to give. "All right," Doon said. "I'm with you."

"Good," said Tick. He held out his hand, and Doon shook it. Tick grinned and walked away.

Doon watched him lope across the field. For a moment he was lost in his thoughts—*food in the storehouse, stinginess, unfairness, figure something out, you're with me. . . .* When he came to himself again and glanced down at his hands, he was startled to see them streaked with blood. Had he scratched himself on the thorns of the vines? It took him a second to realize that what looked like blood was only berry juice, passed to his hand from Tick's.

Lina made a plan. She'd hide among the boxes and crates on Caspar's truck, and she would ride that way to the city. It was only a day's journey away. Surely she'd be able to find a way back. There must be other roamers on the roads.

Of course, she *could* just ask Caspar if she could go with him. But she was sure he'd say no. He was on some kind of important business. He wouldn't want to be bothered with her. It was best to go secretly. Once she had seen the city, she would know if it was the place where the people of Ember were destined to live. She was sure she'd know as soon as she saw it. Then she could hop out of the truck and find her way back. Caspar might never see her at all.

The next day, she tore part of a blank page out of one of the doctor's books and wrote this note:

> *Dear Mrs. M,*
> *I have gone with Caspar and Maddy*
> *on the truck. I will be back in two days*
> *or maybe three. There is something*
> *important I want to find out. Also I need*
> *a change from here. See you soon.*
> *Love, Lina*

Her plan was to wait until that night, when Mrs. Murdo was asleep, and tuck the note between the pages of the ancient, crumbling book she had been reading, something called *Charlotte's Web.* (She kept urging Lina to look at it, but Lina said she wasn't that interested in spiders—it would be better for Doon.) Mrs. Murdo read only in the evening, so Lina would have at least a day's head start before anyone knew where she was.

A few doubts about her plan lurked in the back of Lina's mind. She knew Mrs. Murdo would worry about her. Poppy would miss her. And Lina didn't really like Caspar, or trust him, and she knew that he and Maddy would probably be angry if they found that she had come along. It was a bit of a risky journey she was embarking on. But anything truly important involved risks, didn't it? She had taken a huge risk before, in the last days of Ember, and it had been the right thing to do. So probably this was the right thing, too. She was so sure the city was their destination, and she was so determined to see the city for herself, that she turned her mind away from her doubts. It would be an adventure, she told herself. She would be fine.

She got up before the sun the next morning. She crept out of her bed on the floor one tiny motion at a time. Poppy didn't stir, nor did Mrs. Murdo in her bed on the couch. In the half darkness, Lina put her clothes on and pulled the pillowcase bag she'd packed the night before from its hiding place in the window seat. She tucked her note between the pages of Mrs. Murdo's book. Then, carrying her bag, she opened the door so softly it made no noise and went out into the courtyard.

Just beyond the gate, the truck was standing ready. The oxen weren't attached to it yet; they were down the road, at the barn, to be brought later by the stablehand.

Lina climbed onto the back of the truck. Its metal bottom was gritty with dust and bits of dry grass. It was loaded with four large barrels, two bicycles strapped together, a box full of tubs and buckets, and four big wooden crates made of slats of wood spaced about an inch apart. The crates were taller than Lina and about four feet square—like small rooms, almost. Three of them were full of goods to be sold, but the fourth was empty—its contents had been sold in Sparks. That one would be Lina's hiding place.

Getting into it was easy. First she tossed her bag over the side, and then she climbed up the slats as if they were a ladder and jumped down in. The wood was rough and splintery, but she had prepared for that. She'd brought a small blanket from her bed. She spread this on the bottom of the crate and lay down on it, using her bag of supplies as a pillow. She was sure that if she lay very still, no one would see her.

And she was right. An hour or so later—she didn't know for sure how long, but the sun was now shining through the slats in the crate, and she could feel its warmth on her back—she heard the clatter of the gate latch, and voices. Torren's first:

"But I'd be helpful!" he said in a tearful, desperate wail. "I would! I know how to tie knots, and I can—"

"Now, that's enough," said Caspar. "You're not coming with us, get it through your hard little head. You're not old enough. Roaming is a dangerous business, it's not for children."

"She gets to go," Torren said.

"Of course. She's not a child. She's my partner."

Lina felt a jolt as the box holding Caspar's and Maddy's belongings was heaved up onto the truck. "Here comes Jo with the oxen, right on time," said Caspar.

The truck squeaked and trembled as the oxen were hitched to it. Lina heard the gate latch clatter again, and then the doctor's voice: "When will you be back this way?"

"Not for a while." The truck slanted as Caspar got on. "Several months, is my guess. We've got a big route planned out."

"You should be taking *me!*" cried Torren. "You'll be sorry you didn't! I'll tell on you! I'll tell Uncle!"

Caspar chuckled. "Uncle would not be interested," he said. "He's much too busy. Always has been." There was the crack of a whip. "Goodbye, little brother," Caspar called, and the truck jolted forward.

PART 2

Travelers and Warriors

CHAPTER 14

What Torren Did

All day, after Caspar and Maddy left, Mrs. Murdo wondered where Lina was. Had the doctor sent her on an errand? She asked, but the answer was no. Did Torren know where she was? He said he didn't know and he didn't care. Thinking maybe Lina had gone to the Pioneer Hotel to see Doon, Mrs. Murdo walked down there. But no one had seen her. By evening, when Lina was still missing, Mrs. Murdo was very worried.

She found the note in her book that night. She frowned as she read it. This didn't seem like a good idea to her. It was one of Lina's rash, impulsive acts, and probably it was dangerous. Mrs. Murdo went downstairs, knocked on the doctor's door, and showed her the note. "Can we send someone after them?" she said. "To bring her back?"

But the doctor shook her head. "They're a whole day ahead," she said. "No one could catch up. Even if you could find someone willing to go."

So Mrs. Murdo went back to bed and tried to sleep. She told herself that Lina had survived many dangers before. But still she lay awake worrying most of the night.

In the morning, at breakfast, Torren asked where Lina was and Mrs. Murdo told him. He jumped up from his chair. He threw down his piece of bread, which bounced on the table. *"She went with them?"* he cried. "She went with Caspar?"

"Calm down," said Dr. Hester.

"No!" yelled Torren. "I won't calm down! I hate her! I hate all you cave people! Why did you have to come here and ruin everything?" With a furious swipe of his hand, he knocked over Mrs. Murdo's cup of tea. He kicked backward at his chair, which fell over, and he ran out of the room. Through the window, Mrs. Murdo saw him racing across the courtyard and out the gate.

"Jealous," said the doctor. "He wants Caspar all to himself. Heaven knows why."

"That boy craves attention," said Mrs. Murdo. "I doubt that he cares who it comes from."

"I suppose you're right," said the doctor, looking at Mrs. Murdo with faint surprise.

Torren sped down the river road, full of boiling rage. *He* was the one who should be sitting beside Caspar, not that fat Maddy and not the stupid cave girl. *He* should be there, riding on the truck, going away to be a roamer. But she had snuck off and done it instead, and he hated her for it. It was the worst thing that had happened to him in his whole life.

He ran a long way, his feet pounding the dusty road, his fists pumping back and forth, furious tears streaming down his face. When he stopped, panting, he was way out in the tomato field, not far from the wind tower, where he had been the day the cave people came over the hill. He remembered how they had looked—like a swarm of horrible insects coming down toward the village.

Now the cave people had settled in as if they were going to stay forever. They were eating food that should belong to Sparks people. They were wearing clothes that Sparks people had given them. They walked around in the streets of Sparks as if they belonged here. Torren wanted them gone.

He stomped among the tomato plants, throwing punches at the air. "Get out of here, get out!" he cried, as if Lina and all the Emberites were there to hear him. His thoughts were like flames inside his head. He kept seeing Caspar on the seat of his truck with Maddy on one side of him and Lina on the other. The feeling that went with this picture was like a sharp stick in his stomach.

If only he had one of those giant bombs they had

in the old days! He imagined they were about the size of watermelons. He would shoot one at Lina! *Pow!* It would sail halfway to the city and drop right on Caspar's truck and blow them all up! Then he would shoot another one at the Pioneer Hotel. *Blam!* It would flatten the building and blow up every one of the cave people. He longed to throw that big bomb. He could almost feel it in his hands.

He'd come out at the end of the row of plants now, where a small whitewashed storage shed stood at the edge of the field. Crates of tomatoes were stacked nearby, ready to be distributed. Without thinking, Torren grabbed a tomato from the nearest crate and hurled it against the wall of the shed. It splattered. Red water dripped down the white wall. It felt so good to do this that he did it again. In a fury, he snatched up one tomato after another. *Wham, wham, wham,* he flung them with all his might, until the window of the shed splintered, the wall was a bleeding mess, and a long mound of broken red flesh lay on the ground.

He stopped and took a breath. What would the farmers think when they saw *this*? Two whole crates of tomatoes, smashed. They'd be angry. But they wouldn't know he had done it, would they? No one had seen him.

And that was when an idea floated into Torren's mind. A really excellent idea. He smiled, thinking about it. He threw one last tomato, aiming for the dark, glass-toothed hole of the broken window. There was a satisfying crash as the tomato knocked something over inside. Torren turned and ran, but he didn't go all the way home.

When Doon came through town that morning on the way to work, he found Mrs. Murdo waiting for him by the side of the road. She signaled to him with one finger, and he left the stream of workers and came over to her.

"Lina has gone off," she said. "I thought you should know."

"Gone off? Gone off where?"

Mrs. Murdo produced a scrap of paper from the pocket of her skirt. "Read this," she said.

Doon read. He scrunched up his nose in puzzlement. He remembered Lina telling him something the other day about these people, Caspar and Maddy. What had she said? He tried to recall. He looked again at the note. "'Something important,' she says. What would that be?"

Mrs. Murdo shrugged her thin shoulders. "She gets ideas in her head," she said. Doon could see that she was worried, though she didn't say so.

"Well, she says she'll be back in two or three days," said Doon. "That's not so long."

"The odd thing is," said Mrs. Murdo, "that Caspar, when he left, said he wouldn't be back for several months."

Doon frowned. What was Lina up to? He didn't understand it. But he didn't want to make Mrs. Murdo more worried than she was. "She must have some plan for getting back," he said, handing back the note.

"Of course," said Mrs. Murdo briskly. She folded the note and replaced it in her pocket. "There's no need to worry. I'll have her come and find you as soon as she returns."

She headed back toward the doctor's house, and Doon went toward the fields. He walked slowly to give himself time to think. He was upset about Lina. How could she be so foolish as to launch herself out into an unknown world with two unknown people? But in a way he wasn't surprised. Lina was always eager to investigate new places. Look how she'd gone up to the roof of the Gathering Hall on the first day she became a messenger in Ember. Look how eager she'd been to go down into the Pipeworks. She probably just wanted to see what was outside of Sparks. As soon as she'd satisfied her curiosity, she'd be back.

But Doon was upset about Lina for another reason, too, and it didn't have to do with her safety. He was upset that she had gone exploring without him. All through the last days of Ember, they'd been partners. Now she had gone off on her own, leaving him here.

He was annoyed, and he was hurt. He had to admit to himself that he hadn't been a very good friend to Lina lately. Maybe he'd hurt her feelings by paying so much attention to Tick. But still—it was *Lina* who was his partner in important things. If she had an urgent reason for hitching a ride with Caspar, why hadn't she told him? Why hadn't she asked him to come along?

He trudged toward the tomato field, head down, scuffing his shoes irritably in the dust, and so he didn't notice until he was right up to it that a commotion was going on by the storage shed. Everyone was crowded around it, and Chugger the team leader was yelling. Doon hurried forward to see what was going on.

"Wasted! Wasted!" Chugger was shouting. "Two whole crates, smashed! Who's done this? And the shed plastered with muck, and the window broken!" He glared at the crowd of workers. "Any of you know about this?" he demanded. "Anyone know what mad person did this?"

No one said a word. Doon stared with horror at the mess on the wall. It looked gory, as if it were smashed animals instead of just tomatoes. He could feel the rage of the person who had done it.

"I don't like this," Chugger said darkly. "Nothing like this ever happened before you people arrived. I want it cleaned up right away. Walls washed, window fixed, mess cleared away. Get on it."

"Listen," said someone. Doon turned to see—it

was Tick speaking. "We didn't do this. Don't get all tough with us."

Chugger whipped around. "Who else would do it? Who else but one of you, always griping and grumbling?"

"But we only just got here now—how could we have done it?" someone called out.

"Besides, we wouldn't!" cried someone else. "We would never waste food!"

More and more voices rose in protest. Doon added his, too, saying, "It wasn't us, it couldn't have been!" But Chugger just stood and scowled at them. Finally he yelled, "Quiet! Get to work!" Just after that Doon heard running footsteps behind him and turned to see Torren racing across the field. He was shouting in his shrill, high voice as he came.

"I saw!" he cried, waving his arms. "Last night I was out here, and I saw!" He ran into the midst of the workers and stood panting, his little eyes wild. "I heard a thump, thump, thump, so I snuck up to see, and I *did* see!"

"Well, then," said Chugger, "what did you see?"

"I saw who threw the tomatoes! I saw who made that big mess and broke the window!" He stood with his neck poked forward and his skinny arms held tight to his sides. His whole body was trembling with excitement. His eyes scanned the group of workers. "It was him!" he shrieked, pointing straight at Doon. "It was him that did it! I saw him!"

Doon was so shocked he couldn't make a sound. He stood with his mouth open, staring at Torren. Around him, a few people spoke up. "He did not!" said someone. "He couldn't have! Anyway, he wouldn't." "No," someone else said. "He would never do that."

But Chugger seized his arm and pulled him roughly aside. "What do you have to say for yourself? Is this your doing?"

Doon shook his head. "No," he said. "No. That boy is lying."

"And why would he do that? Why would he take the trouble to come out here first thing in the morning to point to you and lie?"

"I don't know," said Doon.

Chugger released his arm with a push. "I'll be keeping a special eye on you from now on," he said.

"But why?" said Doon. "I didn't do this."

"How do I know that?" said Chugger. "It's your word against his. And he's one of us."

CHAPTER 15

A Long, Hot Ride

Lina lay very still—or as still as she could with the jolting of the truck over the rutted road. Her eyes were at the level of the space between the two lowest slats of the crate, so she could see out just enough to guess where they were—along the road by the river first, and then turning to go around the outskirts of the village. Occasionally she heard someone call a greeting to Caspar, and she heard Caspar's voice returning it. Maddy never said anything that Lina could hear.

After a while there were no more voices. The sun beat down on Lina's back and she began to get terribly hot and uncomfortable. She thought it might be safe to sit up now. The sound of the wheels would muffle any sounds she made, and she was far enough toward the back of the truck so that Caspar and Maddy wouldn't see her moving. So she unfolded herself. She peered out and saw emptiness—vast stretches of dry, brown-gold grass, no people, no houses. It was an enormous space; she had not realized any place could be so big.

Sometime in the afternoon, because of the heat and the rocking motion of the truck and because there was nothing else to do, Lina went to sleep. When she awoke, she could tell right away that it was nearly evening. The air was cooler, and the sun was so low in the sky that she could no longer see it overhead; its slanting rays came between the slats of her crate.

A cramp gripped her stomach. It was partly hunger—she hadn't thought to bring any food with her. But it was mostly fear. They must be close to the city. And when they arrived, what would she do? And what would Caspar do when he found her?

The truck slowed and came to a stop. Lina felt Caspar and Maddy jump down.

"This looks like a good enough place," said Caspar's voice. "Near the water, anyhow."

"Looks all right to me." That was Maddy's voice.

"I'll take the animals down to the stream," said Caspar. Lina heard clanking and slapping sounds as he unbuckled the harness, and then the slow thud of hooves as the oxen were led away.

What was Maddy doing? Lina heard a few footsteps, some rustling among the grasses. Then there was silence. She had to move. Her legs were cramped and she had a pain in her back. Cautiously, she stood up.

She stepped onto the first slat of the crate and then the second, and when she got high enough to look over the top edge, the first thing she saw was Maddy, sitting on the ground a few feet from the end of the truck, leaning against a tree and staring right at her.

"Well, well," said Maddy. "Look who's here."

Lina just stared. She couldn't move.

Maddy heaved herself up from the ground and came over to the truck. She regarded Lina with a look that was half puzzled and half amused. "What in the world are you doing here?"

"I want to see the city," said Lina.

"Don't you know it's a five-day journey? How did you expect to ride in a crate all that time? And not be discovered?"

"Five days? I thought it was one day."

Maddy just shook her head. "What are we supposed to do with you?"

"I don't know," said Lina. She felt a trembling start up in her stomach. She should never have come.

There was a long pause before Maddy spoke again. Then she said, "Listen. It would suit me fine if you came along to the city, if you're sure you want to."

"I do want to," Lina said, though she wasn't really sure.

"Good," said Maddy, "because it looks like you have no choice." She smiled. It wasn't an unfriendly smile, but there was a quirk in it that seemed to say,

What a situation. "Stay there, then," she said. "I'll be back." She stamped away.

Lina watched Maddy heading toward a strip of green grasses and low trees that must border the stream; at the edge of this strip she could see Caspar and the oxen. In all directions, the landscape was the same she'd seen that morning—gently rolling, empty of buildings, covered with brown-gold grass. Here and there stood low, dark green, mushroom-shaped trees. Three of them stood near the truck, their leaves dusty, their trunks thick and gnarled. The sun had gone down behind the hills in the west, and the sky there was scarlet. Though the air was still warm, Lina shivered. She sat back down in the crate, pulled her knees up to her chest, and wrapped her arms around them. Somewhere a bird sang its going-to-bed song.

Then suddenly there were loud footsteps and Caspar's voice coming toward her, and in a moment Caspar's fist thudding against the crate. "Come out!" he said.

Lina climbed out and stood on the truck looking down at him.

"Jump down!" he said.

She jumped down.

Caspar glared at her. "So," he said. "A stowaway. What were you trying to do? Cause trouble? That's your idea of fun?"

"No," Lina said. "I want to see the city."

"What for?" A look of suspicion passed over Caspar's face. "What do you know about the city?"

"Nothing," said Lina. She wasn't going to tell Caspar about her vision of the city, or what the city might be for the people of Ember. "I just want to see it."

"Well, too bad," said Caspar. "Why should I take you there? Why would I want an extra person to feed? A kid to look after? Your ride stops right here. You can go back where you came from."

"One second," said Maddy. "Listen to me before you decide. She could be useful to us."

"Don't be ridiculous." Caspar whacked his two big hands together as if to dismiss the subject.

"Yes, she could," said Maddy. "When you're looking for something in a ruined place—you know how it is. Small spaces, sometimes. Tippy rubble where you need to step carefully. A small, light person could go where we couldn't."

Caspar took a step back and studied Lina, still glowering. Lina tried to look as small and light as she could.

"As for food," said Maddy, "she can share mine."

"Ridiculous," said Caspar again. But he kept his eyes on Lina. She could see he was thinking.

"Come on, Caspar," Maddy said. "Let's take her. We don't have much choice, after all. The only other thing we can do is leave her out here by herself." She turned to Lina. "If we let you come," she said, "you'll have to work for us. You'll have to do what we say."

"All right," Lina said, though she wasn't sure it was all right at all. Maybe it would be better to give up seeing the city and try to get back to Sparks from here. But how would she do that? She'd never be able to find her way. And the Empty Lands frightened her; she didn't want to be alone in such a vast, wild place. "But how will I get back again? Will you take me?"

"You should have thought of that when you climbed onto the truck," said Caspar. "That's your problem, not ours." He turned to Maddy. "Right, partner?"

"Certainly," Maddy said. "Now let's get settled for the night. The first thing we need is some kindling. Lina and I will go and gather it."

Lina followed her out toward the trees. Once they were in among them, Maddy bent down and spoke to her in a low voice. "Don't worry. You were foolish to do this, but I won't let harm come to you. And I'll see you get home again, somehow." She straightened up again. "Now," she said. "Gather up some dry twigs and sticks and a few tufts of dry grass."

They carried the sticks and grass back to where the truck was parked. There Maddy scraped out a shallow hole in the ground with the heel of her shoe. In the hole she set the smallest splinters of wood, arranging them in a sort of square. Over these she placed some sticks, and on top of those she added larger branches. She tucked in some handfuls of dried grass at the bottom of this stick building.

Until this point, Lina did not understand what she was doing. But when she pulled from her pocket a little cloth-wrapped package, unwrapped it, and took out a short blue-tipped stick, she knew. She took in a quick breath and stepped backward.

Maddy held up one of the matches and said, "Have you ever seen one of these?"

"Yes," said Lina.

"You're lucky, then," said Maddy. "They're rare."

She struck the match across a rock and the blue tip burst into flame. She held it to the grass, and the grass sizzled and flared up.

"Come and stand close," she said to Lina. "We need to shield this from the breeze until it gets going."

But Lina stayed where she was, staring. The little flame at the heart of the stack of sticks flickered. It reached for the splintered end of a stick, caught it, set it aflame. The sizzling grew to a hissing, and then to a crackling. Flames jumped, and jumped higher, and there again was the orange hand stretching upward with its pointed fingers, waving, leaning toward her.

Lina stumbled backward. She didn't want to be afraid—Caspar and Maddy weren't. Caspar had come back now and was crouching right beside the fire, feeding it with sticks and grass. But for Lina it was as if the flames were shrieking a message at her: Run, run, run! She stood twenty feet away, staring at the fire with a pounding heart. The wind blew a ribbon of smoke at her, and when she breathed, it stung the back of her throat.

Maddy noticed, after a while, that she was out there. "Come closer, Lina," she called. "It won't hurt you."

But Lina could not get her feet to walk toward that hissing, snapping blaze. It might not hurt Maddy and Caspar; but if she were to stand near it, she was sure it would reach for her with that orange hand, flick its fingers against the ends of her hair or the hem of her shirt, and she too would flare up. "I'm all right here," she said. "I don't want to be near it."

Caspar laughed. Maddy lumbered to her feet and came beside Lina. She put an arm around her. "You're shaking," she said. "Well, never mind. You don't have to be by the fire if you don't want to."

From a box on the truck, she took what they called "travelers' cakes"—lumps a little smaller than a fist, made of Lina knew not what—and she and Caspar stuck them on the end of long sticks and roasted them over the flames. "You have to get fond of these if you're a roamer," Caspar said. "They keep well, that's their best quality. You need them for those long stretches where there's no other food to be found."

They were dry and tasteless, but Lina was hungry,

so she didn't mind much. She ate hers standing up, and she licked her fingers when she was through.

She wondered where they were going to sleep. There was no room on the truck, so she supposed they'd have to lie on the ground. It was quite dark now. A breeze had come up. From somewhere far away, she heard an animal noise: *yip-yip-yip*, then a long wail, then an eerie chorus of wails. "What's that?" she asked Maddy.

"Wolves," Maddy said. "Out hunting. They're not very close, don't worry."

Lina shivered. The darkness here was so enormous, and so full of terrible things. In Ember, except when there was a blackout, people were almost always safe in their beds when darkness came. Lina wasn't used to being outside at night. She thought about Mrs. Murdo, who would be getting into bed in the doctor's attic room right now. Mrs. Murdo would be worried about her. Poppy would be saying, "Where Wyna?" No one would imagine that she was out in this great emptiness, with nothing between her and the sky.

Maddy took some rolled-up blankets from the truck and spread them on the ground. She put two of them close to the fire. The third she offered to Lina. "Put this wherever you want to sleep," she said.

Lina walked over to take the blanket, and as she did, Caspar tossed a big branch onto the fire. Sparks sprayed up. Some flew sideways, caught by the wind.

Lina jumped away, but a few sparks landed on her sock. She stamped her foot frantically, but this only made the sparks burn brighter. The threads of her sock glowed. On her ankle she felt a pain like a fierce bite. "No!" she cried. "Get it off me!" She shook her leg and clawed at her sock with her hand. Panic rose up in her, and she would have taken off running if Maddy had not blocked her path and grabbed her in strong arms. Once she'd stopped her, she bent down and put a hand over the burning place in Lina's sock, and when she took her hand away the glow was out.

But the pain was still there. Maddy took off Lina's shoe and sock and poured cold water on the burn, but it didn't help much. All night, Lina huddled on the ground under the thin blanket, gritting her teeth against the pain on her leg and wishing she had never come on this awful journey.

CHAPTER 16

The Starving Roamer

The next morning, after a breakfast of plums and coarse bread, they set out again. Maddy made Lina a place to sit at the back of the truck, between two of the crates. She took the blankets they'd slept on and spread them on the rough floor of the truck. Lina could sit on the blankets, lean against the nearest crate, and dangle her legs over the truck's back edge. The burn still hurt this morning; it was a reddish, angry-looking blister. After a while, as the sun came up and sweet grassy smells arose from the earth, Lina began to enjoy herself again. She watched the countryside fall away behind the truck, stretches of brown-gold grass as big as the sky, trees like hairy spikes, rocky slopes.

And this is how it was for four more days. At night they would find a place by a stream to sleep, if they could find a stream. They passed other ox-pulled cars and trucks on their way, both going their direction and coming back. They would stop and talk with these roamers and sometimes trade with them for food. Caspar always asked if they'd been to the city. Very few of them had. The ones that had been there just shook their heads when Caspar asked if they'd found any-thing interesting. "It's a waste of time to go there," they said. "Don't bother." Most of the roamers they met had been scavenging in what they called the suburbs, which Lina understood to mean towns that lay around the city.

Caspar and Maddy hardly spoke to her at all dur-ing the day. Around noon they would stop the truck and get something to eat from the chest of provisions they had brought. At first there was dried fruit, but they soon used that up. After that it was travelers' cakes, morning, noon, and night.

Caspar always went to sleep right after he'd filled his belly. He lay back on the ground and snored. Then Maddy would beckon to Lina with a tilt of her head, and they would walk away from Caspar and find a place to sit, often beneath a tree, one of those trees that spread their branches out like the top of a big mush-room. They would sit in the soft grass and look up at the sky through the tree's branches. Sometimes a breeze swept across the land and brought them the scent of dusty earth and dry weeds.

After lunch on their second day of traveling, Lina asked Maddy where she came from.

"A horrible place," was all she said.

"Horrible in what way?"

"Small, cold, and poor. Houses made of old boards. Bad soil for growing things, never enough food. A place that was withering."

"What does that mean, withering?" Lina asked.

"It means shrinking and dying. Things were getting worse there. There was too much sickness, too much hunger, too much unhappiness. People were always quarreling, and a lot of them were leaving. It was ending, the place where I came from. I wanted to be somewhere that was beginning."

"Our city was ending, too," said Lina. She looked up at the blue sky and thought about the sky in Ember: utter blackness, not a speck of light. No lights shone anywhere in Ember now. "There's no one left in our city," she said.

"Sparks is a place that's beginning," said Maddy. "If it can get past the hard spots."

"Hard spots?"

"Yes, like suddenly having to take in four hundred people."

"Oh," said Lina, remembering the conflicts in the village and all the reasons she'd wanted to get away from there. Her heart sank. "Maybe by the time we get back, that will all be over, all that trouble," she said.

"Maybe," said Maddy. "I hope so. Sparks is a whole lot better than where I came from."

"I can understand why you wanted to leave that place," said Lina.

"Pretty badly," said Maddy. "Bad enough to take up with a fool."

"Fool?"

Maddy just tipped her head toward the sleeping Caspar.

"You came with him just to get away?" Lina whispered.

Maddy nodded. "Roamers hardly ever came to our little settlement," she said, "mainly because we had nothing to trade. Caspar was only the second one I'd ever seen. I thought I might never see another, so I grabbed the chance."

"Why couldn't you just leave by yourself?"

"I thought of it," Maddy said. "But I didn't know where to go. I didn't know the roads, or where the settlements were. I didn't know how I'd get food. I guess I wasn't quite bold enough to go alone."

"When you got to Sparks, you could have stayed there," Lina said. "You didn't have to keep traveling with him."

"I would have stayed," said Maddy, "if I hadn't promised to help him on this quest of his. I try to honor my promises, if I possibly can."

That afternoon, as they traveled on across the rolling hills, Lina thought about places that were ending and places that were beginning. She knew

about endings. Now she wanted to be part of a beginning. Maybe the people of Ember could begin again in
the city. If not . . . well, she wouldn't think about that
until she had to.

On the second night, they pulled up beside the ruins of
a town. Not much was left of it, but you could see that
once there had been hundreds of houses. The concrete
foundations, overgrown with weeds, lined up along
curved streets. Here and there a wall or a chimney was
still standing. Caspar stopped the truck just beyond
the outer row of ruins, and Maddy went around to the
back and opened the trunk that held their dwindling
supply of food. They had stopped beside a ditch where
a trickle of water ran. It was green, scummy water, but
Lina drank it anyway. It was all there was.

Caspar seemed especially grouchy. His pink face
was splotched and damp, and his eyes looked
inflamed. He had forgotten to twist his mustache into
points, and it hung down at the corners of his mouth.
He dug a crumbling travelers' cake from the trunk
and glowered at Maddy. "What's the matter with you,
anyway?" he said. "You haven't been very chatty lately."

"I'm never chatty," said Maddy calmly.

Caspar took a savage bite of his cake. "It's like
traveling with a tree stump," he said. "I thought you
were going to be a pleasant and helpful companion."

Maddy did not reply to this. She chewed serenely,

gazing out over the acres of fallen houses. Lina realized there was a certain beauty in Maddy that she hadn't seen before. Her back was straight, she held her head high, and there was something unswayable in her. The bones of her face were strong, and her gaze was firm. There was nothing fluttery about her. You could see that Caspar was finding out that she was not what he'd taken her for at first. She was more than he'd bargained for.

On the third day, near evening, they saw a truck coming toward them from a great distance away. They were on a long, straight road with few trees or buildings to block their view, just the dry brown grass and a few ancient fences leaning over and flocks of birds rising, swooping through the air, and fluttering down again. Up ahead came this dark dot, toiling forward. In twenty minutes or so, the two trucks drew near.

Lina stood behind Caspar and Maddy, looking forward. This roamer looked poor. He had only one ox, a shaggy, swaybacked animal, and on his truck there were only two crates, not four as on Caspar's. The man himself was almost as shaggy as his ox. His hair was long and his beard lay like a hairy brown bib against his chest. As he came closer, he stood up on his truck and shaded his eyes with his hand, peering at them.

"Watch out for this one," Caspar said. "Could be a bandit. Looks bad and mean and dangerous."

When the other truck was twenty or thirty feet away, its driver suddenly hauled on the traces. His ox veered, and the truck turned sideways so that it blocked the road. Lina couldn't tell if he'd done this on purpose. His movements were jerky, as if something was wrong with him. He climbed down from his truck and stood in front of it, his neck tucked down and his shoulders hunched as high as his ears. His eyes glittered in his hairy face. He stood there like that, saying nothing, waiting for them.

Caspar stopped the truck. He stood up and leaned forward. "Out of my way, you ragged wretch! Move that flea-bitten rig!"

The roamer came a few paces closer. His mouth opened—a hole in the tangle of beard—but no words came out.

Lina could see the back of Caspar's neck flush deep red. "I said, *Out of my way!*" He snatched up his whip and sent the long lash curling out toward the man and snapped it a few feet from his face. The roamer let out a howl. He lurched toward them.

All this happened in only a minute or so. Lina's heart was beating wildly. *Was* this a bandit? Was he going to attack them? She ducked down behind a crate and peered between the slats.

Caspar raised the whip again. "Come any closer and I'll cut you to shreds!" he shouted.

But before he could lash out, Maddy grabbed his

arm. "Wait," she said. Caspar tried to shake her off, but she yanked at him so hard he lost his balance and sat down again. "Why not find out what the man wants before you attack him?" she said.

Caspar struggled against her, but she was strong. She managed to wrench the whip out of his hand. Then she jumped down and confronted the other roamer, who had halted just in front of the truck.

"What do you want from us?" she said to him, standing squarely in his path, her hands on her wide hips. "Why have you stopped us like this?"

The roamer backed up a step. He looked at her with his mouth hanging open. He was grubby, Lina saw. His hands and his bare feet were nearly black with dirt. He mumbled something.

Maddy bent closer to him. "What?"

He mumbled again.

She turned to Caspar, who had climbed down from the truck and was approaching with his fists clenched. "He says he's out of cakes." She turned back to the man. "How long since you've eaten?"

The man stared at his hands. He had long, filthy fingernails. His fingers twitched. "Three days," he croaked. "Just crumbs . . . three days."

"Well," said Caspar, "if you think we're going to supply you with food, you're very mistaken."

"Surely we can spare a couple of cakes," Maddy said.

Caspar's face was dark red. "We can*not*," he said. "We are on a special mission, extremely important. We need that food for ourselves—*all* of it."

Lina thought this was unreasonable. "He can have one of mine," she said.

Caspar whirled around. "No!" he said. "You're going to need your strength."

"You're being ridiculous," said Maddy, but Caspar reached out and pushed her. "Back in the truck," he said. "And you"—turning back to the roamer —"get your rattletrap out of my way, if you want to stay alive."

From the roamer came a sound Lina had never heard before from a human being—a hoarse hissing sound, as if he were spitting a stream of fire straight at Caspar's face. He did this twice, and then he turned away and scuttled back to his truck. He pulled on the ox's traces and it moved a few feet along, just far enough for Caspar to drive his truck past it. Caspar yelled at him one more time as he passed: "You shouldn't *be* a roamer if you can't feed yourself!" He cracked his whip at the man and drove on.

Lina climbed into a crate and sat with her head on her knees for a while after this. She was horrified by the starving, filthy roamer. How did he come to be in such a state? Was it his own fault? Was he a madman? But Caspar could have given him *something*, couldn't he? Or were they so low on food that losing any of it really would harm them? Her stomach lurched; she felt queasy. But she didn't know if it was hunger or horror at what she'd just seen.

That night, Lina woke up for a moment and heard the oxen making unsettled noises. She heard a creaking sound, too. But the sounds stopped, and she went back to sleep. In the morning, Maddy discovered they had been robbed.

"Well, well," she said, opening the food chest. "Look here."

"What?" said Caspar, who was wetting his mustache with spit and twisting it into points.

"Someone's been into our food," said Maddy. "I wonder who."

Caspar jumped to his feet. "Into our food?"

"He didn't get much," Maddy said. "Just three or four, I'd guess." She put her hand in the chest and felt around. "But he left us something."

Sputtering with rage, Caspar hauled himself up onto the truck. When he looked into the food chest, he let out a string of furious swear words.

Lina crept out from under her blanket and stood up. "What is it?" she said. "What happened?"

"Our friend from yesterday has been for a visit," said Maddy. "We wouldn't give him what he wanted, so he took it. And left something for us, too."

"Left what?" said Lina. Caspar was shaking with fury. His face was dark red.

"Looks like dirt," said Maddy. "I think he took

what he wanted and dumped a bag of dirt on the rest." She wrinkled her nose. "Might be some ox droppings in here, too."

"The skunk!" Caspar cried. "The miserable rat!"

"In my opinion," said Maddy, "you should have given him a couple of cakes in the first place."

"I didn't ask for your opinion," said Caspar.

"You're going to get it anyway," said Maddy, suddenly fierce. "You turned a crazy old guy into an enemy in less than two minutes. *You* did it. You've done it over and over, I've seen you: you approach people like an enemy and *bam!,* they turn into one, whether they were to begin with or not."

"It's my policy to be ready to defend myself," Caspar said, scowling. "At any moment."

"Fine," said Maddy. "So now, because of your policy, we're out four cakes instead of two, and we have a lot of dirt on the rest." She closed the chest, stood up, and glared at Caspar with a mixture of anger and scorn. "If you ask me, making friends is a better defense than making enemies."

"I didn't ask you," said Caspar.

On the fourth day, they went uphill hour after hour. The heat was terrible. The only water they found was at the bottom of a deep ravine. All three of them scrambled down, half stepping and half sliding, carrying Caspar's biggest pots, and, sweating and gasping, they lugged the filled pots back up so that the oxen could drink.

Then they went uphill some more. It was late afternoon by the time they came to the top of the ridge. Lina was so tired by that time and so hot that she felt like a boiled vegetable, limp and runny. She was a bit dazed, too, only half awake, and so she was startled when the truck jolted to a stop and she heard sharp exclamations from Caspar and Maddy. She jumped down and went around to the front. A tremendous view of land and water lay before her. Such immense water she had never seen—green-blue, glinting in the rays of the late sun, white ripples racing across its surface. To her right, it stretched as far as she could see, but straight ahead she could see the shore on the other side—green trees covering the ground, and hills rising beyond.

"The bay," said Caspar. "This means we're almost there. We go around the end of it and then north."

"When do we get to the city?" Lina said.

"Tomorrow," said Caspar. His wide face broke into a grin, and he laughed his high, weird laugh. He opened and closed his fingers, stretching and gripping, as if he were imagining taking hold of something. "We'll be there tomorrow, and then our work begins."

CHAPTER 17

Doon Accused

Word of the tomato throwing, and Torren's accusation of Doon, spread quickly through Sparks. Some people believed Torren, some didn't. But no one could prove who was telling the truth. Torren said he'd seen what he'd seen in the middle of the night, when he couldn't sleep and took a walk to the field to look at the stars. Doon said he'd been home all night, sleeping, and that his father and the others in his room knew it. But people said he could have slipped quietly out without anyone knowing, couldn't he? He could have gone down there and done his mischief and come back, and they all would have thought he'd been sleeping the whole night.

At noon that day, when he and the others showed up at the Partons' house for their midday meal, no one spoke to them. Martha let them in, and they sat down at the table, where places had been set for them as usual. Doon's father said, "Good day," and Mrs. Polster said, "How are you?" and Miss Thorn and Edward Pocket looked around at the family's stony faces and tried to smile. Ordney put food on their plates (was it an even smaller amount than usual?) and passed the plates to them. Kenny ate tiny mouthfuls. His eyes darted nervously from face to face. But no one spoke.

Finally Doon's father said, "Excuse me, but perhaps there's been a mistake."

Martha looked at him coldly. "I don't believe so," she said.

"Perhaps you're thinking," Doon's father went on, "that my son Doon actually did what he has been accused of."

"In this household," said Martha, "we do not approve of wasting food."

"Neither do we!" cried Doon. "I would never do such a thing! I *didn't* do it." All eyes turned toward Doon. He could feel a red flush rising in his face. "Really," he said, keeping his voice calm. "I didn't."

"Who did, then?" said Ordney.

"I don't know," said Doon.

"No one knows," said Mrs. Polster in her firmest voice. "Certainly we aren't going to believe the word of one unhappy little boy against the word of this young man, who has proved himself so outstanding."

"Why not?" said Martha. "Torren Crane is a decent boy, as far as I know. I don't see why you call him unhappy."

"All you have to do is look at him," Mrs. Polster said.

Miss Thorn nodded. "I do think she's right," she murmured.

"Well, *one* of you people must have done it," Martha said. "Certainly none of *us* would have."

"Nothing has been proved one way or the other," said Doon's father. "It would be unfair to draw any conclusions."

There was an uncomfortable silence. Everyone focused on eating. When it was time to leave, Kenny passed out the food parcels, and as he handed one to Doon, he silently mouthed three words: *I believe you.*

At least one person was on his side, Doon thought. It made him feel better, but only a little.

In the end, because it was one person's word against another's and there was no proof either way, nothing was done. Officially, the identity of the tomato thrower remained a mystery. But the effect of all this was to make the people of Sparks and the people of Ember even more resentful and suspicious of each other than they had been before.

Doon felt unfriendly eyes following him wherever he went. At first he tried to explain when people glared at him that way. He spoke reasonably. "Why would I get up and walk all the way into a field in the middle of the night to throw tomatoes at a wall?" he said. "It doesn't make any sense." But people didn't seem interested in reason. He was one of *them*, and that meant he was strange and might do anything. So Doon stopped trying to explain. He kept his eyes on the ground and ignored the people who muttered darkly as he passed by.

It wasn't just Doon who suffered from the tomato incident. It was all the refugees from Ember. Sometimes the villagers called them names right out loud on the street. It was as if those smashed tomatoes had brought all the quietly rumbling resentments out into the open. The town simmered like a pot about to boil over.

One morning Doon found a crowd gathered in the plaza when he came into town for work. Both Sparks people and Ember people were clustered together, looking at something. He edged between them to see what it was. Across the pavement, someone had scrawled a message. It looked as if it had been written in mud. The sloppy, runny letters said:

THEY MUST GO!

The crowd stared at it silently. A few of the villagers seemed embarrassed. They looked sideways at the Emberites and shook their heads. "Mean," someone muttered. But others scowled. One man, noticing

Doon, glared at him so angrily that Doon felt as if he'd been punched in the stomach. This message was there because of him; he knew it. He put his head down and hurried away.

At the hotel that night, people were upset. They clustered in buzzing groups out by the front steps, talking about the words painted on the plaza. Doon saw Tick striding among them, speaking with everyone, his face flushed and his eyes glittering. When he came toward Doon, he paused. "They've turned against us," he said. "I knew they would. We mustn't stand for it." And he plunged back into the crowd.

A day passed, and then another. The sun blazed down, but Doon felt as if darkness had invaded him. Protests and questions raged through his mind. Why had Torren pointed at him? Was it just at random, or had he singled him out for some reason? Why did Chugger believe Torren and not believe him? Who had written the muddy message on the bricks of the plaza?

Lina did not return, and this added to Doon's glumness. According to the note she'd left Mrs. Murdo, she should have been back by now from wherever she'd gone. Doon's feelings about her were divided between worry and anger. He tried not to think about her, since there was nothing he could do.

Whenever he had a free moment, he holed up with a book and tried to forget about what was happening in the village. Edward Pocket brought him a steady supply. Edward was obsessed with his job. Every now and then Doon would ask him how it was going, and Edward would get a feverish look in his eyes and say, "Ah! It goes by inches, young Doon. By millimeters. I've done this much"—he held his thumb and forefinger a tiny distance apart—"and this much remains to be done." He stretched his arms as far apart as they would go. "It's a gargantuan task. I press forward, but will I finish in my lifetime? It is doubtful." His fingers black with dust, he often came home in the evening later than the workers who went into the village, and he was so tired by then that he usually went straight to bed right after dinner, even though it was still light. Doon would hear him mumbling in his sleep inside the closet. He could make sense of only a few words. "Caterpillars," Edward would say. "Cathedrals. Cattle. Chemistry. Christmas." Then he'd groan and thrash about, banging his bony limbs against the closet door, and go silent for a while. When he muttered again, he'd be on to a different letter: "Hamlet. Harry Potter. Hawaii. Heart surgery. Hippopotamus. Hog farming." Doon imagined that Edward's mind was so stuffed with information by now that there wasn't room for any more, and the excess had started leaking out in the night.

Sometimes Doon passed the Sparks school on his way to work in the morning. It was a small building with a wide, open porch all around it, where the students often sat to do their lessons. The children of the village—there weren't very many of them—went to school only a few hours a day, and only until they were ten years old. Kenny Parton went there. He would wave to Doon when he saw him going by, and before the trouble with the tomatoes, the other children would look at Doon curiously, a few of them smiling. But the first time Doon passed the school after the tomato trouble, he saw fifteen or twenty cold-eyed faces turned toward him. Someone shouted, "Get out of here!" and someone else threw a crumpled wad of paper over the porch railing at him. He walked faster, looking straight ahead. A moment later he heard the teacher scolding the class for rudeness, but not very sternly.

The next day, as Doon and the others arrived at the Partons' for lunch, Kenny peeked out from behind a corner of the house and beckoned to Doon. His eyes wide, his voice even softer and more timid than usual, he said, "You know at school yesterday?"

Doon nodded.

"I was sorry they yelled at you," Kenny said. "They shouldn't. You didn't do it."

"How do *you* know?" said Doon, who was feeling crabby just then at all residents of Sparks. "Maybe I did."

Kenny shook his head. "No," he said. "I don't think so."

"Why not?" said Doon.

"I can just tell," said Kenny. "I can tell about people. You wouldn't." He gave Doon a quick, shy smile.

Doon was touched. Kenny looked like a timid little wisp, but there was something strong inside him.

"I wish you didn't have to leave," Kenny said.

Doon smiled. "We'll be here for a few more months," he said.

"Then what?" Kenny asked.

"We go away and make our own town."

"Where?" asked Kenny.

Doon shrugged. "I don't know. Out in those empty places somewhere."

Kenny looked down at his feet. He stood for a minute in silence. Then he said, "That will be really hard. How will you get food?"

"Grow it, I guess. Just the way you do here."

"But you'll be leaving in the month of Chilling. That's the beginning of winter. You can't grow food in the winter," Kenny said, looking up at Doon with worried eyes.

"Winter?" said Doon. "What's winter?"

"You don't have *winter* where you came from?" Kenny's eyes grew very round. "You mean it's always *summer* there?"

Doon was confused and slightly alarmed by Kenny's tone. "I don't know those words," he said.

Kenny stared at Doon, his face blank with surprise. "Seasons," he said. "They're the seasons. In summer it's hot. In winter it's cold."

"That's all right, then," said Doon, relieved. "We're used to cold."

"But you can't grow food in the winter. It's *really* cold. And clouds come over the sun. And it rains."

"Rains?"

Kenny was so amazed that his mouth dropped open. He flung his arms up and wiggled his fingers like drops sprinkling down. "Rain! When water comes from the sky! And the river rises, and sometimes it floods! And the dirt turns to mud!"

Doon felt as if his mind had suddenly stopped. He stared at Kenny's wiggling fingers and tried to grasp what he was saying. Water dropped from the sky? But—people's clothes would get wet. Everyone would have to stay inside. And if they couldn't grow food . . . "Wait," he said. "You mean the town leaders *know* it will be winter when we leave? They *know* it will be cold and wet?"

"I guess so," Kenny said. He lowered his eyes, then looked up again. "Probably they mean to send food with you," he said. "To get you through the winter. That must be it." He gave a small, hopeful smile. "That must be it," he said again, and he darted away toward the front door and went into the house.

Doon followed. His vision of the future, already shadowed by anxiety, had just grown several shades darker.

One morning a week or so later, as Doon came out the door of room 215, he nearly bumped into Tick Hassler, who was running at full speed down the hall. "Something's happened!" Tick called to him.

"What?" said Doon, breaking into a run himself to keep up with Tick.

"I don't know," Tick said. "But I heard people out in front, shouting."

Tick must have jumped out of bed and not taken time to do anything but throw on his clothes, Doon thought. He hadn't combed his hair, he hadn't tied his shoes, he hadn't even washed his face—there were gray smudges on his neck and below his ear. In the usually well-groomed Tick, these were signs of serious alarm. Doon's heart beat faster. He took the stairs three at a time, crossed the lobby, and, still following Tick, pushed through the front door.

Outside, a crowd stood in the field, staring up at the hotel. Doon ran out to join them and turned around to see what they were seeing.

Someone had scrawled words on the walls of the Pioneer—tremendous black letters, rough and scratchy, as if written with burnt wood. "GO BACK TO

YOUR CAVE," said the message, over and over. "GO BACK TO YOUR CAVE. GO BACK TO YOUR CAVE." The few ground-floor windows that hadn't already been broken were broken now.

Doon stood staring for a minute, feeling sick, and then anger rose in him. This was the work of whoever had slopped that mud message onto the plaza— another ugly message, bolder this time. Around him the others were rushing forward, shouting, staring at the scrawled words. Some of them stood silent and glum, with arms folded or hands in pockets. Others shook their fists in the air and vowed revenge. Tick was more furious than anyone, but he didn't yell. Doon watched him weaving through the crowd, seizing one person after another by the arm, talking in a voice as sharp as a blade but low and steady. His light blue eyes glinted like steel.

"It's what I thought," Tick said. "This shows it. They've pretended to be kind, but their kindness isn't real. Here's what we can know from now on: they hate us." He narrowed his eyes, lowered his voice almost to a hiss, and said it again. "*They hate us.* They want to get rid of us. Well, I'll tell you what." People all around turned toward him. "They want us to leave, but I'm not leaving. Are you?" He scanned the crowd.

"No," said someone.

Doon thought about what Kenny had told him:

winter, cold, rain. Maybe Tick is right, he thought. They *do* hate us.

"Do you *like* being called cavepeople?" Tick cried. "Do you *like* being told to crawl back into a cave?"

And angry voices, twenty, fifty, a hundred of them, cried, "No, no!"

Doon went up close to the wall of the hotel and examined the words scratched there. He pictured the people who had done it, clutching their burnt chunks of wood, writing with big, angry strokes in the dark of the night. Yes, Tick was right. Hatred seethed in those jagged letters. He felt almost as if their strokes had scraped open his skin.

The Second Town Meeting

The three town leaders called a meeting after these unpleasant incidents—the tomato-throwing, and the graffiti on the plaza and on the hotel wall. They met in the tower room of the town hall to talk.

"This is unfortunate," Mary said. "I'm afraid these spiteful deeds will cause bad feelings to get worse on both sides."

Wilmer nodded. "Feelings are already bad," he said.

"These cavepeople," said Ben, "are not as civilized as we are. People who will destroy two whole crates of tomatoes might do anything."

"We don't know for sure that one of them did it," Mary said.

"Come now, Mary," said Ben. "I think it's safe to assume."

"And what about the people who wrote 'Go Back

to Your Cave' on the hotel walls?" said Mary.

"The problem is," said Ben, "we don't know who did that. But I must say that I think they were expressing an understandable frustration. These cavepeople have adversely impacted our way of life. The food we give them comes out of the mouths of our own people."

"We do have a bit of a surplus in the storehouse," said Mary.

"But why should we use it for *them*? It's our protection against hard times." Ben smoothed his beard and went on. "I have a rule to suggest," he said. "I think it would be best if the cavepeople didn't eat in the homes of families anymore. I think it's too hard on our families to have strangers eating with them every day. It would be better if the families simply hand them their food parcels when they arrive. They can eat somewhere else."

"Where?" asked Mary.

Ben waved a hand in the direction of the river. "On the riverbank," he said. "Or at the edge of a field. Or on the road. I really don't care where they eat," he said, "as long as they don't intrude on our households."

"Quite a few people have complained of the inconvenience," said Wilmer. "The Parton family seems the most unhappy."

"That's because they have that evil boy," said Ben. "The one who threw the tomatoes."

"We don't know that he's the one who threw them," said Mary.

"We are as sure as we need to be," said Ben.

So they voted: should they make that rule?

Mary voted no.

Ben voted yes.

Wilmer hesitated for several seconds, his eyes darting between Mary and Ben. Finally he voted yes.

"I suppose this will make things better," said Wilmer.

"I'm sure it will," said Ben. "We need to make it clear that this town belongs to us. This is *our* place, and these people are only here because of our generosity."

"I think we *have* made it clear," said Mary. "We went to all that trouble to make a flag and put it up on the town hall."

"No doubt that will help," said Ben. "Still, we must constantly reinforce the message: if they don't behave themselves, they can't expect to stay here even as long as six months."

"They've just begun to get used to things," said Mary. "They're not ready to leave."

"That," said Ben, "is not our problem."

CHAPTER 18

Caspar's Quest

On the last night of their journey to the city, the travelers stayed in a real house. It was roofless, but most of its walls still stood, providing shelter from the wind that blew strongly off the water. There was no furniture in the house, of course. They sat on the bare floor.

Caspar was excited that night. He talked so much that he almost forgot to eat—his third travelers' cake sat on his knee getting cold. At one point, he turned to face Lina. "Now, listen," he said. "I'm going to tell you something, so you'll understand the importance of what we're doing." He paused. Then he spoke in a low, vibrating voice. "I happen to know," he said, "that there is a treasure in the city."

"There is?" said Lina. "How do you know?"

"Old rhymes and songs speak of it," said Caspar.

"The trouble is," said Maddy, "those old rhymes and songs don't make sense anymore. If they ever did."

"They make sense to me," Caspar said. "But that's because I've studied them carefully and have found out their deeper meaning."

"What do the old rhymes say?" Lina asked.

"Various things," said Caspar, "depending on what version you hear. But they're always about a treasure in an ancient city." He looked into the air and sang tunelessly: "'There's buried treasure in the ancient city. Remember, remember from times of old. . . .' One of them starts like that."

"Why hasn't anyone searched for the treasure before?" asked Lina.

"I'm sure many people have," Caspar said. "But no one has found it."

"How do you know?" Lina asked.

"Because obviously, if someone had, we would have heard about it."

Lina thought about this. She saw some holes in Caspar's logic. Someone could have found the treasure, taken it away, and never said a word.

"Another problem," said Maddy, "is that these rumors never say what city the treasure is in. It could be some city a thousand miles away."

Caspar gave an exasperated sigh and set down his cup of water. He raised two fingers and pointed them at Maddy. "Listen," he said. "Be logical. It's *here* that the rumors are passed around. I've never heard them in the far north, where I was last year. I've never heard them in the far east, either. This talk of treasure in a city—I hear it *here,* and within a hundred or so miles of here."

"Still," Maddy said. "There are at least three ancient cities within a hundred miles of here."

"But only one *great* ancient city," said Caspar. "That's the one we're going to."

"A city is big," Lina said, remembering the myriad streets and buildings of Ember. "How will you know where in the city to look for the treasure?"

A crafty look came over Caspar's face. He smiled, with his lips pressed together and his eyes narrowed. "That's where my careful study comes in," he said. "Many, many hours of study. I've written down every version of the rhyme I've heard—which is a great many, forty-seven to be exact. I've compared them, word for word, letter for letter. *Then*—" Caspar paused. He looked at them in a way Lina recognized— it was the same way Torren looked when he was about to make a big impression. *"Then* I applied my skill with numbers."

"Numbers?" said Lina.

"That's right. What you do is, you count the letters in the words. You count in all different ways, until you start to see a pattern. The pattern is the key to the code, and the code tells you the secret of the message." He sat back, looking highly pleased with himself.

"And the secret of the message . . . ," Lina said, confused.

"Is the location of the treasure, of course!" Caspar slapped a hand on his big thigh. "It's obvious, once you've figured it out. Street numbers, building numbers—it's all there."

"Well, then," said Maddy, "what is the location of the treasure?"

Caspar jerked his head back. "You think I'd tell you?" he said.

"I thought I was your partner in this," said Maddy.

"You'll know when it's time," said Caspar. "Until then, the information stays strictly with me."

Lina glanced at Maddy in time to see her rolling her eyes toward the sky.

That night, Lina couldn't sleep. Animal sounds kept her awake—scrambling and snuffling just beyond the walls, and a strange hooting in the distance. Dark thoughts troubled her, too. Caspar's search sounded all wrong somehow. She didn't want to help him. The thought of it filled her with dread. She lay on the hard floor of the house, staring at the black sky, feeling worse and worse, until finally she decided she must try to think about something else. So she said to herself, over and over for a long time, "Tomorrow I'll see the city, tomorrow I'll see the city."

They traveled the next day, mile after mile, along a road that was nearly straight, though they had to trace a winding path around the places where the pavement was pitted or thrust up or crumbled away. On their right was the vast green sheet of water, bordered by waving grasses where great white birds stood knee-deep in pools and rose like floating paper, and flocks of black birds flew up trilling into the air, their shoulders red as blood. On the left was a forest of trees so thick they hid all but the briefest glimpses of the ruined buildings among them.

Lina's excitement was rising. She rode standing up now. She'd climbed back into the crate and stuck her feet between the third and fourth slats of the side, which put her at the right height for holding on to the top edge and looking forward. She could see over Caspar's and Maddy's heads to the rear ends of the oxen, their sharp hip bones sticking up, left-right, left-right, their tasseled tails switching back and forth. The sun sank lower in the sky until it was directly ahead, blazing straight into Lina's eyes. "We'll be there before night," Caspar said.

The road began to slope upward. Hills rose on either side, and soon Lina could no longer see the water, just the brown humps of the hills, spotted with clumps of trees and scarred here and there by the remains of old roads and buildings. The air was cooler. They rounded a curve—and all at once the city lay before them.

CHAPTER 19

Unfairness, and
What to Do About It

In the days after the hateful words had been scrawled on the wall, Doon went to work grudgingly. He didn't want to work with people who did such awful things. He had to remind himself that they weren't *all* ignorant brutes, and that they *were* still giving the Emberites shelter and food—even though they were no longer allowing them to eat with their lunchtime families, and even though they were planning to send them out to fend for themselves in the winter. But the people who had written those words—no one was trying to find out who they were, no one was punishing them. Who was the one getting the evil looks and being called bad names? *He* was, he who had done nothing! He couldn't stand the *wrongness* of it. He felt it physically, as if he were wearing clothes that were too tight, a shirt that pinched him under the arms, pants that were too short and too snug. Unfair, unfair, he kept thinking. He couldn't *bear* unfairness.

One day he was assigned to clean the fountain in the center of the plaza. Chugger handed him his tools for the job: a bucket, a long stick with a metal scraper on one end, and a pile of rags.

Chugger lifted up one of the bricks in the pavement near the fountain. Under it was a round handle. "You turn this off first," he said. "It shuts off the water coming in from the river." He gave it several turns, and the spouting water in the middle of the fountain dipped and vanished. "Now the water in the basin will drain through the outflow pipe," Chugger said. "It goes back into the river. When the basin is empty, you climb in there and scrub. I want this thing clean as a drinking glass when you're through."

Chugger left, and Doon watched the water level slowly going down. The lower it got, the more green scum was revealed. It coated the inside of the fountain like slimy fur.

He plunged his stick into the water, scraped it along the fountain's inner wall, and pulled it out again. Wet green strings swung from the end of it, and he shook them off into the bucket. He thrust the stick in again, scraped again, brought up more muck. Into the bucket it went. For the next ten minutes, he scraped the bottom and sides of the fountain with his stick and filled the bucket with slippery strands of scum, along with a few apricot pits, dead bugs, and rotting leaves.

The water was about half gone now, but it seemed to be draining very slowly. Probably, Doon reasoned, this was because the outflow pipe was getting blocked up with all the loosened scum being drawn toward it. But because the water was so murky, he couldn't see where the outflow pipe was.

At that moment, Chugger came up behind him. "What the heck is taking you so long?" he said. "If you had any sense, you'd have figured out the drain is clogging up." He grabbed the stick out of Doon's hands and began probing in the water.

"I *did* figure that out," Doon said, "but I couldn't see where it was because—"

"There!" said Chugger, who wasn't listening. He'd pried loose a clump of soggy crud, and the water level was once more going down. He thrust the stick toward Doon again. "Now get busy. And try using your brain once in a while, if you have one." He stalked off.

Doon clamped his teeth together to hold in the rage that boiled up in him. He glared at the retreating back of Chugger and imagined throwing his stick so that it hit him right between the shoulder blades.

I hate being talked to that way, he thought. As if I'm a moron. Why does he get to talk to me like that?

When the water had all drained out of the fountain, Doon took his shoes off, grabbed a handful of rags, and climbed in. On his knees in the green slime that covered the bottom, he wiped and scrubbed. Now and then people came by and peered in at him. "Ugh," they'd say as they passed, or "Yuck." It felt as if they were saying ugh and yuck about him—not surprising, since he was now just about as filthy as the rags he was using. No one said, "Good job!" or said they were pleased the fountain was getting cleaned.

When he finally finished, he opened the inflow valve and plugged the outflow valve, and once again the water leapt from the central pipe and the fountain began to fill. Doon sat down on the rim and put his bare feet in the water to rinse them off. He stayed there for a minute, resting. The cool, clean water felt good.

Chugger came around the corner. "What are you *doing?*" he yelled. He strode toward Doon. "I don't know how you do it where you're from," he said, "but here when we work, we work. We don't sit around gazing at the sky."

Doon started to say he was not gazing at the sky, he was taking a one-minute rest. But when he opened his mouth to speak, the rush of anger that came up through his body was so volcanic that he closed his mouth again and sat there shaking, his face flushed and burning, afraid he would explode if he tried to say a word. *Do not get angry,* he told himself, remembering the advice his father had given him so many times. *When anger is in control, you get unintended consequences.*

"You don't speak when you're spoken to?" said Chugger. "Maybe you didn't hear me. Maybe I need to make it clearer." He took a deep breath. His voice came out in a hoarse bellow: "Get moving, you stupid barbarian! Now!" He seized Doon by the arm and yanked him backward.

That was when Doon felt his rage shooting up like steam, unstoppable.

"Let go of me!" he screamed. "I'm not the barbarian! You are! *You* are!" He tried to jerk away from Chugger, but Chugger held on. Doon pulled harder, wrenching his whole body sideways and slamming against the bucket, which was next to him on the rim of the fountain. The bucket went flying, spewing its slimy contents over a girl who happened to be passing by. She screamed and slapped at the stinking green sludge running down the front of her shirt. People rushed up to her and shouted angrily at Doon, who gave one more frantic pull and finally freed himself from Chugger's grasp.

For a second he and Chugger stood glaring at each other. Doon knew how he must look to the people around him: clumsy, filthy, wild-eyed, and, worse than that—a violent boy, the kind of boy who would waste good food, the kind of boy whose ugly, fiery temper could cause real damage.

He turned and stalked away. No one tried to stop him. He realized when he'd gone a short distance that he'd forgotten to pick up his shoes, but he wasn't going to go back for them. He ran barefoot all the way to the Pioneer.

I've done it now, he thought. I've made everything worse. And yet none of it is my fault. I was trying hard to do my job, and trying even harder not to get angry. But look what happens.

The unfairness of it, the tremendous injustice, felt like a stone in his heart.

"We will do something about this," Tick said to Doon that night. They were standing by the hotel's back stairs, where they'd encountered each other on the way in from the outhouses. "You are being abused. We all are. We mustn't stand for it."

Doon nodded. He had told Tick about winter, and now Tick was more outraged than ever. The look on his face was hard and determined. Doon admired Tick's strength, and the way he always seemed to know what to do. He himself was never so absolutely clear. He saw too many sides of things; it confused him.

"What should we do?" he asked.

"Strike back," said Tick. "They have attacked us, more than once, in many ways. It's time for them to find out that if they hurt us, they'll get hurt, too."

They'll get hurt. Was this the right thing? But it did seem fair. After all, wrong should be punished. "How do we do it?" said Doon.

"Many possibilities," said Tick. He leaned against the wall beside the stairs. He had a red patch on his arm, Doon noticed, that he kept scratching at; it was the first time Doon had seen that Tick, too, suffered from the bites and scrapes that plagued the rest of them. He isn't perfect, Doon reminded himself; he isn't always right about everything.

"We could refuse to work," Tick went on. "But everyone would have to refuse, and I'm not sure everyone would. It would be better to take direct action."

"Action about what?" asked Doon.

"About food. We don't get enough. This is an injustice *all* of us feel. So what about this: we storm the storehouse and take what we need by force."

"Steal food?" said Doon.

"It isn't stealing. It's evening things out. It's getting what should rightfully be ours." There was not a hint of uncertainty in Tick's voice.

Doon thought about this. It did make sense. You had to act against injustice, didn't you? You couldn't just let it happen.

"I know lots of people who'll join us," Tick said. "I'll call them together. We'll have a meeting and make a plan." He started up the stairs and then turned around and looked down on Doon. "But first," he said, "we have to arm ourselves."

"We do?"

"Of course. We need to make sure we'll defeat our enemy."

"What do we arm ourselves with?"

"I'll tell you," Tick said, "when we meet. Tomorrow night, after dinner, out at the head of the road."

CHAPTER 20

The City Destroyed

When the city came into view before them, the three travelers stood speechless, gazing out over ranges of hills standing dark against the western sky. They could see that this had once been a city—to the right, a cluster of tall buildings still stood, tall beyond anything Lina had imagined. But they were no more than shells of buildings, hollow and broken, their windows only holes. Through some of them Lina could see the sky, turned scarlet by the sunset.

All else was a windswept wasteland. Whatever buildings had once been here had long ago fallen and crumbled into the ground. Earth and dust and sand had blown across them, and grass had grown over them, softening their outlines. Here and there traces of ruins remained—they looked from this distance like outcrops of stone, hardly more than jagged places on the smooth slopes. Faint lines of shadow showed where streets must once have been.

Lina stared, trembling. This was far, far from the city she had imagined. Not even the version she'd revised for the Disaster had looked like this. This couldn't be called a city at all anymore. It was the ghost of a city.

Even Caspar seemed daunted. He craned forward, his hand shading his eyes. "It looks somewhat destroyed," he said.

"It looks completely destroyed," said Maddy.

They got down from the truck and stood beside the oxen.

"A trick of the light," said Caspar, squinting harder. He pulled his glasses from his pocket and put them on. "When we get closer, no doubt it will look different."

"How do you plan to get closer?" Maddy asked him, and for the first time Lina saw that a few yards in front of them, the road came to an end. There was an edge of broken pavement, and beyond it a great slab of roadway slanted downward. It had stood on pillars once; you could see a few of the pillars still standing, and rods of thick wire twisting out of them. From here on, the road was a chaos of concrete, gigantic chunks leaning against each other. There was no way the truck could go on.

The sun was nearly down now, and the brilliant red of the sky was fading. Between the ruined buildings drifted a gray mist, and the wind blew more sharply. Some white birds soared high above, screaming.

"It used to be so beautiful," said Maddy. "I've seen pictures of it in books." There was a tremor in her voice. Lina looked up and saw that tears stood in her eyes. "I knew it was destroyed," Maddy said. "But not like this."

"What happened to it?" Lina asked.

"It was the wars," said Maddy. "They must have been . . ." She shook her head. "They must have been terrible," she said.

"What were they about?" Lina asked.

Maddy shrugged. "I don't know."

"And the people who lived here? What happened to them?"

"All killed, I suppose," said Maddy. "Or most of them."

Caspar was frowning at the shadowy wilderness that lay below. "In the daylight," he said, "I'll be able to see how to proceed."

"Proceed!" Maddy grabbed Caspar's arm and wrenched him around to face her. "Are you out of your mind?"

Caspar yanked his arm away. "No," he said. "I am not."

Maddy swept her hand out toward the city. "It's miles and miles of buried rubble!" she cried. "Streets buried under fallen bricks and broken glass! Mountains of concrete and melted metal! Sand and earth blown over it all, and grass growing on it!"

Caspar nodded, his face grim. "Right," he said. "A challenge. You were right about bringing this one along." He tipped his head toward Lina. "Someone small and light, that's what I'll need. Going to have to do some tunneling."

"No, Caspar," said Maddy. "You must give up this idea. You can't find anything there."

"I can," said Caspar. "I can find it, I have the numbers, I have it all worked out." He plunged one hand into his pocket and scrabbled around and brought out a scrap of paper. He snatched his glasses off, put the paper up close to his eyes, and squinted at it. Lina took a step closer to him and peered sideways. The paper was black with scribbling, a tangle of words and numbers and cross-outs. "Forty-seven east," muttered Caspar. "Three ninety-five west." His eyes flicked back and forth between the paper and the dark hills before him, flicked faster and faster. "Seventy-one," he mumbled. "It's just a matter of . . . In the daylight . . ." He caught sight of Lina. "What are *you* staring at?" he said.

"Nothing," said Lina. She felt suddenly sick and frightened. Maddy was right. Caspar *was* out of his mind.

The sun disappeared behind the farthest hill, and darkness fell. Maddy turned back toward the truck. "We'll camp right here tonight," she said. "We still have enough water in the buckets."

They set their blankets on the side of the truck away from the wind, but Lina shivered and couldn't sleep. After days of longing to arrive at the city, she wanted nothing now but to leave. This was a terrible place, full of angry ghosts and sad ones. When she closed her eyes, she seemed to hear their voices— shouts and screams and a dreadful sobbing—and to see flashes of fire in the smoky sky, and sheets of flame sweeping through the streets.

A wail escaped from her. She couldn't help it, she felt so afraid and miserable. A moment later, she heard Maddy's voice close to her ear. "Let's talk for a while," Maddy said.

"Okay," said Lina. She sat up, wrapping her blanket around her. Caspar was pacing up and down on the other side of the truck, muttering to himself. "What about him?" she said.

"Don't worry," answered Maddy. "He's lost in his calculations."

A gust of wind shook the truck. Its loose fender clattered.

"I hate it here," said Lina.

"Yes," said Maddy. "Terrible things happened in this place. You can still feel it."

"Were the people in those old days extremely evil?" Lina asked.

"No more than anyone," Maddy said.

"But then why did the wars happen? To wreck your whole city—almost your whole world—it seems like something only evil people would do."

"No, not evil, at least not at first. Just angry and scared." Maddy was silent for a moment. Caspar's footsteps came closer, crunching on the gravelly ground, and then receded again. Lina inched a little closer to Maddy. "It's like this," Maddy said at last. "Say the A people and the B people get in an argument. The A people do something that hurts the B people. The B people strike back to get even. But that just makes the A people angry all over again. They say, 'You hurt us, so we're going to hurt you.' It keeps on like that. One bad thing leads to a worse bad thing, on and on."

It was like what Torren had said when he was telling her about the Disaster. Revenge, he'd called it.

"Can't it be stopped?" said Lina. She shifted around under her blanket, trying to find a place to sit where rocks weren't digging into her.

"Maybe it can be stopped at the beginning," Maddy said. "If someone sees what's happening and is brave enough to reverse the direction."

"Reverse the direction?"

"Yes, turn it around."

"How would you do that?"

"You'd do something good," said Maddy. "Or at least you'd keep yourself from doing something bad."

"But how could you?" said Lina. "When people have been mean to you, why would you want to be good to them?"

"You *wouldn't* want to," Maddy said. "That's what makes it hard. You do it anyway. Being good is hard. Much harder than being bad."

Lina wondered if she was strong enough to be good. She didn't feel strong at all right now.

"Time to sleep," said Maddy.

Lina pulled the blankets over her head, but still she could feel the wind and hear the oxen making low, uneasy sounds. She heard Caspar still pacing, too, and muttering under his breath.

I want to go home, she thought. And for the first time, the picture that arose in her mind was not of the dark, familiar buildings of Ember but of Sparks under its bright sky. She thought of Dr. Hester's house, and the garden blooming in the sun, and the doctor puttering with her hundred plants. She thought of Mrs. Murdo sitting in the doctor's courtyard, basking in the warmth, and Poppy playing with a spoon beside her. Even Torren was in the picture, proudly arranging his possessions on a window ledge.

And of course there was Doon. He should have

been her partner on this journey. If he were here with her, she'd feel less afraid. She missed him. Maybe when she got back to Sparks, he'd be tired of hanging around that boy named Tick and be ready to be her friend again.

CHAPTER 21

Attack and Counterattack

The morning after the trouble at the fountain, Doon awoke to a clamor rising through his window from the front of the hotel. He looked out, but he could see only the tops of people's heads, all clustered around the front steps. He ran downstairs with his shirt still unbuttoned, flapping around him, to see what was happening.

The doors of the hotel stood open. Through them, he saw that a heap of trash had been dumped on the front steps. He went closer and looked. The pile seemed to consist of rotten vegetables and filthy rags, scattered all over with shiny green leaves and sharp twigs and long creepers pulled up by their dirty roots.

Doon stared at it with the same sick feeling he'd had when he saw the black words on the hotel walls. It wasn't so much the pile itself that made him feel sick; it was that whoever did this hated the people of Ember, and hated Doon himself in particular. This was an act of revenge.

He went outside, edging around the pile. Clary was standing on the step just below it, peering down at the leaves and branches. "Why would they bother to scatter leaves on everything?" she said. "And they're all the same kind, too." She picked up a sprig and looked closely at the bright green leaves, rubbing them between her fingers, sniffing them. "Strange," she said.

But most people were too upset to pay attention to the contents of the pile. An angry buzz filled the air, and now and then one voice or another rose above the rest. "This is an outrage!" It was a clear, sharp voice—Tick's, Doon was sure. Then a high voice: "I hate them, I hate them!" That must be Lizzie—and sure enough, there she was, standing near Tick, dunking her shoes in a bucket of water to get the dirt stains off.

After a while, Tick climbed the steps and clapped his hands. "All right, everyone!" he called. "We've been attacked again—and this is worse than the first time. It's a disgusting insult, and it fills us with rage. But all we can do right now is get this mess off our doorstep. Let's get busy and clean it up."

Everyone did. They picked up armloads of the leafy vines and carried them away. They shoved the garbage down onto the ground and kicked it into the bushes. They brought buckets of water up from the river and sloshed them over the steps until everything was more or less clean. Tick supervised all this, calling out directions—though he didn't do any of the actual work himself, Doon noticed. Doesn't want to get his clothes dirty, thought Doon rather grumpily.

When the cleanup was done, people stood around and argued. Some were for marching down to the town that very minute, confronting the town leaders, and demanding that the vandals be punished. Other people said no, it wasn't good to cause trouble, it would just make everything more unpleasant, and anyway, it wasn't the *whole* village that was against them, only *some* of them.

"But which ones?" someone yelled. "And how do we stop them? They have to be stopped!"

"I'm tired of being blamed and punished!" cried someone else.

"I'm tired of being starved!"

"And what about winter?" someone yelled. The word had spread, and people had added this to their list of grievances.

"Are we just going to sit here and take this treatment?"

"No! No! No!"

Doon could see Tick moving through the crowd, bending to speak into the ear of one person and then another. As people listened, their eyes narrowed and their lips tightened, and they turned to Tick and nodded.

The shouting died down after a while, because people couldn't agree on a course of action. If they didn't go to work, they wouldn't get any lunch. So most of them went back to their ordinary routines: they washed their hands and faces in the river, they ate what remained in their parcels for breakfast, and they headed up the road toward the village.

Doon and his father went, too, though Doon went reluctantly.

"Father," he said, "this is the third time they've attacked us. Don't you think we have to do something?"

"What do you propose to do?" his father said.

"I don't know," said Doon. "But we have to do *something*. We can't just let ourselves be *trampled*, can we?"

"Son," said Doon's father, "I don't know the answer. We're in a tough situation here." He clasped his hands behind his back and walked for a while looking down at the road. "It does seem that something is called for," he said finally. "The trouble is that violence just leads to more violence. So I don't know."

Doon's team was assigned to the cornfield that day. He and his father spent hours on their knees, yanking prickly weeds out of the ground. Doon's arm itched. He kept having to stop and scratch it. Was a mosquito biting him? He scratched and scratched again. It felt like fifty mosquito bites, not one. He had them on his other arm, too. Both arms itched like crazy. Finally he stopped working and held his arms out in front of him. From wrist to elbow, they were carpeted with red lumps.

"Look, Father!" he cried. "I have a rash! What *is* it?"

"I don't know, son," his father said, "but I have it, too."

The itchy rash spread over the arms and hands and faces of all the Emberites who had helped with the cleanup that morning. "What *is* this?" people said as they worked in the bakery and the bike shop, the brickyard and the tomato fields. They itched, they scratched, and the rash spread and oozed and itched still more.

The villagers knew what it was. "Poison oak," they said. They explained about the oil on the leaves, how you only had to touch it to get the rash. "You must have been out scrambling around in the woods," they said. But the Emberites had not been scrambling in the woods. They knew how they'd been poisoned. Someone had done it to them on purpose.

Fury spread among the Emberites like a fire. Those who'd heard about the poison oak raged about it to those who hadn't, and before long everyone knew. Diggers threw down their shovels. Fruit pickers pushed the ladders to the ground and stalked out of the orchard. Someone in the bakery flung a great clump of dough at the supervisor, and someone in the egg shop hurled three eggs at the wall. The terrible itching aggravated everyone's anger, and before long the people of Ember began to gather in the streets and in the plaza, and the gathering became a crowd, and the crowd became a mob.

Doon ran into the village with the other field workers, and he found himself in the middle of this mob. He heard Tick's voice from somewhere nearby: "They gave us poison! What shall we give them?" When there was no response but a confused babble, the question came again, louder: "What shall we give *them*?"

This time an answer came: a crash, and a tinkling of shattered glass. Someone had thrown a rock through the window of the town hall. Cheers arose, and all around him Doon saw people suddenly bending over, looking for rocks to throw. More crashes. More yells.

People started snatching things from the stalls. A jar of jam came sailing overhead. Arms reached up to catch it, but it fell past them and landed a few feet from Doon, smashing open and splattering his legs with sticky red goo and splinters of glass. He saw people stuffing muffins into their pockets, and he saw Tick with his arm stretched backward, ready to throw a rock at the windows of the tower. He saw Miss Thorn running with her hands shielding her head, and the Hoover sisters backing up into the egg shop, trying to get away. He was frightened, suddenly.

At that moment, the doors of the town hall opened, and Ben Barlow strode out. His face was twisted with rage. "Stop them!" he shouted. "Stop these thieves and vandals!"

"You poisoned us!" shouted someone in the crowd.

"We've had enough!" shouted someone else, and threw a potato right at Ben. It hit him in the stomach, and he bent over, his mouth dropping open.

A roar came from the crowd. Tick's voice rose above the others: "Fill your pockets!" he screamed. "Fill your pockets and run!"

There was a mad scramble, and then the Emberites pushed their way out of the plaza and raced down the streets to the river road. Doon ran, too. He saw Tick up ahead of him, sprinting fast, his shirttails flying.

Now we really are thieves and vandals, Doon thought. Was this a bad thing? Or was it exactly what the people of Sparks deserved?

That night, Tick went up and down the corridors of the hotel, knocking on doors and urging people to come to his meeting. They did come—at least a hundred of them, by Doon's count. They gathered at the head of the road as the daylight was fading. Doon saw Chet and Gill and Allie and Elvan from his old class at the Ember school, along with people he knew from the Pipeworks, people he knew from Ember's shops, and others. Most of them were boys and men, but there were women and girls, too. Most were silent, but some whispered excitedly to each other. They formed a semicircle in front of Tick, who had climbed onto a tree stump. Doon saw Lizzie standing near Tick, gazing up at him wide-eyed. The moon shone behind Tick's head; it gave a silver edge to his hair but left his face in darkness.

"All right," Tick said. His voice was quiet, but instantly the whispering stopped. "Our time has come. They have attacked us three times now. Today we showed them a little of our anger. We made them understand that we won't be taken advantage of anymore. They must know that if they hurt us, they will be hurt, too. We will strike back. We are warriors now."

Murmurs of approval rumbled through the crowd. Doon, who was standing at the rear, heard several people echo Tick's words: "Strike back, yes, we have to strike back. We are warriors."

"We must be ready," Tick said. "When the next confrontation comes, we won't be as disorganized as we were today. We'll have a plan. And we'll be armed."

More murmurs, and a ripple of excitement.

"How will we arm ourselves?" Tick asked. He

answered the question himself. "We have what we need right here where we live," he said. "Look in your bathrooms. You'll find strong metal rods there, just the right length, and enough for everyone."

People looked at each other in puzzlement. Metal rods in the bathroom? But Doon knew immediately what Tick meant: the towel racks. Take them off the wall, and you have a sturdy weapon that could do real damage—bruise soft flesh, even break hard bone.

Tick waited until the word was passed through the crowd and everyone understood about the weapons in the bathrooms. Then he said, "There are other ways to arm yourself, too. Did you bring a knife with you from Ember? Are there still slivers of glass left in the windows of your room? Have you noticed that some of the stones by the river are just the size to fit in a fist?"

Again, he waited. All around Doon, people were nodding and whispering. Doon tried to imagine what the uprising earlier that day would have been like if the rioters had been swinging steel rods and striking out with knives and broken glass. People would have been hurt; there would have been blood. But think of the hurt the villagers had inflicted on the Emberites—the pangs of hunger, the humiliation, the name calling, the terrible itchy rash. Didn't one hurt deserve another? Wasn't he simply being squeamish to shrink from it? He would have to strengthen himself, he thought—not just his body, but his spirit, his will.

It would take a kind of strength he didn't have yet to strike another person with the intent to harm.

Tick was bending forward now and speaking in a softer voice. People shushed each other and listened. "Go back now and sleep, my warriors," Tick said. "In the next days, prepare your weapons and prepare your will. Remember how you felt when you saw those ugly words scrawled on our walls. Remember how you felt when the poison rash crawled up your arms. The people of Sparks will wrong us again, we can be sure of that. When it happens, we'll be ready."

After the meeting, Doon walked back to the hotel feeling vaguely uneasy. Tick must be right, but somehow Doon couldn't feel wholehearted about being a warrior. Was it because he was a coward? He didn't want to be a coward. He didn't really think he was one. What was his problem, then?

CHAPTER 22

Discoveries

When Lina awoke the next morning, she thought there was something wrong with her eyes. Everything had gone gray. She sat up and looked around. No, it wasn't her eyes—it was the air that was wrong. It was so thick she could hardly see through it. The truck was merely a dark shadow. The buildings of the city had vanished entirely.

From somewhere in the murk, she heard Caspar's voice. He was muttering to himself, as he had been the night before, but she could hear only a low, growly sound, no words.

A dark shape appeared and moved toward her. It was Maddy. She bent over and whispered, "Don't get up yet. Lie back down."

"What's wrong with the air?" Lina asked her.

"It's called fog," Maddy said. "It comes in off the water. Now lie down. Curl up."

Lina lay down and pulled the blanket up under her chin. Maddy knelt beside her and whispered, "Pretend you're sick. Moan and groan a little. Refuse to get up. I'll explain later."

Lina followed instructions. She stared up into the swirling grayness and whimpered a little. It wasn't hard to pretend she didn't feel good. She'd rarely felt so cold and miserable in her life.

She saw Maddy and Caspar huddling together, two shadowy humps in the fog. They were talking, and their voices rose, but she couldn't make out what they were saying.

She must have gone to sleep again. When she opened her eyes, the fog was thinner. A pale sun like a circle of paper shone through it. Without sitting up, she looked around for Maddy and saw her sitting on the back of the truck, eating. She didn't see Caspar anywhere.

"Maddy," she whispered.

Maddy jumped down and came over to her. "You can get up now," she said. "He's gone."

Lina sat up. "Gone?"

Maddy nodded. "Into the ruins. He won't give up this notion of finding treasure. Something in his mind has slipped, I think. He wasn't all that steady to begin with, and now he's lost his balance." She took Lina's hand and pulled her to her feet, and together they folded the blanket. "He wants you to help him with his search—go into the small spaces where he can't go. I told him you'd help tomorrow but today you weren't well. So he went off to look around by himself. 'Preliminary exploration,' he called it."

"I don't want to help him," Lina said.

"You aren't going to," said Maddy. "We're leaving."

"We are? When? How?" Lina asked.

"Now," said Maddy. "Come and help me."

Maddy climbed up onto the truck, unstrapped the two bicycles, and handed them down to Lina. She opened the food chest and took out some of the remaining travelers' cakes, along with two water bottles, and she wrapped these in blankets and tied them with rope.

"Here," she said to Lina. "This pack is yours, and this bike."

"You mean we're going to ride all the way back to Sparks?" Lina thought with horror of the vast, empty distance, and the blazing heat.

"We won't have to ride all the way," Maddy said. "There are lots of roamers. Someone will help us."

"And we just leave Caspar here by himself?" Lina wasn't sure that even someone as unlikable as Caspar should be abandoned in this terrible place.

"He'll be fine," said Maddy. "He has his truck and all his supplies. He doesn't need us."

So they tied the packs onto their backs. They

walked the bikes across the rubbly part of the road until they came to the place where it opened out into the long downhill curve. Just then the fog lifted and the air came clear. Lina turned around to take a last look at the city, the city she'd had such hopes for, the city she thought might be a home for the people of Ember. In the sunlight, it looked more sad than terrible. Over the rolling, grass-covered mounds, the skeletons of the old towers stood like watchmen. The trees bent their backs before the wind, and the wind swept ripples across the surface of the green water that wrapped around the city's edges. Maybe, thought Lina, the sparkling city she'd seen in her mind was a vision from the distant future, not the distant past. Maybe someday the people of Ember—or the great-great-grandchildren of today's people of Ember—would come back here and build the city again.

"All right," said Maddy. "Let's ride."

Lina flung her leg over the bike and settled herself on the seat. This was a bigger bike than the one she was used to. She gripped the handlebars, gave a push with her foot, and she was off.

From the start, the bike moved so fast she hardly had to pedal. She zoomed forward, going far faster than even her fastest running. The wind in her face swept her hair out behind her, shot through her clothes, nearly peeled back her eyelids. The bumps in the road made the handlebars buck like something alive—she held on with a steel grip. It was absolutely terrifying and absolutely joyful. Down the long hill they went, she and Maddy alone on the wide, empty highway, no need to pedal at all, only steer around broken places or bits of debris. The fast air came into Lina's mouth and buffeted down into her lungs, and she laughed out loud, it was such a glorious freedom. When the slope leveled out a little, she steered the bike in big curves, back and forth, and Maddy did, too. They whooped and laughed and raced each other, and alongside them the white birds swooped, too, screeching in their shrill voices.

Then came a long stretch of flat road and hard pedaling. With many stops for resting and eating and drinking water, they rode all day. Lina's seat was sore and her legs grew tired. Blisters rose on her hands from holding so tight to the handlebars. But Maddy said, "Just a little farther, a little farther, and then we'll stop," and Lina kept going, finding strength when she thought it was gone, until at last, at the end of the day, they came to the place where the water ended and they could begin to turn eastward toward the hills.

Here they stopped for the night. They found a creek with a trickle of clear water running along the bottom. Maddy said the round green leaves that grew on the creek's banks were good to eat, so they had those with their travelers' cakes, along with some wild onions and a few blackberries they found deep in a thicket of bramble. There was no cold wind here, as there had been near the city. The evening was warm and still, except for the chirping of frogs in the creek. They spread their blankets on the ground. Somewhere in the dark, an owl hooted softly and another answered. Maddy was lying on her back with her hands clasped over her wide stomach. To Lina, gazing at her profile against the sky, she looked like a small range of hills, solid and comforting. So Lina dared to ask a question that had been troubling her.

"Maddy," she said, "could there ever be another Disaster like the one that came before? Or even worse? What if every single person and every single animal was killed?"

"Don't worry," said Maddy. "People didn't make life, so they can't destroy it. Even if we were to wipe out every bit of life in the world, we can't touch the place life comes from. Whatever made plants and animals and people spring up in the first place will always be there, and life will spring up again."

Maddy turned over and tugged her blanket around her neck. "Time to sleep now," she said. "More hard riding tomorrow."

In the morning, they were on their way as soon as the sun rose. Lina groaned as she got on her bike again— her muscles were sore from yesterday. But she soon warmed up, and for a long time the road was flat and the riding was easy.

After an hour or so, Lina spotted something moving up ahead of them, a dot in the distance. "Look!" she called to Maddy, who was a little way behind her, and she pointed. "I think it's a truck! Maybe a roamer!"

In ten minutes or so, they had caught up to it. The man driving the truck turned when he heard them calling. Surprise lit up his face, and he halted his oxen and jumped down.

"Greetings!" he cried. "Glad to see some travelers! Haven't met anyone on the road for four days."

He was a short, stocky man with a wild fuzz of black hair that stood out several inches all around his head. Pelton Moss was his name, and he was indeed a roamer, as was easy to see from the crates and barrels on his truck. All his containers were nearly empty, though. He had sold his most recent load of goods to a remote south-bay settlement. Now he was heading back in the direction of Sparks. "I'll take you with me," he said, "if you'll help with my collecting on the way."

And so for five days, Lina got to be a roamer. At every ancient abandoned town, they stopped and combed through the derelict houses. Not much was left; these houses had been picked nearly clean in the last two hundred years. But sometimes, if they looked carefully, they found things the previous roamers had overlooked, or things they had thought worthless.

Lina loved these searches. In some ways, it was like being a messenger back in Ember—she could go everywhere, look in every forgotten corner, and if she was lucky make discoveries. And she was lucky.

She found a silver locket with a picture of someone inside, though the picture was so old and stained she couldn't tell if it was a woman or a baby. She found a small, round pane of glass with a handle. The glass made whatever you looked at appear bigger. "A magnifying glass," said Pelton. "Nice." She found a tiny red truck with wheels that still turned. She found a strip of leather with a buckle and two round metal pieces attached to it. It was too short to be a belt. There were words on the metal circles, but they were so worn she couldn't read them. "That's a dog collar," Pelton told her. "Not very useful, but interesting."

At a house that stood by itself far out in a field, she opened a cabinet on a back porch, where the screen was hanging in brown flaps. In the cabinet was a box that said "Monopoly" in faded letters on its lid. Inside were tiny dotted cubes and tiny bits of wood shaped like houses. "Wonderful!" Pelton exclaimed. "Extremely rare!" There was another box in the cabinet with a picture of a garden on top and a heap of oddly shaped pieces of cardboard inside. And at the back of the cabinet, in a clutter of broken dolls, torn pages from books, and little jars of dried-up paint, Lina found a bar of metal about three inches long that Pelton said was a magnet. "Put it up against the truck," he said. "It'll stick right on there."

Even as she enjoyed the searching, though, Lina couldn't help imagining how it would be for the people of Ember to come out into this empty land and try to start a town. How would they turn the hard, cracked earth into fields of crops? What would they build houses with? What would they eat while they chopped at the soil and put together their shelters? A picture rose in her mind of Ember's four hundred people scattered across the brown fields like a flock of lost birds, scratching in the dry grass for seeds or bugs, huddling for shade beneath the few trees, trying to build shelters of sticks or straw. She shuddered and made the picture go away. It was best to keep her attention on searching.

Maddy didn't do much searching. She didn't care for bending over and creeping underneath things and wedging her large self into small spaces. While Lina and Pelton hunted, she walked around in the fields and the overgrown gardens behind the houses, looking for old fruit trees, wild grapevines, and the kinds of leaves, roots, nuts, and mushrooms that were all right to eat. Lina would look out the window of the house she was poking through and see Maddy wading through knee-high grass toward a gnarled old apple tree. Or she'd see her wide back in among the bushes as she picked berries. Sometimes Maddy simply sat. Lina would see her settled into an ancient lawn chair, gazing across a field or up a street, not moving at all. What was she thinking about? Lina wondered at those times. She looked so serious.

On the evening of the third day, they stopped by a wide, slow part of the river. As the sun went down, they sat on the riverbank, drinking cool tea that Pelton made with mint leaves, and they talked. Pelton told about the places he'd seen, and Maddy and Lina told about Caspar's quest in the city, his mad study of the old songs about treasure.

"Oh, yes," said Pelton. "I've heard those old rhymes all my life, and my father before me heard them, too. It's an old verse, or a song, I think, come down from years ago and scrambled, probably, in the process. Everyone says it in a different way. Something like this." He sang in a sweet but off-key voice:

"There's buried treasure in the ancient city.
Remember, remember from times of old.
What's hidden will come to light again.
It's far more precious than diamonds and gold.

"That's the way I heard it, from an old man who lives up in the mountains near Angel Rock. Then I heard another version from Maggie Pierce, over by Falter. She sings it like this:

"Remember the city, the city remember,
Where treasure is hidden under the ground.
The city, the city, always remember,
That's where the treasure will be found."

Lina stared at him. Her mouth dropped open, her eyebrows flew upward, and her heart thudded in her chest.

He laughed. "What are you looking so amazed at? Think you're going to go find this treasure? Nobody believes those old things anymore. They're nursery nonsense, old jingles made up to put babies to sleep."

"Some still believe it," said Maddy. "But it's only those with a bit of madness in them. And a good measure of greed."

"That's right," said the roamer. "I've known a few like that. One of 'em was sure it was in the old city of Sanazay and spent his whole life digging through the ruins, looking for it. Finally died when a chimney fell on him."

Maddy snorted. "Such nonsense people believe," she said.

Lina was shaking her head. She began to smile. "No, no," she said. "No, you have it wrong." She laughed, she couldn't help it. "It isn't nonsense, it's true. I'm sure, I'm sure!" What she suddenly knew seemed so wonderful and astonishing that she leapt up and clapped her hands and laughed again.

"You're a silly one," said the roamer.

"I'm not silly! The city in that rhyme—it's the city I come from!"

The roamer cast a sideways glance at Maddy. "What's the matter with her?" he said. "Has she got a fever?"

Maddy reached up for Lina's hand. "Calm down now," she said. "Tell us what you're talking about."

So Lina explained. "Sing the first line again, the first line of the second song," she said.

Pelton eyed her strangely, but he sang: "Remember the city, the city remember, where treasure is hidden under the ground."

"That first line," said Lina. "I'm sure it's meant to be 'Remember the city, the city of *Ember.*' That's the name of my home. It was under the ground."

"Not sure I believe *that*," said Pelton.

"I think it's true," said Maddy. "They all say it, all the ones who came from there."

"And what about the treasure, then?" Pelton asked.

"It was *us*!" cried Lina. "We were the treasure, the people of Ember!" She felt a swell of love all of a sudden for her old city. "Sing that first song again, the last lines of it."

Pelton sang: "What's hidden will come to light again. It's far more precious than diamonds and gold."

"You see?" said Lina. "Come to light! We came up into the light! And we were more precious than diamonds and gold because they thought we might be the last people—the only ones left."

The three of them gazed at each other in wonder. "I believe she's right," said Maddy at last.

"Maybe so," said Pelton. He stared curiously at Lina. "You lived *underground*?"

So then for the rest of the evening, Lina told about the city of Ember, and how she had been a messenger there, and how she and Doon had found the way out. It was late when they finally lay down for the night. Lina couldn't sleep at first, thinking of the old songs and what they meant. Someone, long ago, had hoped that at least a few people would survive and had wanted them to remember her city and the treasure it held, the treasure that was most valuable of all— herself, her family, and all the generations of people who had lived in that secret place, their purpose, though they didn't know it, to make sure that human beings did not vanish from the world, no matter what happened above.

The Third Town Meeting

After the rampage in the plaza, the three town leaders
went up to the tower room for an urgent meeting.
They flopped into their chairs and sat without speaking for a few moments, staring down at the mess
below.

"What do we do now?" said Wilmer.

Ben curled both hands into fists and set them on
the table in front of him. "The cavepeople," he said,
"must leave."

"Leave?" said Mary.

"Leave," said Ben. "They must go away from here."

"But they haven't been here six months yet," said
Wilmer.

"They must go now," said Ben. "It's better for them
anyhow, to leave before winter really sets in."

"They won't want to leave," said Wilmer, tugging anxiously at a strand of his hair. "I think they understand now that there's nowhere for them to go."

"They *must* go," said Ben. "We can never feel safe while they are here. If they refuse to go, we will force them to. We have the means to do it."

There was a long silence. Ben and Mary glared at each other. Wilmer's eyes darted anxiously between them.

At last, Mary set the palms of her hands on the table and took a long breath. "You are speaking of the Weapon," she said.

"That's right," said Ben. "We have it for situations of dire emergency. I think we have an emergency now."

"We've never used it before," said Wilmer. "We don't even know how to work it."

"I think it is unwise to use it," said Mary. "We have always tried our best not to repeat the mistakes of our ancestors. Using the Weapon would be the first step down the path they took."

"We may not actually have to *use* the Weapon," said Ben. "All we have to do is threaten them with it. Just the sight of it will make them do what we say— that is, leave."

"What you are proposing," said Mary, "is sending four hundred people to their deaths."

"Not necessarily," said Ben. "The village of Sparks started with almost nothing, why shouldn't they?"

"It's not true that we started with nothing. The founders of Sparks came here from the old cities, in a truck loaded with enough food and supplies to keep them going for months. These people have nothing at all."

"We will send a truck with them, then," said Ben. "With barrels of water, some food, and some basic supplies."

"That would last them about a week," said Mary. "Besides, they have no skills. They haven't had time to learn them."

Ben sighed impatiently. "Are we supposed to subject our own people to hardship and danger because of a bunch of refugees from a cave? Isn't it our job to *protect* our own people?"

"But if they rebel against this order," said Wilmer, "then what?"

"I thought I had made that clear," said Ben. "We use force. It is our only option." He pondered for a moment, frowning into the air above Wilmer's head. "We'll put the Weapon on a truck and take it to the hotel. If they put up any resistance, it'll be right there, ready to use." He thumped a fist on the table. "I say we give them a day to prepare. The day after tomorrow they will leave Sparks. All of them. For good. Shall we vote on it?"

They nodded.

"I vote yes," said Ben. "They must leave."

"I vote no," said Mary.

Wilmer stared down at his hands. He swallowed.

He took a shaky breath. "I . . . ," he said. "I vote . . . I vote yes."

So it was decided. They would make the announcement that very night, calling the people of Ember together after they were through with work and before they went back to the hotel. Ben would be the one to tell them. He would make it clear that the decision was final.

CHAPTER 23

Getting Ready for War

The announcement shocked the people of Ember. That evening, they swarmed through the halls of the Pioneer Hotel in an uproar. People wept and shouted and moaned. In the lobby, Doon encountered a group of people embroiled in a huge argument.

"It's the fault of that Hassler boy," shouted someone. "He was the one who started the riot. He was egging people on."

"No! He stood up for us! He gave them what they deserved!" cried someone else.

"He's a troublemaker!"

"He's a hero!"

Doon started up the stairs. Halfway up, he passed Lizzie. Her face was flushed with excitement. She grabbed his arm. "He won't let them kick us out," she said, "will he?"

"Will who?" said Doon.

"Tick. I'm sure he'll save us. He's so brave, isn't he? He'll make them change their minds." She hurried on down the stairs.

It was many hours before people went to sleep that night. The noise in the hallways went on and on, as some people wailed that they were all going to die, and others vowed to fight, and others gathered up their belongings and stuffed them into sacks. Sadge was so frightened by what was happening that he curled up in the corner with his blanket over his head. But Doon and his father and Edward Pocket sat talking for a long time.

"I don't see how we could make a town from nothing out in the Empty Lands," said Doon. "I don't believe they ever thought we could. We'd starve trying to do it. We *can't* go—they can't make us."

His father, who sat leaning against the wall with his knees up, shook his head sadly. "I don't know," he said. "This Weapon they have—they could use that to force us out."

"But what could it be?" Doon said. "Just one weapon? I don't understand it."

"To be effective," said Edward Pocket in his most learned tone, "a weapon must come into contact with the person or persons it is used against. The question is, how can one weapon be effective against four hundred people? My guess is that it's something very large that could be made to fall on us and crush us."

"But where could they hide it, if it's that large?" asked Doon. "It would have to be as big as a mountain."

"It could be an animal," said Doon's father. "They might have it in a cage in the basement of the town hall. Something very fierce that they would let loose on us."

"Or it might be something like the poison oak, only worse," said Doon. "Some sort of poison that they could spray at us."

His father nodded thoughtfully. "Yes," he said. "That could be it."

"But Father," said Doon, "we have to fight them, don't you think? No matter what the Weapon is. We can't just leave. It's so unfair!"

Edward Pocket, who had been sitting cross-legged on the floor, scrambled to his feet. He clenched both fists and raised them as if ready to pound someone. "I'm not leaving!" he shouted. "Let them try and make me! I'll chain my leg to their big old tree!"

From under his blanket, Sadge moaned.

"Besides," Edward went on, "I have work to do here. They need me. They need all of us!" He sat down again. "Probably tomorrow they'll change their minds."

"I don't think so," said Doon's father. "That Ben sounded serious to me."

"So what do we do, then, Father?" asked Doon. "We fight, don't we?"

Doon's father sighed. He stretched his long legs out in front of him and stared down at his knees. "Think about what it would mean to fight," he said. "Say we barricade ourselves here in the hotel and refuse to leave. They come at us with their Weapon, whatever it is. Some of us are hurt, some die. We go out to meet them with whatever weapons we can find—sticks, maybe, or pieces of broken glass. We battle each other." He ran his hand across his head and sighed again. "Maybe they set fire to the hotel. Maybe we march into the village and steal food from them and they come after us and beat us. We beat them back. In the end, maybe we damage them so badly that they're too weak to make us leave. What do we have? Friends and neighbors and families dead. A place half destroyed, and those left in it full of hatred for us. And we ourselves will have to live with the memory of the terrible things we have done."

Doon pictured all this as his father spoke. He hadn't really imagined before what fighting would be like. "But still," he said. "At least some of us would survive and have a place to live. If we go out into the Empty Lands, we'll all die."

His father just shook his head. "I don't know, Doon. I have to admit, I just don't know what we should do."

"I know what *I'm* going to do," said Edward Pocket.

"What?" asked Doon.

"Go to bed," said Edward. He stamped over to his closet and crawled in. "Wake me up," he said, "when you've got all this figured out."

An hour or so later, the noise of marching sounded in the hallway, and the *thump-thump* of knocks on doors, one after the other. Tick's voice rang out: "Calling all fighters!" he shouted. "All fighters! All those who refuse to be banished! Meet at the head of the road. We must make our plan!" The footsteps passed, and Doon heard the same message repeated farther down the hall, and again farther yet.

He put his clothes and shoes back on. In spite of what his father had said, he still didn't think the people of Ember should agree to go quietly out into the wilderness. Somehow, they must resist—and Tick was the only one with a plan.

The hall was full of people, a few of them murmuring quietly to each other, most of them silent. All were heading for the stairs. Outside, the night was warm, but a restless wind stirred in the trees and scraps of cloud flew across the stars. With the others, Doon headed for the meeting place.

Tick stood in a patch of moonlight, the dense shrubbery behind him. When people had gathered around, he held up his rod, and all whispering died away.

"Listen carefully," Tick said. He spoke in a level voice, not loudly, but every word was sharp and clear. "The day we've been ordered to leave—the day after tomorrow—we will assemble at dawn, at the front of the hotel. Have your weapons with you. There are still many people who haven't made up their minds to fight, and a few who are ready to go meekly into the Empty Lands, following orders. We want to change their minds. Flash your weapons! Shout our battle cry: 'We will not go!' Remind them of the black words of hatred scrawled in mud on the plaza and on the walls of our hotel, and the poison leaves on the doorstep. We will make those cowards ashamed of their weakness. We will make them understand that obedience to evil commands is a disgrace. Most of them, maybe all of them, will join us. And once they have, we will march into the village, loud and defiant and strong, and in the plaza we will confront the town leaders and make our demands."

A few people raised their fists and shouted approval.

"What are our demands?" Doon asked. He was standing at the front of the crowd, just a few feet from Tick.

"They are these," said Tick. "We demand to be made full citizens of this town, not cast out into the wilderness. We demand to be properly fed. We demand decent places to stay. We demand the end to unfair rules and insults."

These seemed reasonable things to ask for, Doon thought. "And if they refuse to agree to our demands?" he asked.

"Then of course we fight."

"But they have this Terrible Weapon they talk about," said Doon. "What about that?"

Others echoed his question. "Yes, what about it?"

Tick smiled. His teeth showed white in the moonlight. "They have one weapon," he said. "We have many. And each weapon, in the right hands, is an engine of power." His voice grew louder. "We will attack them," he cried, "like this!" He raised his steel rod and brought it slashing down so that the air whistled around it. The end cut into the ground. He raised it again and whipped it back and forth, striking tree trunks so hard he gashed their bark. He whirled around and battered the bushes behind him. "You cannot defeat us!" he cried to an imaginary enemy. "Right is on our side! We will have your blood! We will break your bones!" He went into a frenzy of stabbing and slicing, thrashing wildly among the bushes. Leaves flew, twigs snapped.

Something fluttered and fell. Doon saw it. So did Tick. He stopped for a moment and glanced down. At his feet was a half-grown baby bird that must have been huddled deep within the bushes. It flopped onto its side, its beak gaping.

"You see?" Tick cried. "The enemy falls at my feet!" He raised his rod. "With one blow I—"

Doon stepped forward and grabbed Tick's arm. "Don't," he said.

Tick tried to pull away. Then he relaxed and lowered his weapon. He grinned. "Okay," he said. "I think it's dead anyhow." He stuck the toe of his shoe beneath the bird and flipped it away, into the grass. "But you get the idea," he said, turning back to his warriors. "Imagine *hundreds* of us doing that! We'll be unbeatable." His face was alight with glee.

And that was when Doon's vague, uneasy feelings came together into one clear understanding: Tick *wants* war. The thought of war excites him and makes him happy. But not me. The thought of war makes me sick.

Doon's way parted from Tick's that night. He walked back to the hotel and up the stairs slowly, his heart heavy. He still didn't know what he was going to do the day after tomorrow. All he knew was that he did not want Tick for his commander. He would command himself.

PART 3

The Decision

CHAPTER 24

What Torren Planned

Torren heard the news from old Sal Ramirez, who came in the evening to have the doctor look at his infected eye.

"They've been ordered out," said Sal as Dr. Hester stood over him, pulling his eyelid down. "The cave-people. They have to leave. Day after tomorrow."

"That can't be true," said the doctor. She dipped a spoon into a small glass jar full of clear liquid. "Tip your head back," she said. She dripped drops into Sal's eye.

"It is true," said Sal. "Ben told 'em to go."

"But how can they?" said the doctor. "There's no *place* for them to go."

"Some of 'em refused," said Sal. "They said they'd fight." He wiped his eyes. "Ben said he'd bring out the Weapon if they did."

"The Weapon!" The doctor set the jar down on the

table and stared at Sal. "Has Ben gone out of his mind?"

"Don't know," said Sal.

Torren listened from his place on the window seat, shivering with excitement. There was going to be a war, right here in Sparks! And the terrible Weapon would be used at last—on the cavepeople! He had always wanted to know what it was. Now he'd find out.

Sal left, with a bandage pressed to his eye. The doctor sat down at the table and stared out the window at the flame-colored streak in the western sky. "How have we come to this?" she said, but she didn't seem to be asking Torren.

The look on her face caused a little fear to mix with Torren's excitement. He didn't want to be *in* the war, he thought. He could get hurt. The Weapon might accidentally get *him* instead of the cavepeople. He just wanted to *see* the war, not fight in it.

"Where will the war be?" he asked the doctor.

"What?" She looked at him as if she'd forgotten he was there.

"The war," he said. "Day after tomorrow. Where will it be?"

"You're talking nonsense," said the doctor. "If there's a war, it will be everywhere." She stood up slowly, hoisting herself with an arm on the table. Her face looked heavy, and she shuffled to her room without saying good night.

Torren went to bed and lay there a long time with his mind racing. He decided he would get up before anyone else the day after tomorrow, the day the war would begin. He would get dressed. He would take a hunk of cornbread from the kitchen and put it in his pocket. He would take a knife, too, in case the war came close to him. Then he would go down to the plaza and climb to the top of the big pine tree, so high up that he'd be hidden from below. From there, he would be able to see everything.

CHAPTER 25

Dread at the Last Minute

As Pelton's truck drew near the village of Sparks, Lina was more and more impatient. She longed to see Poppy and Mrs. Murdo and Doon. "Another day's travel," Pelton said. "We'll be in Sparks by tomorrow morning."

Lina was too excited to sleep much that night. Her mind galloped forward to the people she would see tomorrow, and backward to everything she'd seen on her journey. She finally fell asleep a few hours before morning, and when she awoke, she could feel immediately that something in the air had changed. A wind had arisen, a warm, gusty wind that bent the brown grasses and rattled in the leaves of the trees. The blue of the sky had faded to a hazy gray, and the heat seemed more fiery than ever. She felt something unsettling in the air, a warning, like the first traces of fever when an illness is coming on.

"Could be nearly a hundred degrees today," said Pelton. "But in a week or two the heat will start to slack off. The season's changing. You can feel it in the wind."

They started out early. After only an hour or so, Lina could see the fields and buildings of Sparks in the distance. She stood up—she was sitting on the front seat of the truck between Maddy and Pelton—and shielded her eyes with her hand to see better. There it was—and now it looked like home to her, the solid little brown houses, the tidy fields around them. When they came to the road that led to the Pioneer Hotel, Lina had a sudden idea. "Let me off here," she said. "I want to tell Doon I'm back. I'll walk the rest of the way."

She thanked Pelton for all his help, and he thanked her in return. "Take a few of the things you found," he said, "whatever you like." She rummaged through the crate until she found the magnifying glass, the magnet, and the little red truck, and she tucked these into her pack.

"I'll go into town and help Pelton with the trading," Maddy said to Lina. "I'll meet you later at the doctor's house."

Lina jumped down from the truck. Her legs strong and springy, her hair flying in the wind, she ran up the road toward the hotel.

She expected to see people at the river, washing, and people sitting on the hotel steps eating their breakfasts, getting ready for work. But the grounds of the hotel were empty, and when she went inside, she found people milling about the lobby in confusion. Some of them were crying—she saw the two Hoover sisters, one wailing, the other trying to comfort her, and she saw old Nammy Proggs sitting on a rolled-up blanket, grumbling to herself. People were arguing with each other—she heard angry voices, and questioning voices, and voices full of fear.

For a second she just stood looking, wondering what was happening. Then someone spotted her. "Lina!" Her name rang out over the hubbub. Faces turned toward her, and people rushed up to her and crowded around her. "You're back! Where have you been? We thought you'd disappeared forever!" She saw Clary's face, smiling, and she heard the voices of friends from school, and Captain Fleery of the Ember messengers, and someone who used to work in the shoe store. "Are you all right?" they said. "What a time to come back! Why did you leave? Where have you been?" Hands reached for her, arms wrapped her in hugs. She saw a red head bouncing up and down as Lizzie jumped in the air, trying to see over the crowd, and she saw Mrs. Polster beaming at her, and Miss Thorn at her side.

"I'm fine, I'm fine!" she said. "I'm so happy to be back! But what's going on here? And where's Doon?"

"I'm here!" It was Doon's voice. There he was, just

coming down the stairs. She broke away from the welcoming crowd and ran over to him. He didn't speak, just reached out an arm and grabbed her hand. The look on his face startled her. Was he angry?

"Come outside," he said.

She followed him down a passage and out a door in the back of the hotel. There was a small concrete terrace there, bordered by a low wall. Behind the wall, the drooping branches of a dusty tree stirred in the wind. Doon sat down on the wall and pulled her down next to him.

For a moment he said nothing. When he spoke, his voice came out in a rough shout. *"Where have you been?"* he said. "Don't you know how everyone has worried about you? Don't you know everyone has thought you were *dead?"*

Lina shrank back. "I didn't mean to be gone so long," she said. "It was a mistake. I thought—"

"Nearly a month you've been gone!" Doon said.

"It was because of the city, Doon. I thought the city would be like those drawings I made. I thought maybe we could go there, all of us, and live there, and . . . and be happy," she finished weakly.

"You could have told me you were going," Doon said. "I might have wanted to go, too. Did you think of that?"

"I didn't really think at all," Lina said, "I just saw the chance and went. But if I *had* thought about it"—

she frowned, remembering—"I'd probably have figured you wouldn't *want* to come. Because you were too
busy with that . . . that Tick."

Doon's face fell. "Oh," he said. "Well, you're right.
I guess I was . . . I thought Tick might be . . ." Doon
stopped, looking flustered. "I'm sorry," he said.

"I'm sorry, too," said Lina. They were silent for
a moment. Then Lina said, "Shall we forgive each
other?"

"All right," said Doon. He smiled.

Lina smiled back. "But what's going on *here*?" she
asked. "Why is everyone so upset?"

"They've ordered us out, Lina! They've told us we
have to leave tomorrow morning!"

"What?" Lina could not take this in. "Who has to
leave?"

"All of us! All the people of Ember!"

"And go where?"

"Out into the Empty Lands. We have to make a
new life for ourselves, they said. On our own."

Lina's mouth dropped open. A wild confusion
filled her mind. "But how can we? What would we eat?
Where would we live?" Again the frightening picture
rose in her mind—the people of Ember scattered like
fallen birds across a vast, dry landscape. "There are
wolves out there," she said, "and bandits!"

"I know," said Doon. "And it will be winter soon.
Have you heard of winter?"

Lina shook her head. When Doon explained, her eyes widened in shock.

"All this time you've been gone, Lina, they've done terrible things to us. The first thing was that boy Torren." He told her about the smashed tomatoes that Torren blamed on him.

"He said he saw you?" Lina said, outraged. "Why would he do that?"

Doon shrugged. "Ask him. I don't know." He went on to tell her what else had happened. "They've thrown us out of their houses! They've written hateful words on our walls. They've poisoned us with leaves!"

"But why? What did we do to them?" Lina said. The wind blew her hair forward over her shoulders. She clutched a handful of tangled strands to hold them still.

"We ate their food," said Doon. "That was the main thing. But other things happened, too." He told her about the riot in the plaza, and about what happened at the fountain. "Now," he said, "they've threatened to use their Weapon on us if we don't leave. So Tick says we'll use our weapons on them."

"Our weapons? What weapons?"

Doon sighed. For the first time, Lina noticed how thin he was. She saw the shadows beneath his eyes.

"There's so much to tell you," Doon said. "And we only have today."

"But I haven't even been home," Lina said. "I have

to see Poppy, and Mrs. Murdo. Are they still at the doctor's? Is Poppy all right?" A scattering of dry leaves blew against her legs. The wind whipped her hair. The whole world had changed suddenly, just in the last half hour. Her throat tightened, and she felt tears threatening.

"Yes, they're still at the doctor's," Doon said. "Come on, I'll go with you. We'll talk there."

"Wait," said Lina. "I brought you a present. Two presents." She unrolled the pack she'd carried all the way from the city, took out the magnet and the magnifying glass, and handed them to Doon. "This one is a magnet," she said. "If you put it against metal, it sticks there. I guess it isn't very useful, but it's interesting. The other one is for making things bigger—I mean, making them look bigger."

"Thank you," Doon said. He examined his presents curiously. He held the glass up and peered through it at the back of the hotel.

"Look at something small," Lina said. "Like a leaf or a bug."

Doon riffled among the leaves on the ground and found an ant, which he set on the palm of his hand. Holding the glass above the ant, he looked through it. "Oh!" he said. "Look! You can see its knee joints! And even . . ." He trailed off, absorbed in looking. Then he raised his eyes to Lina. "It's like a miracle!" he said. He blew the ant from his palm and looked around until he found a beetle. "Look at this!" he cried. "You can see it chewing!" He tried a feather, and a bit of moth wing, and a blade of grass.

"This is such an amazing world," he said finally, putting the glass and the magnet into his pocket. "I love it here, except for the troubles with people."

Lina and Doon went through the village and up the road to the doctor's house. It was still early morning when they got there—when they came through the door, they saw everyone at the table, eating breakfast. Mrs. Murdo was facing the door, so she saw them first. She stood up, her spoon still in her hand. She stared for a second, her eyes round, her mouth open, words trying to come out of it. Then she rushed toward Lina and wrapped her in a hug. At the same time, Poppy jumped down from the bench, dashed toward Lina, and hugged her knees. The doctor stood up and watched this reunion wide-eyed.

Torren leapt up, too, but not to hug Lina. He ran to the door and looked out, and then he cried, "Where's Caspar? Isn't he here, too? Where is he?" But no one paid attention to him. They were too busy fussing over Lina, asking questions and not giving her a chance to answer. "Where have you been? Are you all right? Why didn't you *tell* us . . . Do you know what's happening here?"

Poppy yelled, "Wyna, Wyna, pick me up! Pick me

up!" And the doctor, thrown into a state of even more confusion than usual, murmured, "Some tea? Or . . . let's see. Why don't we all . . . So glad you're . . ." And all around the edges was Torren, pulling at Lina's sleeve, saying, "But why *isn't* he here, where is he? When is he coming?" and getting no answers.

When things calmed down a little, Lina said, "Maddy will be coming soon. She stayed in town to help the roamer for a while."

Mrs. Murdo stopped smiling and grew stern. "Lina," she said, "how could you go off like that and not talk to me first? And just leave that careless little note, which was not, I would point out, true. Three days, you said. It's been twenty-eight! That was a thoughtless, foolish thing to do."

"I know," Lina said. "I'm really, really sorry. I didn't know I'd be gone so long." She explained how, when she overheard Caspar, she'd thought he'd said "a day's journey" when really he'd said "five days' journey." "And then," she said, "other things happened, and . . . it took a long time."

"Yes," said Mrs. Murdo. "And we had a long, long time to worry about you." She picked up Lina's pack, which Lina had dropped on the floor, and set it on the window seat. "And you know what's happened here? You know we've been ordered to leave tomorrow?"

"I know," Lina said. "But I can't believe it's true."

"It's true," said Mrs. Murdo. "It doesn't please me

a bit, but what to do about it I don't know. Come and have some breakfast."

Lina and Doon sat down at the table, where the others had been eating raspberries and cream. Though Lina was so thoroughly sick of travelers' cakes that all real food should have looked good to her, she had no appetite. Her stomach was in a knot.

"I can't eat," she said. "I'm not hungry. I have to— Doon and I have to talk."

"At least take an apple," said Mrs. Murdo.

"First of the season," the doctor added. "From up north."

Lina took the hard red fruit, and she and Doon went outside. The heat was baking now. They went through the courtyard, where the doctor's plant pots were mostly empty, the plants having either been put into the ground or died. The ones still there struggled in the heat, limp or brown. They crossed the road and walked down to the riverbank. Even the river was suffering in the heat—it no longer flowed deep and smooth but ran in streams between the exposed stones. Its edges were yellow-green and smelly.

They sat on the ground. Lina said, "It would take me hours to tell you everything I've seen. But listen, this is the main thing: people had a beautiful city, and they wrecked it."

"On purpose?" said Doon.

"With wars. With fighting. It was horrible, Doon!"

She shuddered, remembering. "That war—it sort of whispered to me. There was a moment when I could hear screams. I could see flames."

"And there's nothing left?"

"Almost nothing."

"And all across the Empty Lands—are there houses?"

"Some. But they're old and falling down. Mostly it's fields and fields of brown grass. There's howling animals. If we had to go out there and try to live—well, we couldn't."

"That's why some people—a lot of people—want to fight." Doon told her about Tick, and the weapons he and his warriors had gathered. He explained the plan—how they would go into the village tomorrow, refusing to leave, prepared to fight. And he told her about the Terrible Weapon the town leaders had threatened to use.

"Yes," Lina said, "I've heard about the Weapon, too. Torren mentioned it one time. But what is it?"

"We don't know," Doon said.

"If it's from the old times," Lina said, "then it is so terrible that Tick's little weapons would be like—like twigs against it. The old weapons could burn whole cities." She clasped her arms across her stomach and bent forward. Everything inside her felt cramped, knotted up. Her hands were slick with sweat. "There can't be war," she said.

"But we can't leave, either," said Doon.

They sat watching the water struggle along between the rocks. The sun blazed down, burning the backs of their necks.

"Don't you think," said Doon, "that fighting would be better than just giving in? At least it's *doing* something."

"I don't know," said Lina. "It scares me." She ran her finger over the glossy red skin of the apple Mrs. Murdo had given her. "I talked a lot to Maddy on my journey," she said at last. "She's wise, Doon. She told me how war gets started. It's when people say, 'You hurt me, so I'll hurt you back.'"

"But that's just how people are," said Doon. "Of course when people hurt you, you want to get back at them."

"And then they want to get back at you. And then you want to get back at them again, only worse. It goes on and on, unless someone stops it."

"Stops it how?"

"You have to catch it soon, Maddy said. As soon as you see it starting, you have to stop it. Otherwise, it can be too late."

"But *how* do you stop it?"

"You have to reverse the direction," said Lina. "That's what Maddy told me. She said that if someone had been brave enough, the wars might not have started in the first place."

"But Lina!" Doon slapped his hand down on the ground next to him. "What does that *mean*? How do you *do* it?"

Lina wasn't entirely clear about this. She took a bite of the red fruit the doctor had handed her. It looked as hard as a polished stone, but the juice that burst into her mouth was sweet. "I think it's this," she said. She chewed and swallowed. "Instead of getting back at the other side with something just as bad as they did to you—or something worse—you do something *good*. Or at least you keep yourself from doing something bad." She took another bite of the apple. "I think that's it. One bad thing after another leads to worse things. So you do a good thing, and that turns it around."

Doon sighed. "That's not very helpful," he said. "How are we supposed to do something good for these people who have done so many bad things to us? Why would we even want to?"

"Well, that's it," said Lina, wiping apple juice off her chin. "You don't want to, but you do anyway. That's what makes it hard. Maddy said it was very hard. It's much harder to be good than bad, she said."

"So what do we do, then?" said Doon. His tone was bitter. "Say we'll be happy to work without food? Say we'll always be nice no matter what they do to us?"

"No," said Lina. "That can't be right."

"Or should we just go quietly out into the Empty Lands and not bother them anymore?"

"No," said Lina. "That can't be right, either." She stared at the water rippling by. She was thinking hard. "We don't want to leave," she said. "And we don't want to fight. Do you think those are the *only* two choices?"

"What else could there be? If we don't fight, they'll make us leave. If we don't leave, we'll have to fight."

Lina discovered a tough part in the center of the apple, surrounding some brown seeds. She picked at the seeds with her fingernail. "There must be some other way," she said. "What if we all just sit down in front of the hotel and refuse to move? We don't leave, but we don't fight? They wouldn't use their weapon on us if we weren't fighting, would they?"

"I don't know," said Doon. "They might."

"I don't think they would," Lina said. "They're not *bad* people."

"But we couldn't sit there forever," Doon said. "Sooner or later, they'd make us leave. They'd pick us all up one by one and load us onto trucks and drive us away."

"Maybe they wouldn't," said Lina. "Maybe we could talk, and work something out."

"I don't think so," said Doon. "Tick and his warriors would never just sit. They *want* to fight."

Lina drew up her knees and rested her chin on

them. Something good, she thought. What good act would turn things around?

"We could volunteer to be roamers," she said. "A whole lot of us, so they wouldn't have to feed us, and we could bring things back to them."

"We don't know how to be roamers," said Doon. "We don't have trucks. Or oxen. We wouldn't know where to go."

"We could say we'll do all the worst jobs," Lina said.

"But that wouldn't be fair," said Doon impatiently. "Why should we? That's no good." He stood up, slapping the dry grass from his pants. "I think it's too late for any of that. None of it's going to work."

Lina stayed where she was, still thinking. She desperately wanted to find an answer, but no answer came to her. Her spirits sank, and she suddenly felt tired. "Well, then, we just have to be on the lookout," she said. "Some chance might turn up. We have to watch for it. I don't know what else to do." She knew how weak and silly this sounded.

But to her surprise, Doon smiled a little. "That's like what my father told me when I was working in the Pipeworks. 'Pay attention,' he said. It was a good idea then. I suppose it still is. Anyway, I guess it's the best we can do."

Lina dropped her apple core on the ground and scuffed some dirt over it, and they trudged back to the doctor's house. Doon stayed there for lunch instead of going to the Partons', and then he headed back to the hotel. Lina meant to spend the rest of the day thinking as hard as she could about the choice she'd have to make tomorrow. She sat on the window seat, sideways, her legs stretched out, and she tried to get her mind to produce ideas. But she kept coming up against the two walls: fight (she didn't want to fight) or leave (she didn't want to leave). A slow fly buzzed against the window. Wind stirred in the grape leaves outside. Think, thought Lina. Pay attention. And then she fell asleep.

CHAPTER 26

The Weapon

Morning came. Doon got up. He had to be ready for anything. So he rolled up his blankets and made a pack for all his clothes, everything he had. His father and the others did the same. Downstairs, out in front of the hotel, the people of Ember were gathering and swarming about, loud and distressed and confused. Tick roamed among them, urging courage, inspiring them to stand up for their rights, telling them the time had come for battle. His eyes flashed with a cold light. His voice rang out like the high, urgent tone of a bell. Very often, the people he spoke to seemed to catch fire from his words and be filled with the burning desire to fight.

Over half the people of Ember joined with Tick to be warriors. Some of them had wrenched the towel racks from their bathroom walls; others grabbed rocks or branches to use as weapons. They started down the road to the village, and the rest of the Emberites followed in a confused mass.

Doon went, too. The morning sun, already hot, blazed down on him; wind riffled his hair and his shirt. His mind was in turmoil, his heart thudding like a fist in his chest. Tick and his warriors, carrying their towel racks, their sink pipes, their shards of glass, strode along roaring their battle cry: We will not go! We will not go! More and more people picked up the chant as they came into the streets of the village, and at doors and windows faces appeared, shocked faces, and people still in their nightgowns. They shouted to each other—Look, the cavepeople are coming! They're coming into town! Other windows flew open, and doors, and people stepped out into the streets, unsure whether to be angry or afraid.

All the people of Ember had come. No one stayed behind to wait for the trucks that would take them out into the Empty Lands. All of them had to know what was going to happen. They had to be there, whatever it was.

They poured into the plaza and stood packed together, the warriors roaring and the others nervous, some of them half hiding in doorways or behind trees, afraid of what was going to happen, not sure if they wanted to be part of it or not.

Tick roared out his challenge. "People of Sparks! We refuse to leave! We are here to make our demands, and if you will not meet them, we will fight!"

"We will fight!" roared the warriors.

Others looked at each other fearfully. Will we?

From a side street Ben Barlow appeared, running. He bounded up onto the steps of the town hall, faced the crowd, and yelled back. "What are you doing here? This is an outrage, this is unacceptable! You are leaving today, leaving here for good."

"We will not go!" screamed the crowd.

"Wilmer! Mary!" shouted Ben. The other two leaders followed him up onto the steps.

"Clear out, now!" they shouted. "Back to the hotel! Move back, move back!" They stood in front of the crowd and tried to press them backward, but it was no use. There were simply too many Emberites. Ben darted at Tick and tried to grab him, but Tick struck him with his rod, and he lurched sideways, clutching his arm. No one had expected the Emberites to have weapons.

Doon was standing on the river side of the plaza, slightly apart from the main crowd. He had the feeling things were right on the edge of chaos, right on the edge between being in control and being out of control. It was frightening—the yelling, the waving of weapons, the people of Ember filling the plaza and the people of Sparks crowding in around the edges, their faces full of rage and fear. Maybe, thought Doon, the leaders will be willing to discuss our demands. Maybe we can talk, and everything will be all right. It was the only ray of hope he could see.

"These are our demands!" cried Tick. "Listen carefully!"

But Ben just screamed back. "We've heard enough from you! We're finished talking to you! No more talking. No more demands!"

When he heard that, Doon felt a jolt of fury. It launched him into action. He sprang up onto the bench next to him and shouted at the top of his lungs at Ben: "At least *listen!*"

That drew the attention of Chugger, who was standing near him. He lunged at Doon, but Doon leapt away. He heard Ben's voice shout, "Catch that boy!" Angry faces turned toward him, arms reached to grab him. He ducked and swerved and wove his way along the edge of the crowd, and as soon as he was in the clear, he ran.

But he didn't go far. He had to stay close to the plaza; he had to know what was going to happen. He ran up the river road and darted behind the town hall, where a few garbage barrels stood by the back door. He paused for a moment. Was anyone following him? From the plaza came a roar and then a voice shouting. What was happening? Doon *had* to know.

He pushed against the town hall's back door. It opened easily and he slipped inside. A hallway led toward the front of the building. On his right was a flight of stairs. Surely, he thought, no one was in here. They were all outside, dealing with the army of Emberites. He ran up the stairs, and at the top, he found himself in the tower room.

It was a square room with windows on all sides. A table stood in the middle, with straight-backed chairs around it. Down below was the plaza, swarming with people. The noise was like the roar of water. Tick was at the front of the crowd—Doon could see the top of his head, like a shiny black stone, and his steel rod glinting in the sun.

Straight below were the steps of the town hall and the tops of the heads of the three leaders. To his right, the windows were partially blocked by the branches of the great pine tree that stood next to the town hall. When he looked out the windows toward the rear of the building, he saw the town hall roof below.

This was perfect. He could see what was going to happen; he could hear, too, because the windows were open. And, he realized, if he stayed here, he wouldn't have to decide whether he was going to fight or not. This seemed a bit like cheating—but it was a relief, too. The thought of taking part in a bloody brawl had filled him with dread.

Standing to the side of the front window, Doon looked down. Right below him was Ben Barlow—he could see the wiry gray hair on the top of his head, and his hands waving furiously in the air. Mary Waters and

Wilmer Dent had stepped up behind Ben. Mary tried to take him by the arm, but he shook her off. He made his hands into a megaphone for his mouth. "We will not be threatened!" he shouted. "We are in charge of this town! It is our place, we built it, we own it!" He yelled so loudly that his voice rasped and cracked. "You are destroying our way of life. You must go!"

The crowd rumbled. They pressed forward. Clouds came over the sun, and a vast shadow swept across the plaza.

"You may try to make us leave!" shouted Tick. "But we are here to stay!"

The air seemed to quiver with rage. Or was it just the wind? Everything was moving—the clouds raced overhead, the branches of the trees thrashed, the Emberites raised their motley weapons. Up on the roof of the tower, the flag of Sparks whipped and snapped on its pole—Doon could hear it, though he could not see it.

He felt the wind whirling through his mind as well. His father's words came back to him. *When the fight is over, what do we have? A place destroyed. People who hate each other.* Standing above it all in the tower, he had the strange feeling of being separate, belonging neither to one side of the fight nor the other. Whose side was he on? Not on Ben's, certainly. But not on Tick's, either, with his warriors calling out threats, eager for a fight.

Ben held up his hand and shouted again. "We warned you! And we're ready for you." His voice was hoarse. "I'll give you one last chance. Will you leave or not?" With his head thrust forward and his hands tightened into fists, he waited for an answer.

"No!" screamed Tick.

His army bellowed it out with him. "No!" "Never!" "No, no!"

Ben dashed to the door of the town hall. Wilmer went with him, and together they darted inside. Doon froze, afraid they might climb up to the tower. But they came out onto the steps again right away, pulling a thing of black metal that ran on wheels. For a moment the clamor of the crowd ceased as they craned their necks, trying to see over each other's heads. Doon had a good view from where he stood, but still he had no idea what the thing was. He knew it must be the Weapon, but it looked almost like a great black insect. It stood on black iron legs. It had a complicated black iron body nearly as long as a truck, studded with hooks and boxes and points. A narrow scarf of ridged metal hung across it. It was ugly, Doon thought, like the skeleton of a monster.

Ben turned the thing so that it pointed out over the crowd. He stood behind it, his feet planted wide apart. "This is your last chance," he shouted at the crowd. "Disperse! Or take the consequences."

Mary Waters dashed toward him. "No, Ben!" she cried. "We can't do this!"

Ben pushed her away. "We agreed!" he cried. "Stand back, Mary!"

Now the crowd in the plaza sensed danger and began to push backward. Tick cried, "Stand your ground!" but Doon saw him take a step back, too.

Ben squatted at the rear end of the Weapon. "Leave now, and take your gang of hoodlums with you!" he shouted. "Or I fire!"

Fire? thought Doon. What does he mean?

It was clear that Tick didn't know, either. "You have one weapon," he shouted, "but we have many!" And he raised the rod in his hand, and behind him his warriors did the same.

Ben gave a furious shout. He was crouched over the Weapon. Doon saw his bent back, and his arm jerking at the machine. Nothing happened. His arm jerked again, harder, and at the same time Mary rushed forward. She aimed a powerful kick at the nose of the Weapon, bumping it upward, and the Weapon, in a harsh machine voice, began to chatter. *Uh-uh-uh-uh-uh-uh-uh-uh-uh,* it went, turning its snout back and forth. People in the crowd began to scream.

Doon couldn't see at first what the Weapon was doing. What was the point of its loud, furious shuddering? The noise was horrible, but the Weapon was staying in one place, not flying out into the crowd. Was it shooting something out of its— Yes! Across the plaza, over the heads of the people, Doon saw a line of holes punching into a wall, splintering a window—

But the Weapon suddenly stopped its chattering. Doon looked down and saw Ben give it a furious shake, and shake it again, pounding on its nose to aim it lower as the crowd yelled in panic and scrambled backward, and Mary shouted and tried to rush toward Ben, but Wilmer grabbed her arm—

And then the Weapon exploded.

No chattering this time, just a spurt of fire that shot from the Weapon's rear end, knocked Ben flat on his back, and toppled the Weapon forward so that it stood on its nose. This made the fire shoot straight upward, a column of bright orange, scattering sparks and reaching toward the branch of the pine tree that hung over the town hall steps.

From his place in the tower, Doon watched, horrified. Where was his father in that frenzied crowd? Where was Lina? Below him, the pine tree was on fire. The building would be on fire, too, in a minute, because the tree stood right up against it. Smoke was already curling through the windows. He had to get out.

And that was when he heard a scream—not from the plaza below, but from somewhere above him. A bird? An animal in the pine tree? A second later, an echoing scream arose from the crowd. Doon heard someone cry, "The tree! Up in the tree! Someone's there!"

Doon was at the door, ready to flee down the stairs. But he heard the scream again, and it sounded close. He darted back into the tower room and ran to the window that faced the tree. The lower branches of the pine tree were a mass of flame. He could hear the rush and roar as the fire raced among the dry needles. When he turned his gaze upward, he saw what the screaming was about: a boy was clinging to a branch a little higher up than the tower roof, hugging the trunk of the tree and screaming in terror as the fire swept upward.

Kenny! Doon thought. Was it? He couldn't tell for sure. But he knew he couldn't leave him there. Maybe somehow he could get him in through the window. He opened it as far as he could—it was the kind of window that swung outward on hinges—and then he grabbed one of the chairs from around the table. Holding it by its back, he thrust it out the window as far as he could.

"Climb down!" he shouted to the boy in the tree. "Climb down, quick!"

The boy saw him—and with a start Doon realized who he was. It wasn't Kenny at all. It was Torren, the one who had started so much trouble, the one who had pointed a lying finger at Doon. For one furious second, Doon felt the urge to leave Torren to his fate and get himself out of the tower as fast as he could. But he pushed that thought away and shouted louder: "Hurry! Get down here!"

Torren clambered down through the branches, down toward the flames beneath him. When he was opposite the tower window, he was still too far away to reach the legs of the chair. He edged out along a branch, but it was a slender branch and bent under his weight.

"Jump!" Doon yelled. "Jump! And catch the chair legs! I'll pull you in!"

Torren crawled backward to where the branch was sturdier. He stood up. Then he froze. He stood clutching the tree trunk, staring down at the flames, his mouth a dark O.

"Jump!" screamed Doon again. Smoke was pouring into the tower room now. "Hurry! You can do it!"

A gust of wind. The flames leapt. Now the branches just below Torren's feet were blazing, and suddenly he made up his mind—Doon could see the moment of decision in his face. He clamped his lips tight. He fastened his gaze to the chair dangling out the window. And then he pushed himself away from the trunk with his hands and flung himself toward the tower. His hands caught the rung between the chair legs, and Doon's whole body was yanked forward. He almost lost his grip on the chair, but not quite. "Hang on!" he yelled. With all his strength, he hauled the chair upward, and when Torren's hands were within reach, he grabbed one of them, and then both of them, letting the chair topple back into the room. One last heave, and Torren was in the tower room, shaking so violently he could hardly stand.

"Now," said Doon, "let's go."

He headed for the door. Over the sill of the window Torren had just come through crept a row of flames like sharp orange claws.

CHAPTER 27

Firefight

Lina was on the side of the plaza farthest from the river when Tick called out his demands and Doon yelled, "At least *listen!*" When she heard his voice, she tried to make her way toward him, but the crowd was so dense and turbulent that she couldn't get through. Tick's warriors were everywhere. The sun flashed off their steel rods and pipes and jagged pieces of glass. She was worming her way among the dozens of shoving and shouting people when Ben fired the Weapon.

She heard the sound, a chain of loud pops, and the people in front of her screamed and scrambled backward. Lina ducked and put her hands over her head. She stayed that way as people pressed past her and stumbled over her, and in a moment the popping noise stopped. Then there was a bang, and more shouts, and when she dared to stand up and look, she saw that the pine tree was on fire.

The flames were small at first, creeping along just one branch, with sudden flashes as dry bunches of pine needles caught fire. But in seconds the flames grew bigger. They leapt and crackled. Black smoke rose in a pillar into the air. The crowd pressed backward, crashing against each other. The people of Ember, for whom fire was a rare and terrible danger, stared upward with their eyes wide and their mouths gaping. Some of them screamed. Some were too frightened to make a sound.

Such a terror came over Lina that she couldn't move, except to stagger a few feet back along with the crowd. Her eyes were fixed on the flames—the terrible orange hands, reaching up into the branches of the tree. A voice in her mind screamed, "Run! Run!" but she couldn't run. Her legs wouldn't work. It was all they could do just to hold her up.

A voice cried out, "Someone's in the tree!" and Lina looked up through the smoke just long enough to see the upper branches thrashing and get a glimpse of something white moving among them. Then she was surrounded again by struggling people. She tripped over a piece of pipe rolling on the pavement and fell to her knees. When she managed to get to her feet again, the mass of people had pressed back behind her, and she found herself near the front of the crowd.

On the steps of the town hall, she saw Ben lying motionless, sprawled on his back. Wilmer bent over him, and Mary Waters shouted, "Fire truck! Fire truck!" The fire had leapt from the pine tree to the town hall tower—flames licked up its wall.

That was when Lina heard a wild laugh from behind her. "Let it burn!" someone cried. "Let it burn! It's their punishment! They deserve it!" She recognized the voice. It was Tick. Others took up the cry. "Let it burn!" they shouted, and a chorus of voices raised a harsh, triumphant cheer.

The people of Ember were packed together at the far south end of the plaza now, as far from the town hall and the fire as they could get. A few ran into the streets to get away, but most of them waited to see what was going to happen. They stayed at a safe distance, hovering between terror and fascination, and watched as the flames streaked up the sides of the tower.

The people of Sparks were running in all directions. Shopkeepers grabbed buckets and ran to the river and filled them with water, but most of the fire was high above their heads, impossible to reach. They flung the water into the air and then stood with empty buckets, watching the tower burn.

The two fire trucks arrived, their drivers standing up and lashing the oxen to make them trot. Water sloshed from the big barrels on the trucks' beds. As soon as the trucks stopped, people jumped up onto them, grabbed buckets, and began dipping buckets in the water.

"Fire line! Fire line!" the cry went up, and the villagers, who must have practiced this many times, formed straggling lines stretching out to the fire from the truck at the edge of the plaza. Burning twigs broke from the pine tree and blew in the wind, and new fires started up here and there. The people in the fire lines flung water in all directions, but for the few flames each bucket of water doused, it seemed ten new ones sprang up.

Lina's heart was beating so hard it drowned out all her thoughts. She wanted to run, to get away from here, but something paralyzed her. Part of it was fear of the fire. Part was fear of something else, fear of an idea that was trying to come to the surface of her mind. She didn't want to hear it. *Pay attention,* a voice whispered to her. She tried to push it away.

Faster and faster, the people on the truck dipped the buckets into the barrels, dipped, filled, and handed the buckets to those in the line, who passed them along from hand to hand. The last person in line, the one standing nearest the flames, flung the water, which hissed and steamed and put out a few flames.

Tick and his warriors, along with the rest of the people of Ember, watched all this as if it were a frightening but fascinating show. Tick and a few others cheered. But most people just gazed goggle-eyed as the flames blackened the town hall. When the wind blew sparks toward them, they shrieked and pressed back farther.

Lina scanned the crowd. Where was Doon? Where was Mrs. Murdo? She didn't see either of them—she could hardly see anything. Smoke filled the air. All she could see was a shadowy tumult of people. Only the flames were bright. The pine tree was a column of fire—within it, Lina could see the tree's black skeleton. When a great branch broke off and fell, crashing into the shrubbery below and setting it alight, a terrified clamor arose from the people of Ember, and now instead of pressing backward many of them turned and ran.

Lina stayed where she was. She felt as if she were being gripped by two huge hands. One pulled her backward, away from the fire, back toward the streets of the town, through which she could run to safety. The other pulled her forward into danger, urging her to do what she suddenly knew was right. It was the good thing. It was what she'd been waiting for. But she didn't want to do it. *I can't,* she thought. *I don't want to. I'm too afraid. Someone else will do it. Not me, not me. I can't.*

At that moment, the tower collapsed. Its walls crumpled, the roof caved in, and flames shot up from the hole. The flagpole came hurtling down like a spear. The blackened walls leaned and toppled.

And then the fire was everywhere. Flaming branches and tufts of needles, blown by the wind, landed in the dry grass at the edge of the plaza, and in the trees by the river, and on the thatched roofs of the market stalls. "There!" cried the people in the bucket line, pointing. "There! And over there!" The lines twisted around, the buckets traveled faster and faster from hand to hand, and those at the front of the lines tossed the water this way and that. But there were too many fires, and not enough people to keep up with them.

It's now, thought Lina. I have to do it. I *will* do it.

Quickly then, before she could change her mind, she ran. She ran with a hammering heart, with her head down and her hands in fists. She ran as if fighting a powerful wind, out across the plaza by herself, and when she reached the nearest bucket line she pushed her way in.

"Traitor!" shrieked a voice behind her. It was Tick's voice, that voice like a cutting blade. Lina heard it, but she paid no attention. "Traitor, traitor!" Tick cried again, and his warriors echoed him. "Traitor!" they yelled, jumping backward when the sparks flew too close.

Doon got out of the tower just in time. He'd had to almost throw Torren down the stairs and then take

them three at a time himself. Torren ran off somewhere as soon as he went out the back door, but Doon
dashed around to the plaza, staying close to the market
stalls, and joined the crush of Emberites at the south
end. Panting, he stared back at the ruin he had escaped
from—the black spine of the pine tree, the smoldering
boards of the town hall. He watched as the flames con-
sumed the building and the tower collapsed. He saw
the fire lines snaking among the scattered blazes, and
he heard Tick's laugh ringing out over the clamor.
"Burn, burn!" yelled Tick, and other voices chimed in
with his. "Let it burn! Serves them right!"

For a moment Doon stood there, stunned, his
mind a blank. It seemed that war surged around him,
but not the war he had imagined. Where did he belong
in this battle? Who was his enemy, where were his
friends? Noise and confusion assailed him. His eyes
stung. His legs were shaking.

And then he saw Lina break away from the crowd
and run across the plaza. He heard Tick and his
warriors screaming, "Traitor!" And he felt as if suddenly his eyes had opened (though they hadn't been
closed) and he had awakened from a bad dream. The
air around him seemed to become clear. Strength
returned to his legs. He edged between the people in
front of him, burst out of the crowd, and ran the same
direction as Lina—toward the fire lines.

And seeing what Lina and Doon had done, others

followed. Clary pushed through the crowd and ran forward, and Mrs. Murdo went after her, taking long, quick strides and holding up her skirts. Then came the Hoover sisters, and Doon's father, and fragile Miss Thorn, and five more people, and three more after that. They ran with their hands before their mouths or their arms over their heads, shielding themselves from smoke and falling embers, and they added themselves to the bucket brigade and began hauling water.

More and more of the people of Ember followed. At last the only ones not fighting the fire were Tick and a few of his men. Wearing half-stubborn, half-frightened expressions, they clustered at the far end of the plaza, shouting, "Traitors!" now and then, with their useless weapons dangling from their hands.

CHAPTER 28

Surprising Truths

Fighting the fire was so hard that Lina forgot to be afraid. Everything but firefighting was erased from her mind. Her hands reached for the next bucket, over and over and over, and when a warning cry arose she would look up to see where the danger was and dart out of its way. The water in the barrels soon ran out, and the rear ends of the lines had to move back to scoop water directly from the river, which meant a longer distance for the buckets to travel. The lines snaked left and right, moving to follow the fires, which sprang up in the dry grass like a crop of terrible weeds.

In the smoke-dimmed air, people looked like ghosts, swarming every which way, shouting at each other. Once Lina caught sight of Doon. He had jumped into the fountain and was bent over, as if fishing with his hand for something at the bottom. He jumped out again, soaking wet, and in a moment the fountain began to overflow, and the water spread, running toward the flames in the grass at the plaza's edge. Oh, Doon, hooray! Lina thought.

She saw Maddy, too, several times, appearing and disappearing in the swarm of firefighters, sometimes calling out instructions or warnings, sometimes just passing along the buckets, her hair flying in the wind.

It was the wind they fought against as much as the fire. It blew in unruly gusts, and the flames leaned and stretched before it, reaching for new things to burn. But there were twice as many people fighting the fire now, and before long the people began to win. The flames became flickers, put out with a shovelful of dirt or a splash from a bucket, and finally no trace of orange remained in sight. The plaza was a landscape of ashy puddles and smoldering black heaps, looking strangely open without the town hall and the pine tree.

Then for a few moments, people just stood and stared at each other. All of them had smoke-darkened faces and ash-dusted hair and damp, grimy clothes. The people of Ember were just as grubby as the people of Sparks; everyone looked more or less the same.

Lina went searching for Doon. She couldn't find him, but she did find Mrs. Murdo sitting on the ground at the north end of the plaza. Her bun had slid all the way off the top of her head and was hanging beneath one ear. Her skirt was dotted with burn holes. "Are you all right?" Lina asked her.

"I believe so," Mrs. Murdo said. "And you?"

"I'm fine," said Lina.

"Yes, you are," said Mrs. Murdo, giving Lina a long look. "Very fine indeed." She held out an arm. "Help me up," she said, "and we'll go back to the doctor's house and get ourselves decent again."

When the fire was out and all the firefighters were exhausted and wet and dirty, Doon discovered that his legs felt shaky again, and he went down through the village streets until he found a shady place under a tree where he could sit for a while. People trudged by him, heading for their homes, and the people of Ember passed, too, going back to the hotel, which that morning they'd thought they might be leaving forever. Doon didn't call out to anyone. He felt too tired even to talk. He just wanted to rest a minute before facing whatever was going to come next.

But he hadn't been sitting there very long before he saw Kenny coming up the road, and when Kenny spotted him he came over and sat down. "I saw you," he said. "You pulled Torren in from the tree."

Doon nodded.

"I knew you were that kind of person," Kenny said. Bits of ash sprinkled his blond hair, as if someone had shaken pepper on his head.

"What kind?" said Doon.

"The brave kind," Kenny said. "The good kind. Not like that other boy."

"What other boy?"

Kenny leaned back against the trunk of the tree and stretched out his legs. "The one who was yelling for people to fight. That one with the pale eyes."

"Tick," said Doon.

"Yes. I knew he wasn't a good one, ever since I saw him in the woods that day."

"What day?" Doon said.

"That day when he was out there with bags on his hands," Kenny said.

Doon turned to stare at Kenny. "Bags? Why? What was he doing?"

"Cutting vines," said Kenny.

"What kind of vines?" Doon asked. His heart was starting to pound.

"Well, I wasn't close to him. I'm not sure. But it was something he didn't want to touch, I guess. Like poison oak."

"Poison oak? Why would he cut poison oak vines?"

"I heard what happened," said Kenny. "About the leaves on the hotel steps. They thought we did it, but I don't think so."

Doon's thoughts were racing. He was remembering things: how Tick had an itchy patch on his arm days before the stuff appeared on the hotel steps; how he led the cleanup but didn't participate himself; how he had smudges on his neck the morning that "GO BACK TO YOUR CAVE" was written on the hotel walls; how he stirred everyone up, fed their anger, by reminding them of those two attacks over and over again.

And as if his mind had been full of clouds but now was clear, he understood. Tick *needed* all that anger and outrage. The more upset people were, the more of them would want to fight. And the more fighters there were, the more people for Tick to lead. Tick wanted power. He wanted glory. He wanted war, with himself in command. He had raised his army by attacking his own people.

Doon was breathing fast. His hands were cold and shaky. He knew, suddenly, that this changed everything. It meant that the people of Sparks had not attacked the people of Ember after all. Their fears and suspicions had made them unkind and selfish, but—except maybe for the muddy words in the plaza—they had not attacked. And if there hadn't been the writing on the wall and the poison oak, there probably wouldn't have been the riot in the plaza. And if there hadn't been the riot, the town leaders might not have decided that the Emberites had to leave.

Doon jumped to his feet.

Startled, Kenny said, "What's the matter?"

"You've told me something important," Doon said. He held out a hand and pulled Kenny up. "I have to—I have to—" What *did* he have to do? He had to talk to someone. He had to explain. "I have to get going," he said to Kenny, and he headed back up the road toward the village center again, thinking about whom he should talk to, and what he should say.

The doctor was standing out in front of her house with Poppy at her side when Lina and Mrs. Murdo arrived. Poppy came galloping toward them. "Wyna!" she yelled. "I saw fi-oh! I saw fi-oh!"

"Are you hurt?" Dr. Hester asked.

"Just tired," said Lina.

"And dirty," said Mrs. Murdo.

"Dirty, dirty," said Poppy, tugging at Lina's shirt and trotting along beside her.

Torren was sitting on the sofa with his feet in a tub of water.

"What happened to you?" asked Lina.

"I got burns on my feet," Torren said.

"On your feet? How did you do that?"

"You didn't see?" said Mrs. Murdo.

"See what?" said Lina.

So Mrs. Murdo told her. "I don't know why Doon was up in that tower to begin with," she said, "but it was a lucky thing for Torren that he was."

Lina raised her eyebrows at Torren. "Doon told me

what you said about him. Aren't you ashamed, now that he's saved your life?"

Torren didn't answer. He stared down at his feet.

"You lied," Lina said. "You blamed Doon for something he didn't do."

Torren slumped down into the sofa pillows.

"He didn't throw those tomatoes!" said Lina. "He would never do such a thing. Why did you say he did?"

"It was a mistake," said Torren in a muffled voice.

"Well, who did it, then?"

"Someone else."

"Who?"

"Just someone. I'm not telling."

"You *are* telling something, though," said Lina. "Maybe you won't tell who *did* do it, but you have to tell that Doon didn't." She shuffled through the clutter on the table and found a scrap of paper. "Here," she said, handing it to Torren with a pencil. "Write on here that you told a lie about Doon. Sign your name."

Scowling, Torren wrote. He handed the note to Lina, who headed for the door. "I'm going back to the village," she said. "Just for a little while. I'll be home by dinnertime."

After dinner that evening, Lina did a lot of talking. Mrs. Murdo and the doctor wanted to know what was out there in the Empty Lands, and how it was to be a roamer, and what the city was like. Maddy, sitting on the window seat with a cup of tea, put in a word now and then, but mainly she let Lina tell the story. Torren sat on the couch with his feet stretched out— the doctor had wrapped them in rag bandages—and pretended not to listen, but every now and then he couldn't help asking a question. Usually his questions had to do with Caspar.

"I don't understand," he said, "why *you two* came back and not Caspar."

"He hadn't finished what he wanted to do," said Lina. "His mission."

"What *was* his mission?" cried Torren. "You must have found out."

"We did find out," Lina said. She glanced uncertainly at Maddy.

"Your brother," said Maddy, "is looking for something he will never find. When he realizes that, he will come home."

"But *what* is he looking for?" Torren said. He reared up on his elbows and glared at Maddy.

"He is looking for a treasure," said Maddy. "But he doesn't recognize it even when it's right in front of him."

"Did he forget his glasses?" Torren said.

"No, no. But he has trouble seeing even with his glasses on."

Lina didn't like Torren any better than she ever had, but she did feel a little sorry for him. So she fetched glasses of honey water for him that evening, and she gave him the little red truck she'd found as a roamer. Poppy seemed to think all this was a kind of party for Torren. She joined in by bringing him things to play with—spoons, socks, potatoes. When it was bedtime, they carried him into the medicine room, and then Lina went with Mrs. Murdo and Poppy up into the loft.

Mrs. Murdo unpinned her hair, which fell around her shoulders in strands clumped together with soot. "I have something to say to you," she said to Lina.

Lina's heart sank. Whatever it was, she was sure she deserved it.

"I saw what you did," Mrs. Murdo said. "You did a remarkable thing, running out alone like that. Quite courageous."

"Well, I had to," said Lina.

Mrs. Murdo raised her eyebrows questioningly.

Lina was too tired to explain about trying to do a good thing to change the direction, and how she had hoped that someone else might do it so she wouldn't have to, but nobody did. So she just shrugged her shoulders and said nothing.

Mrs. Murdo ran a comb through her hair. "I believe a great many of us were thinking of doing the same thing," she said. "But no one quite had the courage. Only you."

"I didn't feel courageous," said Lina. "I felt afraid."

"That makes it all the braver," said Mrs. Murdo.

Lina felt a glow, like a little flame inside her—no, not a flame, a light bulb, that was better. A little light bulb was glowing in her heart.

"I believe I'm more tired than I've ever been in my life," said Mrs. Murdo. "And tomorrow there's more to face."

"Tomorrow?" For a moment Lina couldn't remember what had to be faced tomorrow.

"Well, yes," said Mrs. Murdo. "I suppose tomorrow we'll find out if they're still planning to make us all leave."

The Fourth Town Meeting

That night, the wind cleaned the smoke from the air, and in the morning the sky was a brilliant blue and the air felt tingly. The sunlight was warm, but it had a new quality, thinner and sharper. The season was changing.

A messenger from town arrived at the hotel that morning. Doon, who happened to be the first person up, ran into him on the hotel steps. "Tell your people," said the messenger, "that the leaders of Sparks wish to meet with the people of Ember at noon today. They will come to the hotel ballroom."

Doon conveyed this message to the next several people he saw, and they told others, and soon everyone knew. At noon, they assembled in the ballroom. Doon stood with his father in the midst of the crowd. All around him, he heard uneasy murmurings. Would this be more bad news? He heard Miss Thorn whisper to someone, "I'm so nervous, I have a stomachache."

He was nervous, too; his hands were damp.

At a few minutes after twelve, Mary Waters and Wilmer Dent came into the ballroom. With them were four men carrying a stretcher on which Doon saw a blanket-draped figure. The stiff gray beard jutting up from the chin told him it was Ben Barlow. Dr. Hester walked beside him, and with her were Mrs. Murdo, Lina, and Poppy. Other townspeople followed, lining up around the edges of the room—Doon recognized storekeepers and team leaders (including Chugger), along with many of the families of Sparks. The Partons were there; he saw Kenny trotting behind his parents.

Doon raised his arm and called to Lina, and she came to stand beside him. "Is Ben badly hurt?" Doon whispered.

"I think so," Lina whispered back. "The doctor says he was hit in the shoulder. She said the blast almost blew off his arm."

"Listen," Doon said. "I have to tell you something important." And in the next few minutes, as the town leaders and the men carrying Ben mounted the steps to the stage, he whispered to Lina what he'd discovered about Tick.

"Really?" she kept saying. "*Really?* How *could* he? I can't *believe* it!"

"And last night," Doon whispered, "I went and found Tick, and I told him I knew, and he said—"

But at that moment, Mary Waters held up her

hands for quiet. Doon stopped whispering and turned his eyes to the stage. The men had set the stretcher down and propped one end of it on a chair, so that Ben lay at a slant. A bandage covered one of his eyes. He glared out at the audience with the other.

When Mary spoke, there was a slight quaver in her deep voice.

"We are here to talk of serious matters," she said. "Ben was badly injured yesterday, but he has insisted on coming. We all wish to speak with you face to face." She paused. "First of all, I must tell you this."

Doon felt his stomach lurch.

"We have realized," Mary said, "that we cannot ask you to leave here. Your generosity yesterday has helped us remember our own."

No one spoke, but the people of Ember glanced at each other and let out breaths of relief. Doon bumped his shoulder against Lina's, and they grinned. "Yesterday," Mary went on, "when our Weapon exploded and the fire went out of control, a child of Ember crossed the line that divided us from each other. We are grateful to her for leading the way."

"Lina! Lina!" cried a few scattered voices—Lina thought she heard Maddy's voice among them. Doon startled her by yelling, "Lina the brave!" right in her ear.

"I want to say," Mary continued, "that we have made mistakes and we are sorry for them. We had good intentions, at the beginning. We did our best to help you. But when it got hard, we closed our hearts."

Wilmer Dent smiled apologetically. "We were worried—" he began.

Ben interrupted him. His voice was hoarse and weak, and he seemed to be having trouble breathing. Doon strained to hear him. "We were justifiably . . . concerned," he croaked. "About critical . . . food shortages. Attempting to ensure . . . the safety of . . . our own people." He made a kind of wheezing, gasping sound. "Under . . . standably," he added.

Wilmer shrugged his shoulders, still smiling nervously. "It was just that we were—"

"Afraid," said Mary. "We were afraid, let us say it right out. We were afraid that you would ruin everything for us. We were almost on the edge of prosperity. We feared that you would push us back into deprivation."

There was a silence then in which no one knew what to say.

"So we tried to get rid of the problem instead of solving it," Mary went on. "Fortunately, both our plans and yours were thwarted." She stepped forward and gazed out at the crowd. Her eyes met Doon's and held them for a second. "Just last night," she said, "I learned two things that have changed my picture of what has happened here. The first is this: we still don't know who wrote the muddy words on the plaza—we may

319

never know—but the other attacks on the people of Ember, the ugly writings on the walls of the Pioneer and the poison oak on the doorstep, were not carried out by Sparks villagers at all."

The Emberites turned to each other with puzzled looks and murmured confusedly. "But how could—" "But who would—" "What does she mean?"

"It was young Doon Harrow who explained it to me," said Mary. "I'd like him to explain it to us all, if he will." She nodded to Doon and gestured upward with her hand.

So Doon stood up. He told the assembled people the same thing he'd told Mary the night before when he came to her house late in the evening.

"It can't be true!" someone cried out—Doon thought it was Allie Bright, who had been Tick's right-hand man.

"It *is* true," Doon said. "Tick told me himself last night. He said it was just good strategy. He said he knew there was going to be war, and he needed to raise a strong army. When people are attacked, he said, they get mad, and angry people are the best warriors. So he decided to *make* people angry. He told me he got a good idea for how to do it when he saw those muddy words in the plaza."

At that, a roar swelled up and filled the ballroom. People shouted, "Where is he?" and twisted around to look for Tick. A few of them began barging through the audience trying to find him.

Doon called out, "Wait! Listen! He isn't here."

The commotion quieted down. People turned toward Doon.

"Last night when I talked to him, Tick was stuffing everything he owns into a sack," said Doon. "He told me he was leaving. He said he couldn't live anymore with cowards and traitors. He'd heard a roamer was coming through the village today, and he planned to catch a ride with him. Some others are going, too. They're going to the settlement in the far south, Tick said, where they hope to have a better welcome than they got here."

A great clamor greeted this announcement. Some people laughed, some shouted, "Good riddance," and some just grumbled and shook their heads.

Finally Mary raised her hands again and called, "Please! Quiet! I have more to say."

People grew silent again and listened.

"I said that I had learned *two* things," she said. "The second is this: the incident that set off this chain of violent events did not happen as we thought. It was not Doon Harrow who destroyed those crates of tomatoes."

This came as no surprise to the people of Ember, who had never believed Doon guilty in the first place.

But the villagers at the meeting looked startled. Doon saw Martha Parton flick her eyes toward him, her eyebrows flying upward, and he saw Ordney give him a quizzical look. Behind them, Kenny smiled a sunny smile.

"Torren Crane has taken back the statement he made," Mary said. "He did not, after all, see Doon Harrow throw those tomatoes. He still refuses to say who *did* throw them. We must make up our own minds about that. But I believe we can be sure that it was not a person from Ember."

At that, a cheer arose from the crowd, a loud, disorderly cheer, and Doon was so astonished that he nearly fell over. Lina grabbed his arm. "I made him write it down on paper!" she yelled into his ear. "I took the paper to Mary last night!"

When the cheering subsided, Mary continued. "We should take note," she said, "of how easy it is to bring out the worst in us. The actions of a few troubled individuals fanned resentments into violence. Only an accident kept us from murdering each other."

She turned around to face Ben, whose head was lolling sideways, his eyelids drooping. "Ben has something to say now. Ben? Are you able?"

The doctor, standing next to Ben, nudged his shoulder gently, and Ben opened his eyes.

"Can you make your statement, Ben?" asked Mary.

Ben frowned at the ceiling. The audience waited.

Finally he spoke. "I have been told," he said, ". . . that Doon Harrow . . ." He stopped. Frowned again. "I wish to thank . . . young man named Doon Harrow . . ." He took a shaky breath. "For rescuing . . . foolish nephew."

What? thought Doon. What's he talking about?

Ben scowled. He appeared to be gathering his strength. "Foolish nephew Torren Crane," he rasped, "in the . . . pine tree. Who could have been killed . . ." Ben's voice sank to a whisper, and the audience strained to hear. ". . . By my foolish actions."

Doon stood stunned. Torren was Ben's nephew? That was a surprise. But it was even more of a surprise to hear Ben almost apologizing for what he'd done.

Lina was thumping Doon on the back. Someone behind him cried out, "Three cheers for Doon!" and three cheers rang out in the ballroom. Doon just stood there, with what he thought was probably a silly smile on his face.

Then Mary stepped forward and called for quiet again. Her voice grew steady and businesslike. "Now," she said, "we must look to our future. You will not get everything you want. Neither will we. All of us will suffer, perhaps even be in danger. There will be more mouths to feed—but more hands to do the work, too. And though we may have a shortage of food, we have no shortage of work." She paused. She smiled a little. Her eyes passed over the people in the room, and Doon felt her gaze almost like a reassuring touch. "The main thing," she said, "is this: we will refuse to be each other's enemies. We will renounce violence, which is so easy to start but so hard to control. We will build a place where we can all live in peace. If we hold to that, everything is possible."

Someone clapped. Doon turned around and saw his father, clapping with his hands held high in the air.

"There is much to be worked out," Mary said. "It won't be easy, but we'll talk about it together." She paused for a second, and a change came over her face—the beginning of a smile. "One more thing," she said. "We will no longer speak of 'the people of Sparks' and 'the people of Ember.' From now on, we are *all* the people of Sparks."

A rustle swept through the crowd. Both Doon and Lina felt a pang of sorrow. To call themselves people of Sparks meant leaving behind the last trace of their old home—its name. The villagers, too, felt a pang; for them it was a pang of fear. These were their people now? Could they really live peacefully together?

But the sorrow and the fear lasted only a few seconds. Everyone was tired of sorrow and fear. Whatever lay ahead, they thought, would probably be better. They were willing to try it.

After that, they turned to the practical details.

"Actually," said Alma Hogan, the storehouse manager, "there's a fair amount of food in the storehouse.

It's just that we never like to use it all up. This year, we'll expect to use it all and hope we can replenish it next year. I'm afraid a great deal of it is pickles, though. By the end of winter, we may all be eating more pickles than anything else."

Doon's father mentioned politely that the hotel residents would have to have decent houses sooner or later. Mary said they would start building some of them now out behind the meadow. The best of Sparks's builders would be in charge, and they would teach the Emberites construction. "The houses will be small," Mary said, "and we'll be able to build only a few before the rains come. Most of you will have to spend the winter in the hotel."

Clary stood up to announce that her garden was producing well; in addition to cucumbers, melons, and peppers, she had grown nearly a hundred butternut squashes, which would keep well through the winter. That would help a little. The villagers looked at her curiously. Butternut squashes? They had never heard of them. "I grew them from seeds I brought from Ember," Clary said. "I brought all the seeds I had, all kinds. Next year I'll be able to grow more."

Mrs. Murdo said she had learned a great deal in her time with the doctor. She would like to be Assistant Doctor. "It's clear that this community needs more than one," she said.

"I know something about plants," said Maddy,

speaking up for the first time. "I wish to be Assistant Hotel Gardener, with Clary Laine."

Edward Pocket said he demanded to be made Official Librarian. Mary looked surprised. "We don't have a library," she said.

"Exactly right," said Edward. "You have a disorderly heap of books. I have made great progress with them, however. I invite you to come by and see."

Ben Barlow kept muttering dire warnings about crop failures and vitamin deficiencies and epidemics, but Mary said they would cope with those problems when and if they actually occurred.

Little by little, people began to feel interested in how this new arrangement was going to work. There were endless questions. What if there were arguments? How would they be settled? Would the Emberites go back to eating with their lunchtime families? Would they get enough for dinner and breakfast? What would happen when they needed things other than food, like shoes or soap or hats?

"The trouble is," said Mrs. Polster, "we don't *have* anything. We can't trade for the goods at the market because we don't have anything you'd want."

But Doon saw the solution to this right away. "We do!" he said. Mrs. Polster raised her eyebrows at him. She wasn't used to being contradicted. "We have *one thing* that you need," said Doon. "Matches! We still have a lot left. We could use them to trade

326

with, at least for a while. Two matches for a pair of shoes, say."

People laughed and clapped—it was perfect. Ben said in his opinion a pair of shoes was worth at least *five* matches, but no one paid much attention.

"All of this has to be worked out," Mary said. "It's going to involve disagreement, and it's going to involve hardship. But we have endured hardship before. We can do it again."

Wilmer sighed. "It's just that we hoped we wouldn't have to," he said.

Mary shot him a stern look. "We can do it again," she repeated. "And we will."

CHAPTER 29

Three Amazing Visits

Lina gave up on trying to persuade Mrs. Murdo to move to the hotel. Since they'd all have their own houses sooner or later, they might as well stay at the doctor's house until then. Besides, Mrs. Murdo was so intent on learning to be Assistant Doctor that it seemed unkind to take her away.

Lina and Maddy took on the job of harvesting and preserving the produce from the doctor's vegetable garden. Every morning they picked baskets of tomatoes and beans and peppers and corn and squash. Every afternoon, they sliced tomatoes and laid them in the sun to dry; they took dried beans out of their pods and put them in jars; they cooked peppers and packed them in olive oil; they tied bunches of herbs with string and hung them up to dry. Poppy puttered around their feet, "helping" by sprinkling dry leaves here and there or banging spoons on pots. Even

Torren, whose feet were healing, often chose to hang around with Lina and Maddy. He said he knew how to make a garlic braid, so they gave him a basket of garlic, and he made one.

One afternoon, as she and Maddy were cutting green beans for dinner, Lina heard wheels crunching on the road outside. The next moment, she heard the whuffling of an ox, and then Torren sprang up and limped as fast as he could to the front of the house. Uh-oh, thought Lina. Is it who I think it is?

It was. There was Caspar's battered truck, and there was Caspar just climbing out of it. He looked grubby. His mustache drooped. Torren ran toward him, crying, "Caspar! Caspar!" And Caspar smiled in a tired way.

"Hey, brother," he said. He thumped Torren's back a couple of times. Then he started toward the house. Lina and Maddy went out to meet him.

When he saw them, he stopped and glared. "Deserters," he said. But he didn't seem to have the energy to berate them further. He trudged into the house and plunked down on the couch. Torren plunked down beside him.

"I've been waiting and *waiting* for you," Torren said. "Why didn't you come back with them?" He flicked his hand toward Lina and Maddy.

"I had important work to do," said Caspar. "Which they didn't want to help with."

"And what happened with your work?" asked Maddy, standing by the door. "Did you find what you wanted to find?"

Caspar didn't even look at her. He closed his eyes and slumped against the back of the couch. "My numbers," he said, "need readjusting. They were completely right except for one thing."

"What thing was that?" asked Maddy.

"Wrong city," said Caspar, still without opening his eyes. "I have reworked the numbers. Tomorrow I head north."

Maddy and Lina exchanged a look.

Caspar turned his head toward Maddy and squinted at her. "I don't suppose you want to come," he said.

"No, thank you," said Maddy. "I plan to stay here, where something with real potential is beginning."

Torren tugged on Caspar's arm. "Did you bring me something this time?" he asked.

Caspar opened his eyes. He looked at the ceiling for a while. "Well, yes," he said. "I did."

"What?" shrieked Torren. "What is it? Can I have it now?"

"It's out in the truck," said Caspar. "I found a whole crate of them, very unusual. You can have one."

"One what? Let's go get it!" Torren darted to the door.

Caspar heaved himself up and they went outside. Lina watched as Caspar rooted around in one of his crates. He came up with something she recognized with a start. She hadn't seen one for a long time—it was like seeing something that belonged to an old friend, now dead.

"What is it?" said Torren.

"A light bulb," said Caspar. "I found a case of forty-eight of them, all unused."

"But what does it do?" Torren asked, peering into the light bulb as if he expected to see something alive in there. He tapped the glass with his fingernail.

"It gives light," said Caspar. "If you have electricity."

"But we don't have electricity."

"That's right," Caspar said wearily. "So you hold on to it, in case someday we do."

Torren went to the window seat and sat there turning the bulb around and around in his hands. Lina watched him, thinking about Ember. People had figured it out once, she thought. They could figure it out again.

A few days after Caspar left, there was another visitor to the doctor's house. Lina was out in the courtyard at the time, cracking walnuts with a rock. She saw someone approaching the gate, a bent figure walking slowly and somehow crookedly. She stood up. The person seemed to be having trouble with the gate latch, so she went to help, and that was when she realized it was Ben Barlow. His injured arm was bandaged and strapped to his side, and the jacket he wore was draped over it with the sleeve hanging empty. That was why he looked lopsided.

"Good afternoon," said Ben. "I wonder if Torren is here."

"He is," said Lina. "I'll get him."

She found Torren out in back of the house, sitting under a tree, eating a hunk of bread. "Your uncle has come to see you," she said.

Torren stared at her. "My uncle?" He sounded both excited and scared. He jumped up, shoving the bread into his pocket.

When Ben saw Torren coming toward him, he frowned. Then, as if catching himself, he changed his expression to a smile. "Hello, nephew," he said. "How are you getting on?"

Torren looked wary. "Fine," he said.

"Good," said Ben. He stroked his beard. Lina wondered if that was all he had to say.

Torren filled the silence. "Is your arm still attached to you?" he said.

"Yes," said Ben. "Just barely." He started to frown into the air again and then thought better of it. He sat down on a bench. "Well," he said. "I thought I'd just come and see you. Haven't seen you for a while."

"Years," said Torren.

"Well, yes. Busy life, you know, being a town leader. Many decisions to make. Matters of right and wrong to . . . to grapple with."

"Oh," said Torren. Lina could tell he was thinking the same thing she was: Why has he come?

"Sometimes one makes the right decision," said Ben. "Sometimes not."

"I guess so," said Torren.

Ben readjusted his bandaged arm. Lina saw that his beard was not as neatly trimmed as usual. Probably he had a hard time doing it with his left hand. She was pretty sure Ben didn't have a wife—she'd never heard mention of one.

"Well," said Ben. "You were fortunate, weren't you, getting pulled out of that tree?"

"Yes," said Torren.

"I am forced to acknowledge," said Ben, "that it was my fault. That fire."

"I guess so," said Torren.

"An accident," said Ben, "but one that did not have to happen."

"Uh-huh," said Torren.

Ben got to his feet with painful slowness. "So," he said. "Enjoyable talking with you. No doubt we should get to know each other. You must come by for a visit sometime, though of course I'm rarely home."

"You're very busy," said Torren.

"That's right," said Ben. He made his way toward the gate with his limping step. As he went out, he waved over his shoulder with his good hand, but he didn't turn around. Slowly, he started back toward the village.

"That was an apology," Lina said to Torren when Ben was gone. "He's sorry for doing what he did. I guess he's sorry for not being a good uncle, too—for not taking you to live with him."

"*Live* with him?" said Torren. He made a horrible face.

"Well, I thought you weren't happy living with Dr. Hester," Lina said. "You never *seem* very happy."

"I am *too* happy," said Torren crossly. He sat down on the bench that Ben had just left and pulled the hunk of bread from his pocket. A few little birds were hopping nearby. Absently, Torren tossed them some crumbs. He seemed to be thinking. "I *like* it here," he said to Lina, and he looked up at her with his eyes all round, as if he had only just discovered this himself.

The next day, Doon came to the door of the doctor's house carrying a sack. Kenny was with him, standing slightly behind Doon and peering curiously past him into the room.

"I have to show you this," Doon said to Lina. "I made it with the present you brought me."

"He's kind of a genius," Kenny said. "He already showed me."

Doon set the sack on the window seat. It was only just after dinnertime, but the days were shorter now, and the sun was nearly down. Dr. Hester had already lit two candles. She and Mrs. Murdo and Maddy were sitting at the table shelling lima beans. Poppy was sitting with them, tearing the bean pods into little pieces. All four came over to see what Doon had brought.

Torren came, too. He was actually more interested in showing Doon what *he* had than in seeing what was in the sack. "I got a present from Caspar," he said.

"Great," said Doon, but he wasn't really listening. Lina could see how excited he was about whatever he had in the sack. His eyes shone in the candlelight, and his hands fidgeted impatiently with the string around the sack's neck. When he got it untied, he reached into the sack and brought out a small device made of wood and metal—some sort of machine, Lina thought. It had a coil of wire, and inside the coil she saw the magnet she'd given Doon. There was a handle that looked as if it would make something turn. Lina, not being much interested in machines, was a little disappointed.

It was clear that Torren was disappointed, too. "Want to see my present from Caspar?" he said.

"In a minute," said Doon. "Let me show you this first."

"What does it do?" Lina asked.

"Is it some kind of a can opener?" asked Mrs. Murdo.

"Or maybe it's a sort of mixer?" said the doctor.

"Or a drill?" said Maddy.

"Nope," said Doon happily, and Kenny, his face shining with the shared secret, whispered, "Nope," too. "You won't believe it," Doon went on, "but it makes electricity. I found the directions for it in a book called *Science Projects,* but I couldn't try it out before because I didn't have a magnet. I didn't even know what a magnet was. But then you brought me one, Lina! And just the other day I remembered about this project." He took the machine over to the table and set it down. "What you do is, you turn this crank, and that turns the magnet, and that generates the electricity and runs it down these wires. It's supposed to be enough to light a light bulb. The trouble is, I can't test it because I couldn't find any light bulbs that weren't broken."

Torren started jumping up and down. He pounded on Doon's arm. "My present from Caspar! My present from Caspar!" he yelled. He bolted into the medicine room.

"What's the matter with—" said Doon, but Lina broke in.

"Doon!" she said. "His present from Caspar was a light bulb! Unused!"

Torren came out of the medicine room carrying

the light bulb encased in both hands, walking now, fast but with stiff legs, being extremely careful. "You won't break it, will you?" he said to Doon. "Your experiment won't blow it up, will it?"

Doon gazed at the light bulb as if it was the most wonderful thing he'd ever seen. Gingerly, he reached for it. "I'll be very, very careful," he said. "You can help me, Torren. Hold the light bulb right here." He showed Torren where to put the bulb, and he wound two loose wires around its metal end.

"Now," he said. "Blow out the candles."

Lina blew them out. The room went dark.

Doon began turning the crank of his machine.

At first nothing happened except that the magnet turned around. Doon cranked faster. And faster. And a glimmer appeared in the light bulb, first a glimmer and then a glow, and then the bulb shone with a faint but steady white light.

Lina shrieked. Poppy shrieked, too, because Lina had, and both the doctor and Mrs. Murdo gasped and broke into applause. Kenny beamed, glancing between the light bulb and Doon's face. Torren was being too careful to make a noise, but his eyes grew wide and his mouth dropped open.

For almost three minutes, until his hand got tired, Doon turned the crank of his machine around and around. The doctor wagged her head in wonder, Mrs. Murdo turned her face away to hide her tears, and

Torren held on tight to the light bulb even though it was getting very warm. Lina gazed at the light shining on everyone's faces. Full to the brim with hope and love and joy, she watched the little light bulb shining like a promise in the night.

Acknowledgments

My gratitude to my patient agent, Nancy Gallt, my skilled editor, Jim Thomas, and my unfailingly supportive friend Susie Mader.

JEANNE DUPRAU has been a teacher, an editor, and a technical writer. *The People of Sparks* is her second novel and the sequel to the highly acclaimed *The City of Ember*. Ms. DuPrau lives in Menlo Park, California, where she keeps a big garden and a small dog.